Carmen Reid is the bestselling author of the *Personal Shopper* series, starring Annie Valentine.

She has worked as a newspaper journalist and columnist, but now writes fiction full-time. Carmen also writes a series for teen readers, *Secrets at St Jude's*.

Join Carmen online for all her latest news, competitions and exclusive content, plus Annie Valentine's fabulous fashion blog!

www.carmenreid.com
www.facebook.com/carmenreidbooks

Reasons to love Carmen Reid!

'Sexy and flirtatious. The most fun you can have with the lights on!'   Katie Fforde

'As fun and frothy as a poolside pina colada!'   *Heat*

'Outrageously funny . . . filled with shopaholic fabulousness'   *Now*

'A rollicking tale'   *Glamour*

'A brilliant read that'll be popular with fashionistas!'
Closer

'A sassy little number'   *OK!*

'More heartwarming than an expensive round of retail therapy'   *Daily Mail*

'This is escapist summer reading at its best'
Jill Mansell

www.rbooks.co.uk

SHOPPING WITH THE ENEMY

CARMEN REID

CORGI BOOKS

TRANSWORLD PUBLISHERS
61–63 Uxbridge Road, London W5 5SA
A Random House Group Company
www.transworldbooks.co.uk

SHOPPING WITH THE ENEMY
A CORGI BOOK: 9780552163194

First publication in Great Britain
Corgi edition published 2012

Addresses for Random House Group Ltd companies outside the UK
can be found at: www.randomhouse.co.uk
The Random House Group Ltd Reg. No. 954009

The Random House Group Limited supports The Forest Stewardship
Council (FSC®), the leading international forest-certification organization.
Our books carrying the FSC label are printed on FSC®-certified paper.
FSC is the only forest-certification scheme endorsed by the leading
environmental organizations, including Greenpeace.
Our paper-procurement policy can be found at
www.randomhouse.co.uk/environment

Typeset in 11.5/15pt Palatino by Falcon Oast Graphic Art Ltd.
Printed and bound by CPI Group (UK) Ltd, Croydon, CR0 4YY.

2 4 6 8 10 9 7 5 3 1

For my writer buddies
Kim, Lennox and Shari

Chapter One

London

Annie glams up:

Red and white silk skirt (Donna Karan)
White ruffled chiffon blouse (Gucci)
Vest top underneath as buttons won't close (Sloggi)
Extra control top tights (M&S)
Red patent platform heels (LK Bennett)
Signature red lipstick (Max Factor)
Total est. cost: £560

'Annie, phone!'

Although she was breathing in and trying to tease her skirt zip up over a pair of dangerously over-stretched control top tights, Annie managed to shout back at the disembodied voice of her

7

husband: 'Just blinkin' leave it, will you? I'll phone the fascist dictator right back.'

It was bound to be the hyper-efficient production assistant wanting to talk through some finer details of the next filming schedule. But quite frankly, Annie had been in the TV studios for twelve hours already today and twelve hours every other day this week, plus last weekend, and she needed a night off.

She *deserved* a night off. In fact, if she didn't get tonight off, she, Annie Valentine, stressed-out mother of four, popular presenter of TV's down-to-earth fashion show *How To Be Fabulous*, was going to scream long and loud. Her sister Dinah and her best friend, Connor, were probably already in the bar halfway through their first round and all she wanted right now was for this blinking skirt to blinking do up so she could dash over in a taxi and join them.

There: muffin-top managed. The zip was up, the skirt was on, the ruffled chiffon blouse was tucked in. The blouse didn't do up at the front any more, so she'd put a vest top underneath and left several buttons undone, using a chunky, pearly necklace to camouflage the crime scene.

How she could go to the gym and be tortured once, sometimes even *twice* a week and not shift one pound of post-baby lard was yet another of life's many unsolved mysteries.

She stepped over a pile of dirty football kit, a pair of clapped-out tartan slippers, a bundle of toddler pyjamas and stood in front of her bedroom mirror.

'ED!' she shouted as she pencilled liner round her eyes.

'What?'

'Our bedroom . . .' she began, 'our bedroom is one complete and utter . . .'

She stopped herself and sighed.

Yes, the bedroom was a disaster zone. But looking around she could see that it was just as much her fault as his. When had she last found the time to deal with the overspill from the shoe cupboard? Or thinned out the gigantic collection of lotions, potions, perfume bottles and make-up littering the top of her chest of drawers?

But at least that was her stuff. What gave her teenage son Owen the right to dump his dirty football kit on the carpet? She gave a frustrated kick at the pile of muddy socks, tops and shorts. Hooligan!

And then the babies . . . She looked down at the tangle of pyjamas beside the football kit. The babies slept in here more often than in their own beds and they weren't even babies any more; her twins Micky and Minette were about to turn two!

This room had once been beautifully decorated but now the paint was looking tired, the surfaces cluttered and dusty. Any signs that it had once been a romantic, relaxing haven were long gone. Where there had been tea lights and a speaker system playing jazz, now there were dust bunnies, battered Thomas the Tank Engine books and old cups of tea developing strange new life forms.

The Japanese were into a special kind of mould from the top of teacups, weren't they? Health freakish Dinah had tried to make her drink it once. What was it called again? Kombucha tea ... or something? Good grief. Looking at the row of abandoned mugs on the mantelpiece, Annie wondered if she should set up a Kombucha stall.

The duvet moved.

'Dave ...' Annie growled, 'DAVE!'

She flicked back the corner of the duvet to reveal the shaggy, saggy dog that Ed, Owen and the twins adored. Annie's relationship with this dog was more complicated.

She liked the fact that the family adored him so much, but she couldn't find it in her heart to join the Cult of Dave. The middle-aged mongrel was scruffy, disobedient and almost totally deaf. Despite regular washing, he always smelled and she definitely did not like his habit of nestling down into the marital bed whenever he got the chance.

'Dave, OUT!' she said firmly, pointing to the floor, so he got the idea.

One glance at her face and Dave darted from the bed and high-tailed it out of the door.

'Are you battling with the dog again?'

She turned to find Ed standing in the doorway.

Looking at him properly for the first time today, she took in the untucked denim shirt, the saggy chinos, scruffy squash shoes and his unruly, cheaply cut, curly hair.

Ed was definitely not a fashion icon.

He was a music teacher at St Vincent's, her children's school. Well, in fact, he was head of the Music Department now. But that hadn't made much of a difference to his frugal, down-to-earth personality. He still 'sourced' most of his outfits from the senior school's lost property sale and wore them with the casual disregard of a teenage boy.

She knew that some people found her choice of husband a little inexplicable. But these were people who just saw Ed's scruffy exterior and knew nothing about the very kind, very funny person underneath.

When Annie had first met Ed, she'd been a recently widowed mother-of-two and she had only seen the tweedy jacket, weird trousers and wild hair too. It had taken some time to unearth the lovely man underneath.

Now, several years on, they were married, they had twins of their own and Annie could forgive all sorts of eccentric outfits because the man she truly loved was wearing them.

Ed smiled at her and all that Annie needed to know was in that smile. The smile that crinkled up the corners of his blue eyes and made them lively with merriment. Whatever the situation, Ed was usually mildly amused.

He knew everything about her, every ambition, every crazed little fact and foible and he still totally loved her, which meant everything, especially in this hectic, overworked, chaotic domestic whirlwind they had managed to create for themselves.

'I do not want a dog in my bed,' Annie complained. 'But the door won't close properly, so we can't keep the duvet snatcher out.'

To demonstrate, she pushed the bedroom door shut and watched it ping straight back out of the catch.

'I will fix the door,' Ed promised. 'I'm just waiting for a long, lazy evening when I have nothing to do and can apply my expert handyman skills to it.'

'A long, lazy evening? Your *expert* handyman skills? You're having a laugh,' she teased: 'and if there are ever any long, lazy evenings around here then I want to spend them catching up . . .'

She put her arms around his waist and pulled him in close against her.

'Exactly . . .' he agreed.

'OK, but you have to let me go now because I'm heading out and there will be no catching up right now.'

'When did we last catch up?' he wondered.

Annie frowned, tried to remember and realized she had no idea. Two weeks ago? One month ago? Longer than a month? That couldn't be good.

'Just a minute,' she remembered, brightening up, 'there was that Sunday morning, not last weekend, but the one before that.'

'That doesn't count!' Ed protested: 'we hardly got started, I still had so many good moves to make.'

'It counts,' she decided, pulling out of his arms and turning to the mirror to finish her make-up job.

'Have you heard from Lana?' Ed asked. 'Is she all set?'

'She texted. Two more days at work, then an overnight flight and she'll be here.'

Annie smiled. It had been nearly three months since she'd last seen her oldest daughter, a terrifyingly grown-up 19 now, and she couldn't wait for this visit, had all kinds of little mother-and-daughter treats planned, despite her heavy TV schedule.

'You've got some tricky conversations ahead,' Ed reminded her. 'I know we think it's a good idea for Lana to come back from New York in the summer and start the course over here, but she's already told you what she thinks.'

Annie sighed: it was definitely going to be tricky, but the situation *was* tricky. Annie had a friend, a fabulous wealthy, mansion-in-Mayfair-loaded friend, Svetlana. Now Svetlana, along with her daughter Elena – estranged for years due to a political sex scandal cover-up (life with Svetlana was always several degrees above complicated) – but, anyway, Svetlana and Elena ran a small fashion company, Perfect Dress, and Lana was employed in their New York office.

However, dress sales had slumped dramatically and now Lana was going to have to come back to London, where Annie had signed her up for a fashion business course in the hope that she could go back to Perfect Dress when the situation improved. But Annie already knew that Lana hated this plan and did not want to leave New York.

'It doesn't really matter what she thinks,' Annie told Ed. 'They've got to shrink the New York office and Svetlana agrees that Lana should come home. If Lana doesn't have a job or a work permit, then she has to come back to the nest.'

Ed whistled.

'It's going to be tricky. But don't let it spoil your night out. You deserve a night off.'

'Yeah,' Annie agreed, 'I should go . . . but darlin', is there anything, by any chance, just a little something . . . to eat?'

Ed laughed: 'Oh right . . . Do you mean, in between nappy changing and putting on the latest *oeuvre* by Mr Sponge Bob of the Square Pants, have I been rustling up a little pre-pub guzzle for my life-long companion?'

'Have you?' she asked hopefully.

'No, Annie, I'm not some kind of domestic superman.'

'Oh yes you are.'

'If you go and look in the fridge you might find some of last night's stir-fry in there unless . . .'

'. . . *Owen's got to it first*,' Annie finished the train of thought.

She fussed for a moment about which shoes, then after a squirt of perfume she brushed her hair, tied it up into a not very satisfactory short ponytail and hurried downstairs.

Opening the kitchen door, she spotted her great, gangly son standing just a few feet from the fridge, fork in one hand, plate in the other, putting what looked suspiciously like a last mouthful of chicken noodles into his mouth.

'Owen!' she complained, 'was that the leftovers? Are they completely annihilated?'

He turned, looked at her with a mix of surprise and sheepish apology and said with a full mouth, 'I thought anything under cling film was fair game.'

'Oh no,' she said, opening the fridge door. 'Is there anything left in there at all?'

'Half a tub of hummus,' Owen admitted, knowing just what his mum would think of this.

'Oh hummus, fantastic . . . why don't I just chop up a celery stick and stuff my face?' she snapped.

'*Entschuldigung*,' he replied, looking properly sorry. He even patted her back with one of his big hands.

'Please stop speaking German.'

'*Aber warum?*' he asked.

'It's annoying.'

'*Nein!*'

'What are you doing tonight?'

'*Fussball*,' Owen replied.

'Your football kit, Owen, I have a lecture all ready for you about your football kit and what you should not be doing with it.'

Owen bent down and dropped a quick kiss on his mum's forehead.

'You look lovely,' he began, to deflect the lecture, 'you always look lovely.'

The compliment made her smile – but it was from Owen, a generally charming teenage boy who knew absolutely nothing about fashion.

Really, she was wearing a two-year-old blouse and a four-year-old skirt with tried and trusted shoes. She had a feeling the whole blouse and skirt thing was old anyway. She should probably be doing shorts with a pageboy jacket ... or slinking about in an edgy graphic-print tunic with jeggings. Or maybe a jumpsuit? A leather dress?

She peered at her reflection in the kettle and felt a fresh wave of worry. She was a fashion presenter on TV, must have her finger on the pulse. She was supposed to find the time to read *Vogue*, follow *Women's Wear Daily*, check out Net-A-Porter, be right at the cutting edge, accessorize like Mary Portas.

But lately, if Annie was completely honest, she had begun to feel out of touch. She didn't really (whisper it) *get* this season. She thought the colours were weird and the styles were wacky. She was beginning to suspect that her sense of style, her one true skill, was growing stale.

Chapter Two

London

Dinah dressed up:

Pink and beige floral top (New Look)
Suede button-down skirt (Red Cross charity shop)
Pink wedge sandals (Office)
Purple lace tights (John Lewis)
Faded, frayed denim jacket (Levi's)
Sparkly diamanté earrings (Claire's Accessories)
Total est. cost: £90

'Dinah, wait for me!' Annie shouted, spotting her younger sister ahead of her on the way to the wine bar.

'Hello you!'

Dinah treated her to a hug as soon as she was in range.

There were many differences between Annie and her sister: differences of opinion, of taste – differences of every kind – but they knew each other inside out, enjoyed the differences and got on brilliantly well.

Annie even employed Dinah as her twins' nanny during the week because she couldn't think of anyone who could do the job better. In fact, sometimes Annie had the sneaking suspicion that Dinah cared for the twins even better than she did.

Dinah definitely fed them better. She was the kind of saintly nanny who puréed roasted squashes with sautéed spinach and toasted pine nuts and really, Annie could never hope to keep up with that level of dedication to the job.

'Ever been to this place?' Annie asked, as they looked each other's outfits over appreciatively. 'Nice skirt – you're going to tell me it's Oxfam, aren't you?'

'Red Cross.'

Dinah never liked to spend much money on clothes, but she always dressed in a totally stylish second-handy, chain-store-meets-creative kind of way.

'No, never been here,' Dinah added, 'but it's Connor's choice, so much more flashy than our usual kind of place. You'll feel right at home, though, in your snazzy shirt. Are those interlocking

Gs? Have you been shopping at Gucci?! You are such a bad girl.'

Annie put her hand to the silky chiffon defensively and declared: 'This is *years* old. Honestly.'

'You always say that.'

'But it is. Really. Anyway, I work in television. I'm allowed to blow a teeny bit of my hard-earned money at Gucci. In fact I'm supposed to blow money at Gucci. It's probably in my contract.'

'Annie Valentine,' Dinah began in a teasing voice, 'you know perfectly well you spend just about all of your, in fact, quite modest TV wages on clothes and drive your poor husband completely crackers.'

'I don't spend anything like I used to now that I have *four* children. Anyway, are we drinking posh wine tonight or cocktails?'

'We're with Connor, so it has to be cocktails – or is he still AA? I can never keep up.'

'No, I think he gave up being an alcoholic when he left LA.'

They both stifled giggles, not because they didn't have sympathy for anyone who was genuinely battling the booze, but Connor was an absolutely diva-ish actor and no one had believed his stint in Alcoholics Anonymous had been anything other than one great big pose and networking opportunity.

'How is work?' Dinah ventured carefully, once they'd entered the bar, established with a quick sweep that Connor wasn't there yet and settled into a corner booth.

Annie leaned back against the leatherette bench and let out a heartfelt sigh.

'I'm not going to complain because I'm lucky to have a job, a well-paid and interesting job when times are so tough . . .'

'But,' Dinah prompted.

'I am working very hard – very, *very* hard. I've worked sixty hours since Saturday and it's only Wednesday.'

'I know.'

'But that's television. Once filming starts, the cost of having everyone on set is so gigantic that we just keep going and keep going till everyone drops and the rest of my life just has to wait on the sidelines until the end of the season.'

'I know,' Dinah repeated.

'Without your help and without Ed I would not be able to keep going, you do know that, don't you, my love?'

'Yes,' Dinah assured her.

'Girls! How totally fabulous to see you!'

At the sound of Connor's deep, melodious and quite famous voice, Annie and Dinah's heads weren't the only ones to turn.

The tall, ludicrously handsome, dark-haired man swept over to their table, kissed them both on the cheeks, then took a place right beside Annie. He pinched her on the bum as he sat down.

'Still chubby then?'

Only because she had known him since he was fresh out of drama college and auditioning for bit parts, was he allowed to get away with this with just a mild slap on the hand.

'Not all of us have time for two-hour sessions with our personal trainers every morning of every blinking day,' she replied.

'As if! I am so busy, darlings, I am working my fingers to the bone,' he pretended to complain, throwing off his jacket, stretching his long legs out under the table and making a not-so-subtle check of the room for smiles of recognition and any other devastatingly handsome, available men.

'Your beautifully manicured fingers, I'm sure,' Annie teased.

'Musicals are such hard work, my darlings, you have no idea. You have to eat well, sleep well, gargle with salt, go out and give your all, three hours a night, every single night. It's drudgery.'

'Ha! I think I could cope with a little West End theatre drudgery at what, ten thousand pounds per hour?' Annie chipped in.

'Is that what you think I earn? You must be having a laugh.'

'Don't you be coy with me, Connor McCabe, I know you don't get out of bed for anything less than five figures.'

'Are we having a bad day?'

'Poor Annie, she's just worked five twelve-hour days in a row,' Dinah explained.

'All the flicking through fashion collections, all the getting in and out of lovely outfits, all the time spent in hair and make-up being pampered and beautified ... you must be *exhausted*,' Connor teased. 'What are we drinking, by the way?' he asked as a waiter appeared at his elbow, face lit up with recognition of the man who'd once been a star on Sunday evening's most watched TV series.

'Champagne cocktails, life's too short for any other kind,' Annie replied.

'Agreed.'

Connor placed the order, lined up another round, then turned back to the conversation.

'It is hard work,' he agreed. 'It is so demanding to give yourself, your heart and soul to an audience one hundred per cent of the time. They want it all, they want to suck you dry. At the end of every performance I feel like a husk.'

Dinah had to gulp her drink to stop herself from laughing out loud.

'We need to shut up, Connor,' Annie decided. 'You've spent too long in luvvie-land. Lots of good people work much harder than us for a lot less, but . . . OK, I'll have just one more rant. It's the clothes! The clothes they want me to work with this season are just *impossible*!'

'Ooooh listen to you, Ms Annie Valentine,' Connor retaliated, 'you sound like one of those divas on *MasterChef* complaining about slightly soggy shitake mushrooms.'

'Shut up!' Annie warned. 'It's fashion this season. I don't get it. I can't understand anything that's in fashion right now and I can't work with any of it.'

'Soggy shitakes,' Connor repeated.

'Shitake youself. Can we be serious for one tiny moment?'

Dinah saw the concerned look on her sister's face and put down her glass.

'I really think I might be losing my touch,' Annie confessed, 'in fact, I might already have lost it. The last time I was standing next to the woman I was meant to work my magic on, I just stared and stared at all the pieces on the entire clothes rail and I couldn't see anything I liked. Not one single idea jumped out at me. That has never happened to me before. We took a break and I had to ask one of the junior assistants to help me out.'

'You were just stressed,' Connor decided. 'You

24

tensed up and you found it hard to be creative. No one can be creative when they're stressed.'

'So am I supposed to ask the director to massage my shoulders then? Or maybe my feet?' Annie snapped, *'Could I have a lovely foot massage please, then I'll feel so much more focused?'*

'There's no need to snipe.'

'I'm sorry. But I am so het up about this,' she admitted, 'If I've lost the fashion touch, the makeover magic, then I am over. Finished. And who's going to foot the mortgage-slash-school fees-slash-daughter's airfares to New York then?'

'Shhhush now,' Dinah said soothingly, the way she might to a sleep-deprived toddler, and patted Annie gently on the hand. 'This season is definitely a challenge, it reminds me of all the bad things we used to wear when we were teenagers. You're probably traumatized. I mean, lacy tunics, fingerless gloves, peachy neutrals and dayglo – there are even leg of mutton sleeves!'

'Oh God, I hate them!' Annie exclaimed.

'Exactly. You're having flashbacks to the late Eighties.'

'But how can I get over this?' she asked. 'And by tomorrow, please. In fact, we have a live event in front of an audience coming right up. I'm already having nightmares about it.'

'You probably just need to recharge your fashion

batteries,' Dinah replied. 'It's like when Jamie Oliver got fed up with food. Remember?'

'Huh?'

Annie had as many Jamie Oliver cookbooks as the next person, but she wasn't quite as devoted a fan as her sister.

'Don't you remember? He was pole-axed after his School Dinners nightmare. He was spent, half dead, didn't even want to open a tin of beans. So what did he do next?'

'I don't know, Dinah. Did he retire to his vast mansion for a spot of light gardening?' Annie asked sourly.

'No. He got into a camper van and set off for Italy because in Italy everyone loves food, everyone loves to cook, he was surrounded by passion for food and for eating and so he got his cooking mojo back again.'

'And a whole new TV series, clever man,' Connor pointed out.

'You need a break, Annie,' Dinah said. 'Maybe you need to go to Italy in a camper van and relight your passion for fashion.'

'Italy *would* be very nice,' Annie agreed, a little wistfully. 'Italy is the birthplace of style.'

She paused to consider the wealth of Italian labels: Pucci, Gucci, Armani, Fendi. Italy was the land of the leather handbag, the spiritual home of the shoe.

'But in a camper van? No,' she said firmly. 'Shudder. If I'm going to Italy then it's staying in a lovely hotel with 300-thread-count sheets and room service or nothing.'

'Well, just go to Italy,' Dinah said, making it sound so simple.

Annie gave a deep sigh: 'Dinah, sweetheart, I have another six whole weeks of twelve-hour days before the first break in the schedule. There's not one spare moment, let alone one spare penny, to take me swanning off to Italy.'

'You'll have to find your fashion mojo,' Dinah warned, 'or how will you man your show with all the required energy, enthusiasm and sparkle?'

'All my energy, enthusiasm and sparkle is going to be needed to persuade lovely Lana to give up her cushy little number in New York and come back to London to start the Retail Business course at Dagenham Technical College.'

'Oooooh,' Connor winced. 'Give up Manhattan for Dagenham? That is evil, Annie. She is going to hate you.'

'It's a really good course,' Annie protested, 'I've done the research!'

'She will *hate* you!'

27

Chapter Three

New York

'Floor 47?' the elevator attendant asked, obviously remembering that this was where Lana worked.

'Yes, thank you.'

It didn't matter that on floor 47, Lana, Elena and Gracie shared the smallest office that three people

28

could possibly squeeze into. The important thing was that the teeny tiny office was a foothold in this dizzying skyscraper right at the heart of Manhattan's famous Fifth Avenue.

It meant that fledgling fashion company, Perfect Dress, had a Fifth Avenue presence, a Fifth Avenue letterhead and that all-important, Fifth Avenue address.

In the mirrored elevator wall, Lana checked herself over discreetly. Her long, dark hair fell smoothly past her shoulders, although there was now a perky new fringe cut high above her elegantly tweezed eyebrows. She was fully made up, but in the light and glossy way of the super-groomed New York girls she was making a huge effort to copy. Lana was deeply in love with every single detail about New York. She planned to stay in this amazing city *for ever*.

Today, she was wearing a bright white blouse and a puffy above-the-knee skirt with the highest heels she could bear and sheerest tights. April was drawing to a close and it was already warm enough to go bare-legged, but no high-aiming New Yorker would risk bare legs at the office. Way too unprofessional.

Opening the door to the office, Lana saw that Svetlana's 23-year-old daughter, Elena, was already at her desk, on the phone, firing off questions in her distinctive Eastern-Europe-meets-Manhattan accent. Just like her mother, Elena was unfairly blonde and beautiful, but unlike Svetlana, she didn't exploit her looks. She always wore sober, professional outfits and pulled her golden mane into chic ponytails or grown-up chignons.

'Yes of courrrrrse . . . do you have some time to speak with our PR manager?' she asked the caller and looked at Lana with a smile.

As it was a pocket-sized company, with only three people actively involved in the day-to-day running, they all pitched in with the PR, design, product development and sales, although Elena was definitely the boss.

'All set,' Lana said, reaching for her phone.

'Well?' Elena asked once Lana's call was over, 'did she go for it?'

'Um . . . she's thinking about it,' Lana admitted, immediately worried that she hadn't given the journalist at the other end of the line enough of a dazzling sales pitch to get a Perfect Dress featured in her fashion spread.

'Please don't worry. Really, I hate that magazine,' Elena told her. 'We just move on and find some-where else. There are always new opportunities: my mother say this, I think she hear it from one of her husbands, maybe Igor.'

Lana smiled. Igor was the most famous of Svetlana's ex-husbands. He was the father of Svetlana's two boys, owned gas fields in Russia and was richer than anyone could imagine, so his nuggets of advice were usually followed.

'Oh my goodness, Gracie has been busy,' Lana exclaimed, spotting the pile of clutter strewn across the third desk in the cramped office: drawings, photos of models, photos of dresses, clippings of fabric and everything stapled, scribbled on, clipped together. A creative frenzy had obviously been going on since Lana had been in the office yesterday.

'Yes, we were here until late last night putting together the plans for the big presentation to the mothers in London. I am very serious about our new ideas,' Elena added. 'The latest sales figures came in yesterday and in New York, London, Paris and Milan we are 20 per cent down for the last two months and according to Svetlana, our new autumn/winter collection will look like this–'

Elena held up several pages of drawings and pulled a face.

Lana went over to study the sketches.

'But don't these dresses look just the same as last year's? Some are even in the same colours.'

'Exactly!' Elena exclaimed. 'They are all exactly the same as last year. We can't do this, people will laugh at us. This is an all-new old collection. But Svetlana says: "everything is classic, everything is vvvvonderrrrful." She just wants to put out the same dresses season after season. It will never work.'

'I can sort of see the point of running the black, the navy and maybe even the gold silk one again,' Lana ventured. 'You know, classic colours, very classic styles. They could probably run for a few seasons, but . . . the purple?'

Elena shook her head: 'Purple is no good for next season. Dove grey did not sell the first time round, so why would we do it again? And sea green? Sea green is finished! Our ideas are much, much better.'

For several weeks now, Elena, Lana and newest member of the team, Gracie, had been putting together ideas for a dramatically new and different Perfect Dress collection. It was about wild new colours and prints, bold shapes, and all sorts of edgy styling details.

The problem was – they hadn't told the Mothers, Svetlana and Annie, about these new ideas yet.

But Lana and Elena were about to travel to London to make a dazzling – and, they hoped, persuasive – presentation to their bosses. If they could just get the Mothers to agree, then they were sure they could turn the Perfect Dress situation around.

Lana knew what would happen if they didn't turn the situation around: she would be on a plane back to London and her exciting New York life would be over, possibly for good.

That just couldn't happen! She would not allow it. Lana would do whatever she had to do to save Perfect Dress and her New York career.

'Svetlana's boring ideas are for ladies who lunch,' Elena declared. 'This is the problem! We need a much bigger market. We need everyone who can afford lunch, not just the ladies pushing sushi round their plates. Plus, I believe that the ladies who lunch are bored with safe dresses and tasteful elegance. I think the ladies who lunch might want to be much more daring if we could just convince them.'

'Something beautifully made, but much more edgy?'

'Ya. Gracie wants studs. She thinks we should put studs round the collars of the dresses and maybe on the pockets and cuffs. Punky stud detailing.'

'Studs?!' Lana asked with her eyebrows raised: 'you want to put studs on a silk dress which costs $400? Oh my. That is . . . that is . . .'

She was thinking of presenting this idea to the Mothers and the words 'scary' and 'terrifying' came to mind.

But Elena chipped in with: 'Genius. It is a genius idea, no?'

'Do you think we can get them to agree? I mean, we have to, Elena, otherwise I'm not going to be working here any more.'

'We have to make them agree. This is our mission

in London. The Mothers must try something new and bold and exciting,' Elena said, looking very serious, 'or very soon it won't just be you leaving – our whole business could be finished.'

The sombre silence that followed these words was broken by the sound of the door opening. Gracie burst into the room, a riot of cheerfulness and colour.

'Hi!' she exclaimed, 'it's another beautiful day for fashion! Is my outfit not a triumph?'

The petite girl with the snowy skin, cropped fringe and curly orange hair held out her hands, gave a quick pirouette and turned to them both for approval.

As usual, Gracie looked amazing. Every day, from a wardrobe made up of second-hand finds, sale bargains, scraps of materials and home-sewn creations, this 19-year-old fashion whizz managed to conjure up a new, fresh and entirely original look.

Today her dainty figure was swathed in a bright green ballet cardigan, leggings, silver ballet shoes and a skirt, puffed out with netting, which looked as if it had been cleverly created from a 1950s curtain.

A pair of earrings in the style of large, boiled sweets dangled from her lobes.

'Wow!' Lana laughed, 'brilliant!'

Once again, her own attempt at a fashion-forward outfit faded into the background. But she didn't feel jealous, just in awe, because it was impossible not to love Gracie.

'Please tell me you have more of that skirt material,' Elena said. 'Maybe we can make dresses from it.'

Gracie shook her head: 'Found it in a trash can. But what's to stop us creating a totally awesome pattern inspired by it?'

Her eyes flashed with enthusiasm. She darted over to her desk, set down her shiny tote bag and pulled out her notebook, a fuzzy blue pencil case, scraps of paper, magazine snippings, then a foil package which Lana knew would be a wheat-free bagel filled with tofu and vegetables.

'Have you heard of Parker Bain?' Gracie asked, opening her notebook and unzipping the pencil case.

Elena and Lana shook their heads.

'He is uh-mazing,' Gracie said, closing her eyes and stretching her fingers wide to make the point. 'He's this totally cool graphic artist, young, like ... fresh out of college, but his work is so strong, so distinctive that he's already got magazine commissions and I was thinking maybe we could ask him to design some fabrics for us.'

'Our own fabrics?' Elena asked. 'This will be too expensive, no?'

'I don't know, I thought if we kept to one or two

colours, found a small factory . . . I guess I wanted to ask him for ideas. Then we get costings and see what might be possible. I mean: our own patterns – that would be really something. Get us talked about, get us noticed. And Parker Bain, he's on the radar, he's the really cool, edgy, out there kinda guy we could team up with to make a splash.'

Elena's eyebrows were raised, she was obviously considering the idea.

'Sounds cool,' Lana agreed.

'I hope you don't mind,' Gracie went on, 'but I've kind of asked him to come up and see us. Like . . . this morning . . . like in fact kind of . . . now.'

'Now?' Elena frowned.

'I checked your diary and knew you didn't have anything scheduled till 9.30. Plus, I just think you're going to love him. He's seriously cool and more than a little bit handsome.'

Lana gave a snort.

Elena looked stern: 'This is why you want him to work with us?'

'No!' Gracie protested, 'I love this company, I would only suggest someone if I thought they were fabulous.'

'OK, OK, we will speak to Mr Bain for a few minutes,' Elena agreed then turned back to her computer screen.

After that, everyone was busy. Lana and Elena

made fresh calls, Gracie began a new sketch, colouring in energetically, then the intercom buzzed and Gracie jumped up from her chair to answer.

'Whoa, this is cosy!' Parker Bain stepped into the office then manoeuvred himself and his bag into the only available space in between the three desks.

Elena smiled, Gracie grinned and Lana found herself looking hard at Parker Bain and agreeing completely with Gracie that he was more than a little bit handsome.

Parker was tall and thin with long arms and legs. His black jeans and dark striped shirt were tight, making him look even longer and thinner. He was that heady cocktail of both cute and cool.

His hair was inky black and just the right mix of short but tousled, and his skin was a soft, light olive. He had a beautiful mouth, beautiful hands with long fingers. Even the battered leather bag slung over his shoulder was the kind of bag that looked vintage and just right – as if it had been taken up mountains and lashed with rain.

'Hi, I'm Parker, by the way,' he said in a husky voice, 'Gracie asked me to come over because you might like to talk about designs . . . which is totally great, by the way. I love fabric designs. I am all about fabric designs.'

As he reached over to shake her hand, Lana tried to remember that she had just ended a bad relationship with a cool cat New York guy and had promised herself time to get over it, but it wasn't much use. As Parker's eyes met hers, she felt the undeniable sizzle of attraction.

Here was yet another reason why she *had* to stay in New York.

Chapter Four

London

Lana shopping with Mother:

Red silk jumpsuit (Banana Republic sale)
Cropped white leather jacket (on loan from Elena)
Orange peep-toed heels (Primark)
Skull pendant (last bad boyfriend)
White plastic sunglasses (Topshop)
Severely cropped fringe (did-it-herself)
Total est. cost: £105

'No – not working.'

Lana's hand shot out from behind the pink velvet curtain holding an exquisite silver satin dress.

'I don't like these either,' she added as a pair of lacy lilac leggings appeared over the top of the curtain.

'OK. Right, well, I'll see what else I can find,' Annie said, her enthusiasm wilting. It felt as if Lana had already tried on every outfit in the entire shop and she still wasn't happy.

And in The Store too! Did Lana really have to have a great big, stroppy, fashion identity crisis right in the middle of the achingly chic department store where Annie had worked as a personal shopper for years?

Less than an hour ago, Annie had swept in through the doors of The Store in a blaze of glory. She'd greeted, smiled and air-kissed her way through the perfume hall and handbag department and all the way up to the second floor.

'Hello! How are you doing, sweetheart?'

'Back to see us again, superstar!'

'Oooh look at your girl, she's so grown up and gorgeous.'

It had been music to Annie's ears. She loved to come back to The Store and she'd so looked forward to bringing Lana here. Annie had been waiting for this day for weeks. To be in The Store, shopping with Lana, who'd come all the way over from New York and was looking so fashion and so totally grown up. It was supposed to be a perfect day.

Once upon a time, Annie had been The Store's number one personal shopper, who had guided customers through this elegant white and glass slice of fashionista heaven teaching them Miu Miu from Moschino and Calvin from Cavalli. Her client list had ranged from Persian princesses who lived for Chanel to new mums in search of the outfit which could lift them from frazzle to dazzle.

Now that her day job involved doing client makeovers on TV, she still held to the belief that everyone deserves to dress beautifully because a gorgeous outfit makes life just that little bit better.

She'd helped so many people find their dream outfit, their brand new look, their 'wow is that really me in the mirror?' moment, so why could she not work her magic on her own lovely daughter?

'What are you ideally looking for?' Annie ventured.

'I need a jacket, for summer,' Lana replied, 'something cool but girlie, just not too . . . you know?'

'Right.'

Annie squared her shoulders and took a calming breath. She was prepared to go out there on to the shop floor once again to search high and low for exactly the right jacket. But she felt well and truly despondent now. In all honesty, she was out of tune with Lana's new look.

Two days ago, Lana had burst through the arrivals gate at Gatwick airport looking as if she'd got five years older in the space of three months. She was thinner, taller, paler. The slightly gothy teenage thing had gone, to be replaced with something much more angular.

Annie would once have known exactly what to buy Lana: jeans, trainers, chiffon blouses, ruffled miniskirts and distressed leathers. Darkest hair and kohl-rimmed eyes, those had completed the Lana vibe.

But the glamorous girl who'd rushed up to her, arms wide, at Gatwick . . . well, Annie had done a double-take. This girl had caramel streaks through her hair, a severely short fringe, pale make-up, heels, a pencil skirt and a Markus Lupfer sweater with a giant pair of glossy lips embellished across the front.

'Wow!' Annie had breathed, slightly shocked. 'You're stunning!'

Now, she toured round the rails in search of something she hadn't brought in to Lana yet. Marc by Marc Jacobs? Maybe there was something for the new Lana here? She began to look, but the colours . . . the cuts . . . she couldn't blame Mr Jacobs, it was everywhere she had searched today.

Things weren't right this season. There was a sludginess, a bagginess . . . dirty pink baggy tops tucked into teeny grey shorts, saggy trousers with narrow cuffs, manly leather ties, weird jangly bangles, checked pork pie hats. It all felt off.

'So what did she think of the silver satin?' Paula,

a former colleague of Annie's, appeared on the other side of the Stella McCartney concession.

'It wasn't her thing. To be honest, I'm not quite sure what her thing is. She wants a summer jacket, but nothing I've brought her has been right.'

'What about . . . Come over here and tell me what you think of this? I mean I LOVE. I've got one in cerise.'

Paula beckoned Annie to a rail where silky blazers were hanging in a variety of bold colours: dark pink, cobalt blue, black and white.

'Ooooh,' Annie agreed, 'very New York.'

'Yeah – wear during the day then bling up for evening. You don't even need to go home and change.'

'The blue,' Annie said, without hesitation. Her daughter's eyes were a startling, forget-me-not blue and in cobalt silk her eyes and her pale skin, would look amazing.

'I've found this,' Annie told the velvet curtain back in the changing suite. 'It's fabulous and I think you're going to love it.'

'Good, because this is hopeless.'

Lana stepped out of the changing room in the strange, pale green, wispy dress she'd insisted on trying on even though Annie had told her it wasn't her colour.

'No,' Annie agreed, 'I mean, it's nice, but you could be so much lovelier.'

Lana scowled, as if she wasn't convinced.

'Maybe I should be wearing the Perfect Dress collection at all times,' she said. 'I'm guessing you've seen the latest sales figures?'

'Yes, I've seen the figures,' Annie told her daughter cautiously, 'but Svetlana says we shouldn't get too het up, because it's a difficult time. Sales of everything are down. Even toilet paper. I wish I didn't know that fact but it's lodged in my brain and I can't get rid of it.'

'Yes, but we've had a nearly 20 per cent fall,' Lana countered, 'Spring/Summer is down nearly 20 per cent on last year's Autumn/Winter. That is huge. If we take another drop like that, end of story. The next collection will have to pull something incredible out of the bag – which is what Elena and I are going to talk to you about when we have the meeting.'

'You know Svetlana's feelings: stay classic and stay true to the original idea, a really wearable elegant dress that works for day and night,' Annie said. 'Classic and elegant. Those are her watchwords, darlin'.'

Lana scowled again.

'Classic and elegant didn't work last season. There's no guarantee it will work next time.'

'Women always want classic and elegant,' Annie

protested. 'That's why the label began: to fill a gap in the market. It's all about the timeless, wear-anywhere, any-time dress: a classic.'

'Well, even classics need updating, I bet the Yves Saint Laurent tuxedo gets tweaked every season.'

'Tweaked maybe, completely changed and revised, never. But Lana . . . you know you have to come home in the summer, no matter what happens with Perfect Dress.'

Annie hadn't exactly wanted to have this conversation right now, but here it was, raising its awkward head.

'Am I?' Lana asked, eyes flashing. 'You can't make me.'

'You're too young to give up studying. There's this course I wanted to tell you about, I think it'll give you a perfect grounding in the fashion business.'

'What? And working for a fashion label won't?' Lana protested. 'Where is this course?'

'Look, I don't want to get into all the details now, this isn't the right place to—'

'Where?' Lana repeated, her eyes narrowing.

'Dagenham Tech—'

Annie wasn't allowed to finish the sentence.

'WHAT! Dagenham? I've never been to Dagenham and I've no intention of ever going!'

'Oh be quiet, Lana, I'm sure there are lots of nice

things about Dagenham . . . and anyway, the course is perfect. No other college has anything like it: retail fashion and business – it's totally suited to you.'

'Mum! Who, just who in their right mind would give up a job in New York for a course in Dagenham? No one!' Lana stormed, hands on her hips, 'Not one single person on the face of the planet. This is my life, Mum, can you please stop trying to completely ruin it?'

'Lana!' Annie felt properly rattled now, 'how can you say that? I would never try to ruin your life, I'm just trying to help. Look, we are not going to talk about this now.'

She glanced around the changing rooms, but apart from Paula, there was thankfully no one else within earshot.

'Not going to Dagenham,' Lana said firmly, 'not ever. Right, let's see this jacket you've found for me then.'

It sounded like a challenge.

Annie had been hiding the cobalt blue with its silky sleeves and shiny gold zips out of sight, but now she brought it forward with a flourish.

'Da-nah! Isn't that adorable?' she enthused, trying to lighten the mood, 'The perfect shade of blue for you and your beautiful eyes.'

'Muuuuuuum!'

Lana's brows scrunched together in a frown: 'That

is hideous! Even some disco diva from the 1970s would think that was totally lame!'

Oh.

Annie tried to swallow her disappointment.

'Mum, what is going on with you? You always had such amazing taste.'

Annie didn't like the sound of this. There was a nasty, critical feeling in the air. Lana had one hand on her hip and a look on her face.

'You used to have such brilliant style,' Lana went on.

Used to? Annie's stomach clenched.

'And you were really arty and creative and just had a knack for putting things together . . .'

'Oh!' Annie couldn't help gasping out loud.

'What is going on? You just don't look as together as you used to.'

The concern in Lana's voice, mixed in with the criticism, made Annie really upset. She held her breath. This was horrible. Why was Lana doing this? Well, that was obvious: because Annie was pulling the plug on New York and bringing her daughter home.

'Maybe you need a change of scene, Mum. Maybe I'm the one who should be making you over.'

'Just get changed,' Annie snapped and swished the curtain closed on her daughter.

'Fine!'

Rooted to the spot, her pride seriously dented,

Annie felt a lump in her throat and drew her lips tight into an unhappy line. She turned to Paula, who was trying to back tactfully out of the changing area, and shrugged helplessly.

Paula gave her a sympathetic smile and Annie felt her lump grow even bigger.

'It's a tricky age,' Paula whispered. 'What about knitted shorts? We have some Missoni, they are going down a storm?'

'I don't know,' Annie whispered. So Paula came over and put one of her endlessly long arms over Annie's shoulder.

'A tricky age,' Annie repeated and swallowed.

Paula walked Annie away from the pink velvet curtain and added, 'I know I was a complete nightmare for my mum when I was her age.'

'Right . . .'

Annie wasn't sure if this was helping. She looked up and caught her reflection in the huge mirror in the heart of The Store's changing suite. She'd stood here so many times in the past admiring, tweaking and perfecting the lovely new outfits she'd cooked up for her thousands of happy customers.

It didn't exactly help that Annie was standing next to Paula – a six-foot-plus, stunning, black girl with the figure of an Olympic athlete. It was hard to stand in front of a mirror next to a woman like that and not look yourself over critically.

Two years since the twins had been born and Annie was still considerably chunkier than she would have liked. Her blonde hair was at the unfortunate stage of growing out from short and she'd bundled it into a stubby ponytail at the back of her head, which looked OK from the front, but – *help* – comical from sideways on.

Her skirt, top and shoes were . . . well, nice, nice enough, but they didn't scream *fashion, happening, style setter, follow my lead!* the way she would really like them to.

'Let's face it, Paula,' she wailed, 'I thought it was fashion that was off this season, but maybe it's me.'

Chapter Five

London

Ebeny is fashion:

Creamy chiffon and lace blouse (D&G sale)
Navy-blue velvet waistcoat (Camden market)
Teeny denim cut-off shorts (Levi's)
Tights with skull print (Leg Avenue)
Rubber-heeled purple boots (Camper)
Enamelled flower necklace (New Look)
Total est. cost: £210

Annie peered out from backstage, took a deep breath and let it out slowly. The live fashion event, in front of an audience of 5,000 and cameras, was almost over – just one more item to go.

So far, she thought it had gone well. There had

been a high street fashion show, with glammed-up models rocking the latest chain store looks. Then armed with a table full of samples, she had talked everyone through the latest lingerie fashions.

Two teenagers had been let loose on a rail of clothes from Primark and now, as the final event, Annie was to do 'the Ultimate Fashionista makeover' live on an audience member.

'Ready to go back out there?'

At her elbow was Tamsin, the show's producer, her ultimate boss and the woman who had made Annie the minor TV star she was today. Annie smiled as confidently as she could.

'Live events wreck my nerves, darlin', I'll be sinking at least one bottle of fizz as soon as this is over.'

'You're great out there. Stop worrying.'

'Do you think? I get the feeling the audience isn't really livening up today.'

'You're doing fine,' Tamsin assured her. 'All set?'

Annie nodded, but she felt her pores open despite the thick blanket of powder on her face and layers of antiperspirant all over her body. If all those people who longed to be on TV knew how nerve-churningly awful it could be, maybe they would reconsider.

The music started up and, big smile set on her face, she walked out on to the set again.

'Hello! Welcome back to my favourite part of the

show: the Ultimate Fashionista makeover. Darlings, right behind me is a rail of the most fabulous clothes: silks, satins, cashmeres, labels to die for, prices that would kill you! But one lucky person here today is going to be dressed from head to toe in the ultimate outfit. Ready to play an elimination game so we can find our lucky winner?'

There was loud applause.

'Ladies, hands up if you are a size 12.'

Annie looked out across the raised hands. Somewhere in the audience, she knew, Lana and Elena were watching but she hadn't been able to locate them.

'Keep your hands up if you're over thirty-two but under thirty-seven.'

The number of hands halved.

'Keep your hands up if you're blonde.'

Again, the number lowered.

'Keep your hands up if you have children ... if you're wearing something blue ... if your name begins with any letter in the alphabet that comes after h.'

There was only a scattering of hands left now.

'OK ... only keep your hands up if you're not wearing heels.'

A pause. The audience looked around and began to clap: only one hand was left in the air.

'And we have our winner! Come on down!'

As the audience clapped and whooped, the winner stood up, picked her way through the crowd, heading towards the stage. Blushing frantically, she was hooked up with a microphone.

Several minutes later, Nancy from the audience was standing right beside Annie, panting with nerves and looking as if she might cry.

Annie immediately put a calming hand on her arm: 'Well done, you're going to be fantastic ... deep breaths, inner calm,' she whispered, away from her mic.

As Nancy answered a handful of questions about herself, Annie sized her up and tried to think through the items on the designer rail. Nancy was obviously not a fashionista; in fact, some might even describe her as a little frumpy, but she was not the worst case Annie had seen. Not that Annie ever really thought of anyone she helped as a case. To her they were all clients in need of personal attention and helpful coaxing.

Nancy was somewhat solid looking with a terrible frizzy blonde bleach job and a tendency to blush deepest red. But Annie was looking for the good points: delicate skin, a chiselled nose and rose-bud mouth, plus the kind of muscular behind that Beyoncé would be proud to shake, and eyes intriguingly between blue and green.

Lots of cooling colours, Annie was thinking:

soothing blues, gentle greens, cool greys. With a stream of friendly questions, Annie chatted to Nancy, then led her over to the clothes rail as the cameras closed in on their faces.

'I know it's hard, but try to pretend that the cameras aren't here,' Annie whispered. 'Just smile and relax.'

Nancy's face tensed up into a tight-lipped grimace as they began to look through the selection together.

'Now, what gorgeous things have we got here, Nancy, my lovely?' she said, trying to sound bright and breezy. 'And everything is your size, so don't be shy. If you see something you like, jump on in.'

But as Annie's hand moved efficiently through the items, there was bright red, orange-red, pink, yellow, here was hot pink and more bright pink . . .

Ebeny, the stylist who'd helped Annie to make the clothes selection was standing by proudly. She was grinning from ear to ear looking delighted with herself, in her teeny cut-off denim shorts with some complicated blouse and waistcoat thing going on.

Fashion, high fashion: that was what Annie wanted. She and Ebeny had picked all the most cutting-edge items from the most cutting-edge designers. But now, Annie went through the rack again. Nancy was looking at Annie for inspiration and Annie felt the stirrings of panic. Would anything here work for Nancy?

Lana's words at The Store came ringing back into Annie's mind: 'You always *had* such amazing taste . . . You *used* to have such brilliant style . . .'

Annie could feel the sweat breaking through. Her hands searched the rails: a fuchsia-pink silky blouse by Preen, a golden metallic jacket, kaftans spun from heavy satin – how was any of this going to work for Nancy?

Nancy was wearing jeans by M&S, a faded black cotton cardi and clutching at a handbag that was frayed at the edges with use. She was a lovely, mumsy person who needed a trip round John Lewis, not a Haute Hippie maxi-dress.

Amazing taste . . . brilliant style . . .

Still Lana's words were haunting her. Fashion. Annie was supposed to know all about fashion. This was the ultimate fashionista makeover. C'mon!!

'Right.' Annie began to make her choice – a sea-green metallic blazer, a multi-coloured silky top, vertiginous heels and the woven, cashmere Missoni shorts which Paula had promised were going down a storm . . . and which probably alone cost £800.

'OK – let's get to the changing room and see how quickly we can turn you into a runway sensation.'

There was clapping, the music started up again and Annie guided Nancy from the stage.

They were only meant to take a few minutes, so before Nancy knew what had hit her, her clothes were off and thousands of pounds' worth of silk, cashmere, satin and suede were slipped, wrapped, pulled and buckled on to her unsuspecting frame.

Hair and Make-up dived down on her in a frenzy of blusher, hairspray, gloss, tweezers and mascara.

Then Nancy was up on her feet, suddenly six foot tall and impossibly wobbly in sand-coloured sandals with skyscraper heels.

The skin of her legs was so white between the sandals and the cashmere shorts that Annie could only think: tights! We need tights! But there was no time. The entry music was already playing. The audience had begun to slow-clap with anticipation.

Nancy looked . . . Nancy looked . . .

The metallic blazer was stunning, it gleamed blue-green like a bluebottle. The silky top and the cashmere shorts . . . well, not one of the happiest pairings, Annie had to admit. But too late to change anything now.

And wasn't this fashionable clashing? Wasn't everything meant to clash and mismatch? She kept seeing combos on the catwalk that she wouldn't have dreamed of making. This was now. Annie could hit her fashion stride again. She just had to be bold.

The jacket gaped because Nancy had a much

more generous bosom than was ever seen on the catwalk. Her cheeks were deeply rouged and her hair was now in spiky points instead of frizz.

'All set?' Annie asked, big smile in place.

'I haven't seen myself,' Nancy protested.

'You look amazing!' Annie assured her.

'Yeah ... ummm ... wild!' Ebeny seemed to agree.

'Are you sure?' the make-up girl asked.

'I can't walk,' Nancy protested.

'Take my hand, I'll lead you in.'

To the beat of the music, Annie and Nancy strode on to the set. For a moment or two, the clapping sped up, but as they made it to the front of the stage the claps trickled off and were replaced with a ripple and then a wave, a loud, crashing wave of laughter.

What?!

Heat burning her cheeks, Annie's smile froze. And just at that moment she spotted Lana in the audience; her daughter's face the picture of shock.

Annie turned to look at Nancy and of course, clear as day, scales falling from her eyes, she could see that Nancy didn't look good: she didn't scream fashion or channel cool, Nancy looked utterly, unmistakably *ridiculous*! And even worse – she had begun to cry.

Chapter Six

London

Svetlana at home:

Yellow python-print blouse (Chloé)
Cream woollen trousers (Yves Saint Laurent)
Cork and leather high heeled wedges (Jimmy Choo)
Double four-carat solitaire ring (first husband)
Solid gold and ruby rope necklace (richest ex-husband)
Total est. cost: £42,000

'So then what happened?'

'Well, we got off the stage as quickly as we could,' Annie admitted, the horror of the event hideously fresh in her mind, 'I apologized to everyone for making such a complete balls-up, then I went and hid in my dressing room ... and cried. Finally, my boss, Tamsin came in and told me I was to take a week's holiday. Starting immediately.'

'This is not good,' Svetlana said, shaking her immaculately coiffed head. 'Not good.'

'It wasn't so bad. Tamsin promised me I wasn't sacked and I wasn't in trouble. She said I was just overworked and in need of a break. She's very professional, but she's human. She pointed out that the show's ratings are good, they just need me to get back on form.'

As she waited for Svetlana's words of wisdom, Annie let her eyes wander around the splendour of the room. She was perched on a priceless mahogany chair in the exquisite 'salon' of Svetlana's four-storey Mayfair home, aka: the divorce settlement.

Hanging from the silk-lined walls were pieces of art that Annie recognized as important, gallery-worthy and unimaginably expensive. Those hand-embroidered curtains alone must have cost up in the five figures.

But despite the vast difference in wealth, Annie no longer found it difficult to think of Svetlana as a friend. They had begun their relationship as personal shopper and favourite client but after several adventures, shared business interests, plus young daughters who worked together, their friendship had been firmly cemented.

Svetlana was also seated on a spindly, but nonetheless antique and hand-crafted chair. Annie glanced at her beautiful pale, high-cheekboned face. The Ukrainian face and figure, which had made Svetlana her fortune, were impressive. Svetlana admitted to forty-ish, looked not one day over 33, but Annie suspected she must be more than 45 by now.

The surgically enhanced cleavage and flat stomach were tucked into tight, bright Chloé and Saint Laurent. Svetlana's luscious blonde hair was teased, tousled and piled into a Brigitte Bardot style half beehive and the nipped skin was taut all around her jawline.

'Tschaaaaaaaa!' Svetlana said at last, her favourite expression of exasperation, 'I need to think how I can help you, but now we have to go to the sitting room upstairs and watch this presentation our daughters want to make for us.'

Twenty-five minutes later, Annie was sitting in the first floor drawing room listening to the sound of Svetlana's manicured nails being tap, tap, tapped impatiently against a mahogany armrest.

This was her clue that Elena and Lana, standing in front of them with expectant, impassioned looks on their faces, had not made their PowerPoint case entirely convincingly.

Svetlana and Annie had watched as image after image flashed up on the screen. They'd seen the charts, which showed that sales of Perfect Dresses were going down in all the major fashion capitals.

They'd seen images of all the designs, which Svetlana had approved for the new season. Then Lana had shown them drawings, photographs and mocked-up toiles of the new direction they were hoping to take.

With fascination, Annie had seen the ideas unfold: red leather, stud detailing, colour clashes, colour blocking, ruched hemming, mismatched buttoning . . . it was so different from Svetlana's first pure and simple idea of a dress company which made elegant, feminine shirt-dresses that could be worn day to evening.

It was obvious that their daughters cared deeply about the new ideas.

'If we don't change direction, we won't have a business in another year,' Elena said firmly, looking from Svetlana to Annie.

Svetlana said nothing, she just continued with the fingernail tapping.

Elena turned to Annie: 'What do you think about our new ideas?'

Annie squirmed on her Chippendale. She didn't want to speak first. Yes, she was a partner in this business, but she was a small partner. Svetlana was the one who'd put up most of the money.

'This is mainly Svetlana's company,' Annie said gently. 'I think it's important to know what she has to say first.'

Elena and Lana's eyes immediately turned towards Svetlana.

'I've already been talking to buyers about these ideas and they really are interested,' Elena added, her voice a mixture of impatience and pleading.

There was an agonizingly long pause.

Annie watched the drumming fingernails and found herself trying to place the blood-red shade of varnish. Chanel, surely? Svetlana would only use Chanel polish – or was she more of a Dior woman?

'Elena . . . and Lana.'

Svetlana's deep voice finally broke the silence. Everyone straightened to attention with the feeling that this was going to be important.

'When I start Perfect Dress, I have a simple plaaaan,' Svetlana said, in the melodious accent which many years in London had only mellowed slightly: 'elegant dresses in beautiful fabric which an elegant woman can wear anywhere. Day or night.'

Elena was nodding, almost too hard.

'Elegant and simple. No giiiimicks. I did not want one thing this season, one thing the next. I wanted black, navy blue and other true colours in wool jersey, silk jersey, taffeta. It was a simple idea: quality at a price above the high street, but below designer label. This is my simple idea. And now that we have had one season of slow sales, you are in panic and you want to *ruin* my business.'

Oh, that sounded harsh. Annie could feel her stomach clench with the tension building in the room.

'We would still run a line of the classic Perfect Dresses,' Elena protested, 'but we need fun, fashion and young ideas here or it will not work.'

'One season, Elena. We already have three very successful seasons behind us,' Svetlana went on, 'we have one not so good season and you are in a panic. If you change now, just as we start to get a name, you will ruin everything.'

'I am not going to ruin this label!' Elena countered, eyes flashing. '*You're* going to ruin it. Nothing in fashion stands still. You can't make the same thing year after year and hope people will keep on buying. It's impossible!'

'You are being impossible!' Svetlana fired back. 'Just stick with my plan and it will work. I know how much my friends love these dresses. Some of them will not wear anything else.'

'Oh yes, your friends. Well as long as we have your friends buying our dresses we will all be fine, won't we!' Elena snapped.

Annie cleared her throat. She didn't know exactly what to say, but she would have to intervene before this got too personal and ugly.

'My lovely girls,' she began brightly, 'you are both so clever and so talented, you don't need to fight about this. Fighting is not going to help us to move forward.'

As Svetlana and Elena turned their angry faces towards her, Annie found herself looking into two sets of identical glaring grey-green eyes and felt unsure of her next move.

'What do you think, Annah?' Svetlana asked. 'You have worked in fashion for a long time, we could not have started this business without your help . . . so what do you think?'

'Yeah, Mum, can't you see we've got some great ideas here?' Lana asked.

Annie knew her input was important, but the problem was, she just couldn't decide. She'd been feeling so 'off' lately: in the changing room with Lana – then at that terrible, haunting live event.

She couldn't decide. She honestly didn't know. Some of the ideas looked exciting and radical, but should the label stick with simple and elegant or go for a much more fashion look? She had no idea.

Annie's internal fashion radar, the one that had bleeped *Yes, it's a hit* or *No, disaster, steer clear!* and guided all her choices was out of service. It wasn't sending out any message at all. The battery was flat. Or the mechanism had stopped working altogether. Maybe her life in fashion was over. Help!

Diplomatically, she began: 'I like lots of your new ideas.'

She saw Lana's shoulders sag. Obviously, Annie's tone of voice had given her away. She did like the ideas, but she couldn't leap on them, get excited about them. They didn't convince her enough.

'But like me, you think we stay with our original formula,' Svetlana finished the sentence brusquely.

'She didn't say that!' Elena protested.

'Muuum, come on. We know what will sell in New York better than you do!' Lana insisted.

'I don't know,' Annie admitted.

'If Annah is not convinced, it will be very hard to convince someone else,' said Svetlana with an air of finality.

'Maybe we need to try one more season with the originals and if we really don't feel it's working—' Annie began.

'Too late. You will be too late!' Elena exclaimed. 'Someone else will produce dresses which fill this gap in the market and the opportunity will be gone. This is our one chance to jump in. If I could just make you see it!'

She gave a little shriek of frustration. Snapping her laptop shut, she marched out of the room.

Svetlana called after her in Ukrainian.

Elena shouted something back in their mother tongue, which sounded very angry.

'Tschaaaaaah!' Svetlana vented her annoyance.

'I can't believe you, Mum!' Lana exclaimed, 'How

many more fashion disasters do you have to have before you realize you're wrong? I mean that TV event – that was terrible! You're stale and if you don't watch out, you're going to be over!'

'Lana . . .' Annie warned. But she had the feeling she was too late. This was not her little girl any more; a grown-up, self-possessed adult was standing opposite her, demanding the right to be taken seriously and treated equally.

'No. You don't get it,' Lana stormed on, 'I'm not coming back to London. We're not just going to let this dress company die. I will not come back to do some stupid course in stupid Dagenham. I'm going home! To Manhattan!'

'Ah! They will come to see that we are right,' Svetlana promised. 'Children always want to run before they can walk. They want to rush out a line for the summer. Impossible! It is already May. If you rush something like this, you always make big mistakes.'

She took a sip from her crystal flute of champagne and insisted that Annie do the same.

'No running after your daughter, Annah, you are too much a – what-is-it? Mother hen. Even if she runs all the way to New York, stay strong, in the end she will run back to you.'

'Do you think so?' Annie asked, totally upset by

the big row. 'Elena too? Do you think she will come running back?'

'I know so.'

There was a discreet tap at the door.

'Come in Maria,' Svetlana replied.

Annie couldn't help giving a tiny sigh of envy. Svetlana had domestic staff. There was Maria, the stalwart Filipino maid who cooked, cleaned and looked after the boys when they weren't in school. There was also a part-time tutor and a part-time chauffeur and a gardening service.

No rushing round throwing together ready meals at 7 p.m. after a hard day's work for Svetlana. Annie knew her friend arranged herself elegantly in her drawing room, sipped at a cocktail and waited for Maria to announce the evening's menu.

'Miss Wisneski?' Maria asked, standing in the doorway, smoothing down the front of her blue and white striped work dress anxiously.

'Yes? Has the tennis coach arrived for the boys?' Svetlana asked.

'Yes. But he has forgotten the password.'

Just the tiniest of creases at the side of Svetlana's eyes gave away the fact that she was frowning.

'Do you know the tennis coach? Do you recognize him?'

'Yes,' Maria replied, 'I'm sure it is him. But maybe the boys can look out of the window here and check.'

'Maria, you worry too much,' Svetlana said, but nodded. Her two young sons, Michael and Petrov, walked into the room immaculately dressed in full tennis whites, carrying their rackets.

'Hello boys,' Annie said with a smile as they walked past. They were beautiful children with Svetlana's fine features, length of limb and their father's shiny black hair and dark eyes. Always so sombre and well behaved. And how did Maria keep them so neat? Annie wasn't sure if she'd ever heard either of them so much as giggle.

'Hello, Miss Anna,' Petrov, the younger boy replied with a smile which seemed more polite than sunny.

'Hello, how are you?'

'Very well thank you,' he replied with a curt nod of his head.

'Say hello, Michael,' Svetlana ordered.

'Good morning, Miss Anna,' he said, complying. 'That is Yann,' he confirmed as he approached the window, 'so we're not about to be kidnapped, Maria, we are in fact going to play tennis. Boring.'

'Michael, you can be very ungrateful,' Svetlana complained.

Michael just shrugged, turned and followed Maria and his brother out of the room.

'Bye-bye, Mama,' Petrov said and blew his mother a kiss from the door.

'So what's that all about?' Annie asked when she was once again alone with Svetlana. 'Are they really in danger of being kidnapped?

'Very rich children are always a target, but my number one problem is that Igor wants the boys to go to military academy in Russia,' Svetlana replied, her voice dark.

'Oh no.'

Annie knew this meant trouble. Igor, Svetlana's most recent ex-husband, was by far the richest, most powerful and most terrifying of her exes. Plus Michael and Petrov were the sons and heirs to Igor's vast fortune. Igor had tried to take the boys out of the country before and if he now wanted them to go to school in Russia, he would do all he could to make this happen.

'St Petersburg,' Svetlana added. 'Igor wants the boys to go to the military academy there like he did. Pah!' she spat the word out forcefully. 'Turn them into vicious robots just like him.'

'What are you going to do?'

'I will stop him,' Svetlana said simply. 'I am taking Harry's advice and we are being careful.'

'Thank goodness for Harry,' Annie said. She didn't just know Svetlana's calm and sensible English husband well; she had introduced them to each other. Svetlana had been in need of London's best divorce lawyer and via a high-powered client at

The Store, Annie had managed to get hold of him.

Suddenly Mayfair mansions, Chippendale chairs and maids didn't look quite so appealing to Annie if it went hand in hand with kidnap threats and tennis coaches who had to use passwords.

'Anyway, enough about my little problems,' Svetlana said. 'Come upstairs, come to my dressing room, I want to show you some of the clothes I am thinking of buying for the new season.'

In the pale blue dressing room, home to snowy white, ornately carved wardrobes and a vast, glittering chandelier, Annie tried to look with knowledge and appreciation through the clothes which had been brought here on approval by the swankiest boutiques in London. But faced with another row of mini tunics and a putty green double-breasted blazer, Annie finally had to blurt out: 'I don't understand it any more.'

'What?' Svetlana demanded.

'Fashion!' Annie blurted out.

Svetlana turned cool eyes on her.

'But Annah, fashion is your business, fashion is how you make your money. You need to understand fashion every single hour of the day. You need to know. You need to be way ahead of the rest of us.'

'I know it's urgent, it's completely critical, my love,' Annie exclaimed, 'but right now ... I just don't get it. I honestly can't see. I'm looking at

70

shoulder pads and lacy inserts and I just feel burnt out, I don't know where to begin.'

'Annah you have been working too hard,' Svetlana warned her. 'How can you be full of good ideas when you are working so hard for everyone? Filming all day long, looking after your family, helping me with my business – you are working too much.

'In your week off, you must go away for a proper holiday,' Svetlana insisted. 'If you've lost your feeling for fashion then it is the most important thing to rest completely, Annah, or you will lose your job. The television people will find another presenter. I will find another advisor for Perfect Dress. If you are not in fashion, if you are not *au courant* then you are not in work.'

'Oh for goodness' sake, I know that!' Annie snapped. 'Don't you think I'm completely stressed out knowing I could lose everything? How can I go away on holiday in that frame of mind? How am I supposed to relax for one second?'

Svetlana shook her head, wagged a finger at Annie and gave a knowing smile. 'But this is exactly why you need to get away. As soon as you rest, all will come flooding back. Your powers will return. This is how it works.'

Svetlana turned to the full-length Louis XIV mirror at the end of the room, checked her reflection and tucked a stray strand of hair behind her ear.

'How many high-powered, all-important rich men have I been married to?' she asked.

Annie couldn't quite remember . . . Was Harry her fifth husband? Or her sixth?

'I drag them from their business life, kicking and screaming in protest – then two days in a penthouse suite in Monaco and their perspective returns, four days in penthouse suite in Monaco and they are once again ready to conquer the world. I was very good wife,' she added thoughtfully, 'but it was never appreciated. I was always traded in for younger model.'

'You are a good wife,' Annie reminded her, 'and Harry will never trade you in.'

'No. Harry is a different kind of man. Just good, honest, hard-working millionaire. But I can afford to be married to a nice man now.'

Annie couldn't help smiling.

'You need a proper holiday,' Svetlana repeated, 'so this Friday we fly to Milano, fashion capital of the world, and we make a five-day visit to a spa hotel so expensive even I can only go there once a year. OK? So you need to go home and pack.'

Chapter Seven

London

Night-time Annie:

Men's striped nightshirt (Bonsoir – bought for Ed years ago)
Thick layer of anti-ageing serum (Estée Lauder)
Towel on head (M&S)
Chipped pink toenail polish (Mac)
Total est. cost: £130

'New moves ... I think I was promised some new moves.'

Annie stopped towelling her damp hair and looked over at her husband who was lying in bed with a smile that could only be described as expectant.

'Let me see,' she began, 'I've been ordered off the set by my boss, I've driven my daughter back to

New York in a fury and you happen to think now is a good time to mention new moves? You must be completely barking mad. The only new move you're about to get, my sweetheart, is a karate chop to the nadgers.'

'Annie . . .' Ed smiled and held out an arm, 'come over here and cuddle up. Your boss has ordered a holiday because she thinks you'll get over it. Despite her big, flouncy tantrum, I can absolutely promise you that Lana will get over it and in the meantime, you need cuddling, you need massaging and I think I could work with you.'

He patted the bed encouragingly.

'I miss Lana . . . we used to phone every single day. I've had two texts since she's gone back.'

'I know you do and I'm sure she misses you too. But she'll come round. You're both good people and you will get over this. Just give it a little time. C'mon, over here.'

'You really think you could work with me?' Annie asked. She couldn't help smiling at him.

'Yeah, I know you're trying very hard to put me off with that shapeless flannel nightshirt thing, but I can see past it.'

'Really?'

'Yes, really, so why don't you just take it off and come over here and see me?'

With that Annie pulled the nightshirt up over her head and let it fall to the floor.

'Now that is much better. That is 100 per cent better.'

'Really?'

'Yes, really, now get over here.'

As she approached the bed, she wondered if now would be a good time to mention Svetlana's offer.

'I might like to ask you for a very big favour . . .' she began.

'That sounds good,' he said, putting his warm arms around her and pulling her in towards his fuzzy naked chest, 'sounds very, very good because if you have a favour to ask me, then I'm definitely . . .' he paused to kiss her mouth, 'going to ask for one in return.'

Slowly, they began to kiss with intent, with concentration and with roaming hands, focusing on how to make this as enjoyable as possible for each other.

'It's been too long,' Annie murmured as Ed kissed the base of her neck, 'liking that, definitely liking . . .'

More very good moves were played and Annie was on her back, being licked, being touched and explored. Her foot was dangling from the bed, the sensations from her toes, travelling up her legs, adding to the complete, all-over body pleasure.

'Oh yeah . . .'

But . . . but . . . how was her foot being licked while Ed was very busy elsewhere?

Annie ignored the question for another moment or two, but then raised her head from the pillow.

'Wait a minute!' she blurted out.

'What?'

'It's the dog!' she complained.

'What?'

They both sat up now and looked over the side of the bed.

There was Dave. The dog promptly sat down and looked up at them a little guiltily.

'He was licking my foot!' Annie explained, freaked out. 'I thought it was you.'

'But I was—'

'I know where you were . . . it was completely weird! I do not want a dog licking my foot while I'm trying to concentrate on you . . . and new moves and trying to have a good time.'

'Fair enough, I wouldn't want the dog licking my foot either . . . Well, I don't know – was he good? Was he better than me?'

Annie gave Ed a playful smack on the shoulder.

'Dave! Out!' she ordered.

The dog just cocked his head to the side.

'Out!' she yelled and hurled a pillow in his direction.

Dave saw the pillow coming and high-tailed it towards the open door.

'Annie, he's a nice old boy,' Ed complained, 'don't frighten him.'

'Go to the door and wiggle the knackered handle until it closes. Please,' Annie asked.

'OK, OK . . .' Ed ran his arm over her shoulders and tried to soothe her.

'Stupid blooming dog. Now I'm all distracted.'

'Honestly, lie down, focus, I can take you back . . . just give me a chance here.'

Annie glanced at the door.

'He's still there!' she complained. A grey muzzle and two beady eyes were poking round the edge of the door.

'Dave, buzz off!' Ed said, getting out of bed and waving his arms in the direction of the animal, 'I have work to do here. I'll see you later.'

He pulled the door closed and played with the handle until there was a click.

'Right,' he said, heading back to the bed with an eager smile, 'where were we?'

But as the kissing got going again a ghostly wail drifted towards the room.

'Waaaaaaaaaaaaah . . .'

It was the sound of Micky, tireless cot escapologist.

'No prizes for guessing who that is,' Ed began wearily. 'You or me?'

'I'll go,' Annie replied, 'you take the dog downstairs. Then we'll see if there's any chance of reviving the situation in here.'

'Muuuuuuuuuuuuuuummmmmmmmyyyy!'

The little voice sounded tragic now.

'And up we get,' Annie said, stepping from the bed and wrapping a dressing gown around her naked body. She got to the door ahead of Ed, turned the handle and it came clean off in her hand.

The spindle fell to the floor on the other side of the door and she was left staring at a firmly closed door with a hole where the handle used to be.

'Ed!'

'Oh fuddle.'

Years of teaching had left Ed with a remarkably muted swear vocabulary. He got out of bed to assess the situation. He examined the hole where the handle had been with such a bewildered expression it would almost have been comical if the wailing from the twins' bedroom wasn't growing louder.

'They're both awake now. You have to do something.'

'Yes, I had noticed,' Ed said dryly.

He pushed his finger into the hole the handle had left and felt around a little. He tried to pull the door open. But the catch was still holding firm.

'We're locked in!' Annie exclaimed, beginning to feel slightly panicked now. The crying was reaching fever pitch and she was desperate to go and console her children. 'What do we do now? Let's get a coat hanger and poke it about, we've got to open the door.'

'Good idea.'

Ed hurried over to the wardrobe and brought out a thin wire hanger.

With Annie urging him on, he tried various attacks: he poked the wire about in the hole, he poked it at the catch. Nothing worked.

'MUMMMMY!'

That was definitely Micky's voice and it was growing louder.

'He's out of his cot,' Annie said, really worried now. What if he fell hard on to the floor? What if he came out of his room and tumbled down the stairs?

'Oh for Pete's sake,' Ed exclaimed, poking at the catch again.

'Mummy?'

The voice was definitely coming closer and sounded not so much upset now as questioning.

'He's coming to the door . . . Micky! It's OK, but Mummy and Daddy are stuck in the bedroom.'

There was no reply.

'Micky? Are you there?' Annie asked, face pressed against the hole as she tried to scan the landing for any sign of her son.

There was a snuffling sound and then Annie saw

Micky's great big blue eye pressed against the other side of the hole.

'Micky!' she said, smiling with relief.

'Mummy?'

He sounded smiley too.

'Can you help?' Annie asked in her most encouraging voice. 'Do you see the funny knob with the stick on the floor?'

Micky's eye moved away from the hole.

'This will not work,' Ed hissed.

'It's got to be worth a try.'

'Stick,' Micky declared. This was followed by a heavy clatter against the wooden floor.

'What was that?' Annie asked.

Ed smacked his hand against his forehead: 'Probably the doorknob falling off the spindle.'

'The spindle? You're very technical for someone who's made a complete balls-up of fixing our door,' she snapped.

'You can take this all out on me later, but right now it is not helping,' Ed whispered fiercely.

'Later? Later as in when the fire brigade are here trying to work out how to open this door? Do we even have a phone in our room so we can contact them? Where will Micky be by then? He'll probably have gone down to the kitchen and turned on the gas.'

'Not helping . . .' Ed reminded her.

Annie put her eye to the hole to see what Micky was up to and immediately gave a yelp of pain.

'Owwww!'

She pulled her head away, hand clutched over her eye.

The spindle plopped through the hole and on to the carpet.

'Clever boy!' Annie managed, despite the tears streaming from her poked eye.

'I don't believe it!' Ed exclaimed. 'Are you OK?'

'I think I'll be fine,' she said, hand over her eye again.

Ed slotted the spindle halfway through the gap and turned it. The catch pulled back and the door popped open.

'You clever boy,' Annie cooed, 'you clever, clever boy!'

There stood Micky in his blue babygro with an unusual, concentrated look on his face. Before Ed or Annie could quite register what it meant, he opened his mouth and hit them with a gush of projectile puke.

It was almost an hour later when Ed and Annie finally fell back into bed, soggy, still smelling slightly of toddler puke and far too tired for any romantic rekindling.

'You know some time ago you promised me a mini-break, far away from the domestic mayhem,' Ed complained. 'A mini-break, Annie, where is my mini-break?'

'I did. I totally did, babes. We will go on a mini-break. Just you and me to a lovely place far, far away from the madness.'

'When is this happening? And where?'

'I will book us a mini-break. I promise.'

'Please do . . .' Ed turned and landed a kiss on her forehead, 'because it may be our only chance to have sex this decade.'

He turned out the bedside light but just as they settled down to sleep, he remembered: 'What was the favour you wanted to ask?'

Annie hesitated. It was one thing to ask your husband for a huge massive favour when he was all blissed out and contented post-sex. It was quite another when dogs, puking babies and general exhaustion had got in the way of the big romantic reunion.

'Well . . . I dunno . . .' she began, 'it's a crazy plan. Don't know if I'm even close to pulling it off. In fact, let's not talk about it now.'

'What? Tell me,' Ed insisted.

'Well, it's just Svetlana . . . she knows I'm on a forced holiday, and she's offered to take me on a spa break with her but you know . . . it's really not fair

. . . there would be too much to organize if I went away.'

'When? Right now? While you're off?'

'Oh honestly, I don't think it's going to work. This weekend-ish. Well, in fact, leaving on Friday morning.'

'Friday?!' Ed sounded incredulous.

'It was a very last minute offer. But she has said she'll pay and it's a very famous place. Legendary, in fact.'

'Go,' came the simple reply.

'Go? But how? But who?'

'Dinah and I will share it out between us,' Ed replied, 'but there are two conditions.'

'OK . . .' Annie wondered what was coming now.

'One, you have to come back with a spring in your step, the girl we know and love . . .'

'Well, I can try, babes.'

'Two, you have to promise me that we will go away on our mini-break. We have to go away. I have to get one night, maybe even two of uninterrupted time with you or I am going to . . . burst!'

'It's a deal.'

Chapter Eight

New York

Fabian posing hard:

White linen suit (from Dad via Brooks Brothers)
Pink shirt (same)
Suede lace-ups (Gap)
Cream trilby hat (thrift store)
Green hair dye (drugstore)
Total est. cost: $470

Although the Perfect Dress office had closed for the day, Lana was striding through all the most interesting streets of Manhattan, camera phone in hand, still hard at work.

Ever since she'd flounced back from London, ahead of Elena, with her fate and the fate of the dress label unresolved, Lana had spent the hours between work and bedtime roaming the streets, supposedly in search of inspiration.

She wouldn't admit to anyone, not even herself, that she was lonely. Since she'd ditched her last guy, Matt, she'd found that she didn't particularly want to see anyone from the little circle of friends she'd made through him because it was still awkward.

Gracie was usually busy in the evenings with her friends, her family and her long-standing boyfriend, 'Beefy' Bingham. A nice guy, Lana had thought when she met him, but somehow not exactly the cool, fashiony, finger-on-the-pulse kind of man Lana had imagined Gracie would be with.

So in the evenings, Lana stayed out, away from the apartment phone that never rang now that she and her mother weren't calling each other. Instead, Lana walked the streets and took pictures all over Manhattan, dreaming up inspiration and ideas for a project that now might never get off the ground.

She snapped cool girls with funkily styled outfits, edgy shop window displays, unexpected patterns, clashing colours, anything that might inspire a dazzling new collection of clothes.

'East 28th Street,' Lana whispered, but with determination. She was heading there because that's where Parker had advised them to look for the very hottest store windows and the very coolest New Yorkers.

She was also going there because: 'I like to hang out there myself . . .' he'd told them, 'there's this one place, Blonde Tobacco, it's immense: low key, laid back. If I have any free time, that's where I like to be. Plus it's real close to the hallway-with-a-camp-bed which I call home.'

Although it was almost two weeks since she'd first met and last seen Parker, Lana couldn't get him out of her mind. He was the most attractive and most fascinating person she'd met in a long time. She'd tried to shake the memory of him off, but little details – his scruffy trainers, the clunky watch which slid around his smooth, olive wrist – kept flashing about in her mind.

So now, like a possessed person, she was walking towards the bar he was sometimes in when he had the time. Even though she knew he was not going to be there and she would be wandering around like some minor, wannabe stalker.

But still the street and the bar – Blonde Tobacco – were calling to her, luring her on.

As she turned and began to walk down East 28th Street, she tried to look nonchalant and relaxed but really felt as self-conscious as if she was wearing a T-shirt with the words: *Hello Parker, I am sooooo crushing on you.*

He won't be here, she reminded herself. So she would just walk down the street, take photos of the shop windows and maybe of some of the people sitting around outside in the evening sunshine and then she would go.

No harm done.

Parker would never know.

She raised her camera phone and focused on a small group of Manhattan's coolest sitting in a knot at a tiny metal table.

There was a guy in a small cream-coloured porkpie hat with bright green hair sticking out from underneath it. This was good; this had to be the kind of inspirational image Elena and Gracie would want.

Lana held up her phone then hit zoom because she didn't really want the cool dude in the hat to know she was taking his picture. She looked at the screen and saw a pattern which made her eyes widen: black with a pink and orange stripe?

She looked up and saw Parker – right at the table with the man in the hat – looking straight at her. It was such a heady surprise she fumbled her phone in fright, letting it fall with a clatter. She dropped down to pick it up. When she glimpsed up through her hair, hoping Parker hadn't noticed, he was waving in her direction.

Lana put the phone into her bag and took a

calming breath. He was a cool guy so she would have to play it cool too. She would just go over and say hello. No big deal.

As she approached his table, she set a smile on her face and tried to give off the natural born confidence of a New York girl.

'Hey,' Parker called out.

'Hey,' she replied.

'You meeting someone here?'

She shrugged and said: 'Maybe later' . . . proud that her voice sounded incredibly close to casual even if her heart was beginning to race. 'Right now I'm just walking about, getting inspired. Can I take a picture of your friend? I'm crazy about his hat.'

She gave the guy with the green hair her charm offensive smile.

'Fabian, you have to meet—' Parker began.

'Lana,' she said, holding out her hand.

'I know, you don't have to tell me,' Parker said with a lazy grin, 'So do you have a blog where we can see your photos?' he asked.

'Not yet . . . but I might set one up.'

'You should. I'd love to see them. "Lana from London's blog." Think about it. Fabian, Lana really is from London, how cool is that?' Parker asked.

'Honoured to meet you,' Fabian said in a deep, drawling voice as he extended his hand.

'Fabian is from the South and he's working a

whole Truman Capote but with green hair kind of thing,' Parker added. 'Would you like to sit down and have a drink with us? We're only drinking lemon tea, because we both have to work later.'

'Lemon tea would be lovely,' Lana said, pulling up the chair between them and trying to keep the grin across her face under some semblance of control.

'*Lovely?* Now, isn't that so English and so pretty?' Fabian asked. 'You're probably related to Kate Middleton, right?'

Lana laughed: 'I don't think so!'

'OK, so let's call the waitress over and order you a tall lemon tea, then you can tell us all about London,' Parker said, 'which we love by the way and want to move to like tomorrow . . .'

'Really? But New York is better, so way better,' Lana promised.

'But this is how it is,' Parker said, turning his lively eyes on her: 'you've lived in London, you know London, so you love New York. We know New York, so we want something new and we can't wait to move to London.'

'In London, right now, it may be May but it is cold and rainy,' Lana warned. 'No one is sitting outside sipping at lemon teas, believe me.'

'Right, but in New York we have the coldest winter you can imagine for six months of the year,' Fabian countered.

'Who cares about weather?!' Parker exclaimed. 'Forget weather! You have the East End. Every artist, every photographer I've ever heard of lives or exhibits or creates art in the East End.'

'But you have Brooklyn and Willamsburg and NoHo,' Lana reminded them, 'and trust me, New York is way cooler.'

'Do you think you'll stay in New York or move back to London?' Parker asked.

'No contest, I'm staying in New York,' Lana declared, 'even though my mum's trying to get me to go back and even live at home again. As if!'

'Uh-oh ... know all about that,' Fabian sympathized: 'my hair was the final straw. I still don't know if it's because she didn't dig the grassy green or because I ruined not just one but three white towels in the process.'

The lemon tea arrived and the playful New York versus London argument went on. As Lana kept up with it, she felt her heart skipping about in her chest. Now and then her eyes met Parker's and their legs underneath the tiny table were definitely touching.

She could hardly believe how well this was going. He was interested, she was completely sure he was interested. Any moment now and he would ask when they could meet up again.

Finally, the tea glasses were drained. Parker checked his watch then looked slightly panicked.

'Whoa, we have to shoot. Like ten minutes ago,' he said, pulling out a couple of bills from his wallet and putting them down on the table, 'but Lana, on Saturday there's this club opening, the Spider's Nest. Big party, really excellent party and I'd love it if you would be my guest.'

'Sure! Fantastic!' Lana said, completely forgetting to be cool.

'OK, let me take your number,' Parker patted his pockets and found his phone, 'and I'll message you with the details.'

For several minutes after Parker and Fabian had gone, Lana had to stay on at the little table smiling to herself. He so liked her! He must like her because he'd asked her to the opening: 'be my guest,' he'd said.

But then the doubt began to set in. Be my guest? How many guests would he have? Did that mean she would be his plus one? Did that make it a date? Or were other people coming?

If she was one guest of many, then that wasn't a date. No. Surely she was his plus one? That was what he'd meant.

She glanced down at her phone, wondering when his message would come in. For the sake of something to do, she clicked to Facebook and scrolled down the posts.

Owen was writing in German. The nutter. Gracie

had changed her profile picture to an image of an adorable pug puppy in a shiny PVC coat. As Lana's eyes travelled across Gracie's latest post, her heart sank like a stone.

'Spider's Nest opening, Sunday night. Going with my new best friend Parker Bain. Woo hoo!'

Chapter Nine

Milan

Svetlana travels:

Multi-coloured wrap dress (Missoni)
Pale suede blazer (Gucci)
High cork wedge sandals (Jimmy Choo)
Huge sunglasses (Chanel)
Selection of diamond rings (selection of ex-husbands)
Huge gold and emerald earrings (Bvlgari
Co-ordinating luggage (Hermès)
Total est. cost: £74,000

'And here is our car,' Svetlana purred.

Annie's eyes travelled beyond the glass doors of the airport towards a stately, old-fashioned, luxury-mobile, gleaming in the bright Italian sunshine.

'You have got to be joking.'

'I never joke,' Svetlana replied in a dark, Ukrainian-laced deadpan voice.

Annie was already in a deeply woozy state. She'd woken up very early and made breakfast for her twins before squeezing, kissing, hugging them goodbye and catching her cab to the airport.

As soon as she'd located Svetlana at Gatwick, standing with her chauffeur in front of the check-in area, Annie had been whisked into the world of first class splendour.

There had been no queuing, no waiting, no grumpy-faced check-in girls. Just a flick of tickets and passports, then she and Svetlana had been rushed to the First Class lounge, where glasses of Bucks Fizz had been pressed into their hands although it was only 7.20 a.m.

In the calm and rarefied atmosphere of the first class cabin, Annie had soaked up a little more champagne because it helped with the worries which were racing round her head, even though she was now officially on holiday.

Would Ed and Dinah cope with Owen and the twins? Would she feel any better when she got back? Would her passion for fashion really return as Svetlana promised? Would Tamsin definitely want her back? And as for Lana . . . Annie and Lana had still not had a proper phone conversation.

When was that row finally going to blow over?

Svetlana didn't talk much on the flight, she just issued occasional instructions: 'If you are nervous, drink more champagne. Champagne is wonderful for nerves.'

So here they were in Milan airport, where bright sunshine sliced through the windows, promising a beautiful day outside.

'It's summer!' Annie declared with surprise. May had been so gloomy in London, she'd almost forgotten.

She trailed in Svetlana's Missoni clad, Bvlgari sparkling, Annick Goutal scented wake and even pulled Svetlana's matching, wheeled luggage alongside hers.

'Hermès?' Annie had asked appreciatively when the bags appeared first, of course, ahead of the queue, alongside her slightly more practical Samsonite.

'Yah,' Svetlana had confirmed, 'Louis Vuitton is vulgar. For footballers and Russians.'

They began to walk towards the hotel's car, identifiable by the hotel crest emblazoned on the doors. A smiling, uniformed chauffeur with white gloves and a peaked cap was approaching them, eager to relieve them of their luggage.

'Is this a Rolls-Royce?' Annie asked.

'No. Much better. Is a Bentley, like my car,'

Svetlana assured her, 'but this one is vintage.'

'The hotel's *Bentley* . . .' Annie was very impressed as the door was opened and she slid into the deep, leathery comfort of the back seat. In front of them was a fold-down table set with crystal glasses, bottles of champagne and sparkling water.

'But now, no more champagne,' Svetlana instructed. 'Is best to begin the spa programme from the moment we enter the car.'

'The spa programme?'

'Five days of very pure, very clean living, Annah.'

Suddenly Annie felt a twinge of doubt. This was going to be a luxurious, pampering mini-break, wasn't it? There wasn't any chance that Svetlana had signed her up for some kind of military fitness boot camp, was there?

No, she smiled at the thought. Boot camps wouldn't have crystal glasses and Bentleys.

But then again, Svetlana's figure was flawless, Svetlana's exercise regime was relentless, Svetlana's beauty drills were not for the faint-hearted. Svetlana looked astonishingly good because she worked at it every waking moment.

Her idea of 'pampering' might be very different from Annie's.

'This spa's programme is legendary,' Svetlana began, settling back in her seat, 'one of Europe's best-kept beauty secrets. Every famous, beautiful woman in the world comes here once or twice a year. Here they can take 10 kilos from you in five days and ten years from your face at the same time. It is truly astonishing. One of my secrets.'

'Really? You do know how much I appreciate you taking me with you?' Annie said, although she had already thanked Svetlana at least one hundred times. '*Ten* kilos in *five* days? *Really?!* Do you think they could do that for me?'

'If you stick with the programme,' Svetlana assured her, 'the whole programme.'

Annie might have heard something of a warning in those words if she hadn't been in such a frenzy of excitement.

'Ten kilos?!' she repeated. 'Isn't that even more than 20 pounds?'

'Twenty-two pounds,' Svetlana confirmed.

'In five days?!'

Annie looked down at her baby bulge, or should that now be her toddler tum?

'If they can get rid of this in five days, it will be a blinking miracle. The Pope will have to be informed. He'll have to make the programme director a saint or something.'

Svetlana smiled: 'They will try everything they can for you.'

'So what does the programme involve?' Annie asked, pouring out two glasses of water.

'The spa gives you a total detox. They serve a pure, clean diet that will make you thin and make you glow. You will be clean from the inside out. You will love it.'

'Right.' Annie sank back into her seat. A total detox ... well, that didn't sound so bad. She'd detoxed before. It was all about dairy-free, wheat-free, sugar-free stuff. Eating quinoa, rice and vegetables for a few days, that couldn't really hurt anyone, could it? Plus, she knew it was what she really needed.

Although Ed and Dinah lectured her constantly, Annie was perfectly aware that her daily diet still revolved almost completely around buttery toast, chocolate bars, endless cups of milky coffee and large glasses of wine.

Svetlana took her mobile from her tiny alligator clutch bag and looked at the screen a touch anxiously.

'Everything OK?' Annie asked.

'Yes. Yes I think so. Harry and Maria know exactly what the boys are doing over the weekend. There is no chance of anything happening to them. I know this. I know this, but still the worry rises up, now and again, that Igor will try to take them.'

Svetlana's sunglasses covered most of her face, so it was difficult to read her expression. Annie felt that if she was in this situation, she'd find it hard to leave her children alone for a moment, but Svetlana always managed to handle the high-powered problems her high-powered life seemed to bring.

'Why is Igor so desperate for the boys to go to his old school, anyway?' Annie asked.

'In his opinion, this is the best way to train the body and mind for the future,' Svetlana replied, shaking her head. 'But I think if you go to military school, you turn out like Igor: always at war. He is at war with me, at war with everyone who does business with him, at war with himself. This is result of military school.'

'But he is a phenomenal success,' Annie pointed out. 'Maybe he wants his sons to be a success just like him and he thinks—'

'They need to be like him,' Svetlana interrupted. 'This will never happen. Michael could be like him, if he went to Russian military school, so I will not let him go. Petrov is a totally different child: quiet and sensitive. Petrov will never, ever go to military school. If Igor tries to do this – I will kill him.'

For most people this was simply an expression, but when Svetlana said it, it sounded like a terrifying threat.

'How long will it take Igor to accept this?' Annie asked.

'I don't know. He has never given up on anything ever before. Tschaaaaa!'

The Bentley had purred smoothly from the airport autostrada, past the motorways encircling Milan and out into the glorious Italian countryside. As they drove by terracotta tiled houses and dark cypress trees set against a bright and blue sky, Annie wished Micky hadn't yanked both arms off her only pair of sunglasses three minutes before her taxi had arrived.

She shaded her eyes with her hand and gazed out of the window until Svetlana noticed the problem, clicked open her clutch and offered up a spare pair of vast black Chanel shades.

Another half an hour or so into the countryside and the Bentley slowed, indicated, then waited in the road to make a right turn. Two black metal gates set between carved stone gateposts began to part. The Bentley swung through the gates and began to move up the driveway, gravel crunching under its tyres.

'I could get used to this,' Annie told Svetlana, 'being driven about in my Bentley, through my electronic gates, up my driveway. Do *you* have other houses?' she wondered. Maybe Svetlana had a castle or two like this tucked up in a tax haven.

'Ah ... so many other houses when I was Mrs Wisneski, I lose count, but now just a farmhouse in Portugal,' Svetlana replied. 'I've not been there since 1984 when it was fashionable to play golf.'

She gave a little snort: '*Golf?!* Can you imagine?'

'You've not even been there since 1984?' Annie could hardly take this in. 'But why don't you sell it?'

'It's rented out; it makes some money. Anyway, from Igor I learn if you keep property for long enough, you always win.'

'But how long is long enough?'

'For ever. The best length of time to keep real estate is for ever.'

The Bentley purred up the driveway, through jewel green lawns studded with bright flower beds, towards a beautiful old building. This Italian-style stately home came complete with pale stone columns, ornately carved balustrades and balconies overflowing with flower displays.

The towering front entrance with studded wooden doors was wide open and a smartly uniformed doorman was waiting for them.

'Look at this place!' Annie exclaimed, pushing the sunglasses onto her head to take a better look. 'Just look at it! Isn't it breathtaking?!'

Svetlana gave a little smile in agreement.

As the car pulled to a halt, Annie jumped out, almost gaping at the views. Over there was a huge, vibrantly blue swimming pool surrounded by a stone terrace with a view right out over the most beautiful lake she'd ever seen.

The water sparkled in the sunlight; she gazed at

the hills in the distance and bright, bright blue sky above. This was heaven. Sun loungers were set out around the pool and as the guests basked in the sunshine, a waiter hovered at their elbow serving tall drinks. She couldn't wait to be lying there, Svetlana's sunnies in place as she sipped at a cooling, brain-numbing cocktail or three.

But the rumble in her stomach warned her that hours had passed since the First Class breakfast – surely it was time for a gorgeous cappuccino with thick creamy froth and a dusting of grated chocolate? Or was it too early for lunch ... something beautiful, Italian, fresh and salad-like but nicely substantial? She definitely needed something before she stripped off and dived into the pool.

As the doorman took charge of their luggage, Annie followed Svetlana into the hotel's hall; except 'hall' wasn't quite the word. 'Reception room', 'stately welcoming space', 'marvellous room of gorgeousness' would come closer.

From the marble mosaic floor to the sublime frescoes, from the ornate marble fireplace to the stuccoed plaster ceiling, it was a magnificent, unbelievable hall.

A handsome, dark-haired man in a black suit moved forward to greet them.

'Our long-time friend, Mrs Wisneski, an honour as always,' he said, taking Svetlana's hand with a little bow.' And Ms Valentine, it is a pleasure to meet you for the first time. I am Carlo Moretti, the hotel manager.'

Annie shook hands with him too.

'We hope you will be comfortable and will feel at home. You must let us know what you want or need and we will provide this for you.'

Annie felt her shoulders drop away from her ears. She was smiling, she was relaxing; finally, she was getting into the holiday spirit.

'Mrs Wisneski, you will follow me to the Junior Suite . . . Ms Valentine, Lucca will take you to your room. Relax and make yourself at home then we will bring you to Dr Decatoso so you can have your consultation and begin your programme as soon as possible.'

From a window, Annie cast a sideways glance at the pool and thought for just another tiny moment about cocktails. She would be there, she would be sipping cocktails on the sun lounger very soon; she obviously just had to get through the Doctory bit first.

This was, after all, a spa and these places always needed your medical details: health and safety, insurance policies, all those pesky things. But then again, if 10 kilos were supposed to evaporate in five days . . . not many cocktails could be involved, could they? Maybe they made an extra light, or even slimming cocktail. Some sort of herbal, but slightly alcoholic tonic?

Lucca, smartly dressed in his doorman's uniform, let Annie step into the lift first. As soon as the doors closed, her stomach rumbled loudly.

'Sorry,' she said, 'I'm hungry. I woke up very early to travel here today.'

Lucca just smiled.

'When is lunch served? Or could I order something up to my room?'

Lucca smiled again and shook his head: 'You need to consult with Dr De Catoso before we can give you any food.'

'Really? I can't just munch a little sandwich first – or a salad? Something very small, maybe a croissant?'

Lucca shook his head once again.

The lift opened, she followed him along the corridor and with a gasp of admiration, entered her room.

The windows were slightly ajar, causing the white muslin curtains to swish in the breeze. Outside there was nothing but blue, lake meeting sky and the burst of vibrant pink from a blaze of flowers on the balcony.

'Stunning!' Annie breathed.

She was going to love it here. In fact, she already loved it here.

Only when she'd fully soaked in the view did she turn to examine the room: pink floral wallpaper, a white and gold bed, a huge bouquet of roses, lilies, stocks and gardenias on the dressing table. It was heaven: a girlie, princess heaven. She was going to be all alone here at night. For a moment, she felt a little pang ... no Ed to snuggle with, no babies crawling in pre-dawn, no dog trying to nuzzle under the blankets.

Then an uplifting feeling spread through her chest, as she thought that through properly. She would be all alone in here at night ... no Ed, no babies, no dog ... she was going to sleep for ever, like an angel. It was going to be wonderful.

Once Lucca had gone, Annie threw herself onto the bed, a huge smile in place. This was the life. This was the five star, first class, full-on luxury, Svetlanatastic life!

Annie had been weighed: *urgh!* She'd been measured round all her saggy, flabby bits: arms, thighs, boobs, stomach – more uuuuurgh.

Then the drop-dead gorgeous doctor – surely some younger Italian relation of George Clooney's? – had asked about a typical day in the life of her diet. She'd looked past his thick eyelashes, into his deep brown eyes and tried to be as honest as possible, but as his eyebrows had shot up higher and higher, she'd edited down the coffee count and decided to change 'best part of a bottle of wine' to 'just two or three glasses'.

Dr Decatoso – or as Annie was now thinking of him, Dr Delicioso – had written notes in Italian, so she couldn't read them, then he'd taken her blood pressure and delved into her medical history.

Finally, he'd leaned back in his chair to make his pronouncement.

'You are overweight,' he began.

Annie felt her shoulders sag. Well, it was sort of obvious. Even though she was good, OK make that best, friends with the elasticated tummy tuck knicker and she went to the gym and she had good posture, the scales and the tape measure could not lie.

Still, it felt like rather a punch in her by now ravenous stomach to hear a doctor come out with it so bluntly.

'You drink too much alcohol and coffee,' he added, once again stating the entirely obvious, but it still stung.

'And you eat very little nutritious food.'

Ouch.

'Your body is crying out for detoxification.'

Yikes.

'We will put you on the spa's cleanse regime and although the first two or three days will be uncomfortable, by day four you will start to feel much better. If only you could be with us for two weeks,' the doctor mused, 'we could begin to renew you from the inside out. In five days, we can make big improvements – but in two weeks, we could perform a transformation. Can you perhaps lengthen your stay?'

For a moment, Annie considered: a *transformation*! A brand new body?! It was tempting, it was very tempting. She tried to imagine herself 10 kilos lighter . . . ten years younger. Wasn't that what Svetlana had promised?

Ten whole kilos . . . *ten* whole years!

It would be astronomically expensive, she didn't even want to think about how much it might cost. Probably thousands of pounds per day. Maybe even thousands of pounds per hour. But she had brought a credit card . . . or two.

Then she remembered the critical date in her diary next week: the twins' second birthday. No, she couldn't miss that: not even for ten years and 10 kilos.

'I'm sorry, I can't stay on,' she told the doctor, 'but maybe I can come back very soon.'

'This is a good idea. We will give you as much help as we can to keep pure when you return home.'

'So what does the detox programme involve?'

'It is very simple: all day long, water, water, water, beautiful mineral-enriched water from our own spring. It has special cleansing properties. Once a day, a cocktail . . .'

Annie's ears pricked up: and there was the cocktail! No diet could be so bad if cocktails were allowed.

'Of carrot, cucumber, beetroot and celery juice.'

Oh.

'Once a day, you will eat a bowl of potassium-rich vegetable broth. Once a day, drink fresh coconut milk, full of vitamins and minerals.'

Water, water, beetroot juice, coconut milk and vegetable broth? This didn't exactly sound like the kind of five course lunch then dinner her stomach had now decided on. It gave a loud rumble of protest.

'Your stomach has problems with acid, yeast and wind. We will cure all this for you,' the doctor said, pointing at her bloated middle.

'Once a day, there will be a yoga class, also once a day, a full body massage. Finally, the most important part of the programme: two times a day . . .'

Yoga and massage . . . Annie was listening and considering. It didn't sound so bad. Maybe she could manage on vegetable juice and broth if she was being massaged for hours in between them. And now, what could the most important part of the programme be? Diet tips from a nutritionist? A lovely seaweed wrap? A thermal mud treatment – mmm, delicious – a detoxing sauna?

'You will have coffee enemas.'

'Enemas?!' she repeated.

'Yes, the most important part, encouraging the bowel to move, to cleanse.'

'Coffee?! Coffee enemas?'

She wanted to make sure she'd heard this properly.

'Coffee??'

Dr Delicioso nodded.

A finest Colombian colonic? A Java blend up the . . . ?

'You have got to be joking!'

Chapter Ten

New York

Gracie rocks vintage:

Floral pink, blue and white summer dress (thrift store, but altered)
Wooden sandals (Dr Scholl's used but scrubbed)
Large basketweave handbag (market stall)
White plastic sunglasses (Claire's Accessories)
Sparkly hair clips (same)
Total est. cost: $35

'Oh my gosh, I am so, so sorry about London!'

As soon as Gracie saw Lana come through the door of the Perfect Dress office, she jumped from her seat and rushed over to give her a welcoming hug.

'Yeah, me too,' Lana admitted, 'it was horrible.

Terrible! Our mothers . . . well, you know. I just had to get back as soon as I could.'

'I'm so sorry. All our plans . . .'

'I know. Bummer. Total, total bummer.'

They both sank into their desk seats.

'I've been sitting here, answering calls and going through the motions, but really, I just feel . . .'

'I know,' Lana understood immediately: 'gutted. Totally gutted.'

'How about you and your mum . . . OK?' Gracie ventured.

'No,' Lana protested. 'Of course we're not OK. She was part of it. She and Svetlana sat there, heard the whole thing and just said no. It felt as if they didn't even consider any of it for longer than a minute. Just said no. I'm not talking to my mum. I don't think she even cares. She and Svetlana have gone off on holiday.'

'*Really!*'

Gracie looked surprised.

'Yeah. They couldn't care less. Perfect Dress doesn't matter nearly as much to them as it does to us.'

'Oh boy. But now what?'

As Lana gave a shrug, the phone on her desk began to ring.

She picked it up and gave her most professional: 'Hello, Perfect Dress, how may I help you?'

'Hi, you're back. Are you OK?'

Lana recognized Elena's voice immediately. 'Hi, Elena. Yeah, I'm OK. Still really angry about everything that happened.'

'I know, me too.'

'What are we going to do now?' Lana wondered.

'I guess we'll just have to make the Perfect Dress classics as amazing as we can,' Gracie suggested, trying to sound positive. 'Maybe some of our ideas can go into the catwalk show . . . or into the packaging, or – the website?'

'Is Gracie with you?' Elena asked, 'Is she saying something?'

'Yes, Gracie's here,' Lana replied, 'she's trying to be upbeat, she's saying we'll have to make the classic dresses beautifully and maybe use our other ideas for the packaging and the website.'

'Pah!' Elena exclaimed, 'Packaging?!! We can't let everything we've worked for go to waste on the packaging!'

'Do you want me to try and speak to my mother again?' Lana offered.

'Let's face it, Svetlana said no and your mother didn't do anything to try and persuade her. I don't think she was very impressed. She didn't make any positive noises.'

'So what can we do now?' Lana asked.

'I've been thinking about it very hard. I mean, we

112

could resign . . .' Elena said, but she didn't sound convinced. They all knew how inexperienced they were and jobs in fashion didn't exactly come knocking at the door every day.

'We could threaten to resign,' Lana said.

'Or . . . we could make up just a small Summer Collection of the new dresses, call them NY Perfect Dress, send them out to our favourite buyers and when we get a wonderful reaction, maybe our problem will be solved,' Elena said, her voice low, as if there was a chance she might be overheard.

For a moment Lana said nothing, then she asked: 'You really think we could make the dresses ourselves?! Would that even be a good idea? I mean, what kind of budget would we need? And where would we get the money?'

Lana looked over at Gracie and they raised their eyebrows at each other.

'Well, I have a credit card, you have a credit card, Gracie has a credit card,' Elena replied, 'we could buy the material on credit. Then we withdraw some cash on the cards and pay the making-up costs. Obviously we'll get the money back as soon as the dresses sell.'

'If the dresses sell,' Lana said warily.

'Of course they will sell. They are going to be fantastic.'

'A summer collection?' was her next question, 'But it's already May.'

'I have people I've been talking to who are willing to rush through some orders as long as we provide the fabric and the cash.'

'How many dresses?'

'I want to make fifty dresses. That would be enough to get people looking – and talking. To make up fifty dresses we need about $8,000. But we have to be quick. We need to have buyers loving the new dresses when there's still time to make a full collection for winter.'

'But, Elena, what about when the Mothers find out? They'll be furious.'

'We make sure they don't find out. They only find out when the dresses are a big success with the buyers. Then they'll be delighted with us.'

Lana hesitated. It sounded risky. What if the buyers didn't like the new dresses? Then they'd all have debts, disappointed customers and two seriously cheesed off mothers.

'What does Gracie think?' Elena asked.

As Lana outlined the plan to her, Gracie's cheeks flushed and she gave a clap of excitement.

'I think that's a yes from Gracie,' Lana told Elena.

'I'm in, Gracie's in, Lana you have to be in too. We can't do NY Perfect Dress without you. Please say yes,' Elena urged, 'it's time to show the Mothers just how much they underestimate us.'

'Is it still going to be NY Perfect Dress?' Gracie asked, once the call had ended.

'Yeah. I hope it will work, it has got to work!'

'We will make it work,' Gracie assured her, 'the three of us, we're a great team.'

'Elena can borrow $4,000, so she needs us to come up with $2,000 each. I can do that on my card, what about you?'

'Just checking online,' Gracie said, staring at her computer screen. 'Oh – not quite,' she added, 'I've got $1,400 left before I hit my limit.'

'So we need another $600.'

'We can do that,' Gracie said. 'We can raise $600, can't we?'

'Can we?'

Lana chewed at the skin around her fingernails as she tried to work out how to raise $600. Gracie nibbled at the tip of her pencil.

'Maybe we could hold a stoop sale.'

'A what?'

'Happens in Manhattan all the time. People get stuff they don't want any more, bring it all out onto the front steps of the building and sell it off to people walking past.'

'But what will we sell?'

'What do you have that you don't wear any more

or don't use any more? I always have a ton of stuff. Vintage jewellery, the little felt purses that I make, I'm sure I can find a lot of things to sell on my stoop.'

'Really?' Lana asked, but she was beginning to think – why not? She could rummage through her belongings and find items to sell. Maybe Elena could give them some things too.

The phone rang; both girls rushed to pick up, but Gracie got there first.

'Good morning, this is Perfect Dress, how may I help you?'

'Oh hi . . . hi Parker Bain, how are you?'

At the unexpected mention of this name, Lana coloured up as her stomach flipped about. Although she knew that Gracie was going to the club opening on Saturday night with Parker, she somehow hadn't got round to mentioning that she would be there too. Maybe because she was still disappointed that it definitely wasn't a date.

'Elena's got your designs, I emailed them to her. They are amazing, by the way,' Gracie was telling Parker with full-on enthusiasm. 'We're just trying to raise some money and then we're hoping to get a summer collection made up really quickly . . . Yeah . . .'

Lana tried not to listen. She looked back at her to do list for the day and tried to focus on the next task.

'Our fund-raising ideas . . . well, so far, Lana and I are going to run a stoop sale. Do you want to come by? Yeah, tomorrow . . . I'll message you the address. That would be cool.'

'Yes, OK . . . Lana?'

'Yeah?' Lana's head snapped back up.

'Parker wants to talk to you.'

'Oh . . . me?' she asked with a rush of nerves, 'Right.' Lana picked up the phone on her desk and hit the connect button. 'Hi,' she managed, as calmly as she could.

'Hey, Lana from London, you are still going to come tomorrow night, aren't you?'

The sound of his voice was having an unsettling effect on her.

'Well, I'm not sure . . .' she began, turning away from Gracie's questioning stare. 'We're going to be really busy getting this new collection together and fund-raising for it.'

'Lana from London, this is the hottest ticket in town tomorrow. There is nothing you can be doing tomorrow evening that would be better than this. So you have to come. I'm not listening to any excuses. Plus I want you to come . . . I want to see you.'

She smiled. He was impossible to resist.

'OK,' she said, 'I'll come. I'll see you there.'

'I can't wait,' he replied.

Her smile widened into a grin. 'See you tomorrow,' she said.

She turned around and put the phone down, still with the goofy grin on her face.

'Oh, are you going to the club opening too?' Gracie asked lightly. 'That was nice of him, to invite you.'

'Yes.'

Lana wasn't sure why, but suddenly the air between them felt a little strained. 'So you're going to go?' she asked, trying to keep it breezy.

'Yes.'

'And is Bingham coming too?'

'Ummm . . . no. I think he has other plans,' Gracie shrugged.

'Oh. Right.'

Chapter Eleven

Milan

Inge the chambermaid:

Pink and white striped dress (hotel uniform)
White lace-up plimsolls (Aldi)
Simple leather-strapped watch (gift from Mother)
Total est. cost: €12

Annie pulled the towel turban lower over her eyes, then took the big wooden ladle and heaped more cold water onto the bowl of hot stones in the centre of the sauna.

A dense cloud of steam hissed up and enveloped the small, cedar-clad room. It swirled around her and the two skeletal American women lying on the wooden benches opposite exchanging fascinating gossip.

Annie knew she wasn't supposed to be in here. She was supposed to be in her room awaiting the nurse who would take her to the medical suite for her first ever enema experience.

But as soon as she'd woken up this morning, ravenous after a dinner of broth and a vegetable cocktail, she'd remembered about the appointment and decided that she just couldn't.

It was too grim. She didn't want anyone going anywhere near her with a little hosepipe. She shuddered at the thought of what might go in and what might come out.

So now, after a breakfast of hot lemon juice and a mere sliver of melon, she was hiding in the sauna listening to gossip and the frantic rumblings of her poor, starved stomach.

'So are you going to Betty's benefit when we get back to town?' the woman rocking the teeny Prada bikini, although she must have been approaching 60, asked her friend.

'Oh no,' her friend replied, nonchalantly rolling her swimsuit down and revealing a pair of boobs so spectacularly perky that Annie instantly decided to start saving for the surgery. 'Breast cancer is so old hat. All the best parties are being given by the Testicular committee. You know that. Your daughter is doing a marvellous job there.'

'Nice of you to say, but Ellen is such a lamebrain,

I don't think the success of any dance is down to her.'

'Oh dear ... so I take it she's still determined to marry the poet?'

'Not just a poet, a Communist poet. He occupied Wall Street. Can you imagine? And people know. People talk. There are already places where I'll never be able to refuse a canapé again.'

'Daughters! You have so many hopes and dreams for them when they are small and then they just turn around, grow up, and have all these crazy ideas of their own. It's tragic.'

The woman's words rang in Annie's eavesdropping ears. Daughters with their crazy ideas: was it really tragic? Wasn't it just natural? Mothers might think they knew best, but weren't daughters entitled to ideas all of their own? No matter how crazy?

Annie hadn't had the long heart-to-heart with Lana that she knew she should. She still wasn't sure what to say.

'We have to go. It's Pilates next. In a few more minutes, they'll be coming round, checking we're not hiding in the sauna and missing our treatments.'

The woman cast a pointed look at Annie. Eeeek!

Tightly wrapped in her dressing gown on the bed in her gorgeous pink room, Annie listened to the knock on the door.

121

She sat tight and didn't make any response.

'Mizzzzzz Valentina?'

Annie pulled the dressing gown tighter. If she just sat quietly, the nurse would go away, wouldn't she?

There was a second knock. *Go away!* Surely you were allowed to refuse an enema? If you didn't want one, they couldn't make you have one, could they?

Annie shut her eyes and counted slowly to ten. No other knock followed. The nurse must have gone away. Now she could be left alone to deal with her all-encompassing hunger and pounding headache.

She'd tried asking for paracetamol tablets at lunch but she'd been turned down. Headaches were apparently a normal part of the detoxification process and she was assured that she would feel so much better after her afternoon enema.

She gave a shudder at the thought. Help! This was worse, much worse than she'd imagined. Yet every other guest here appeared so cheerful. At lunch, they seemed to sip at their veggie cocktails with relish.

It felt as if she was the only person who could actually kill for a cake and a cup of coffee. She was beginning to hallucinate food: a few moments ago, she could have sworn she saw a breadbasket filled with crispy white rolls on her bedside table.

But no: it was a basket of flowers and not one of

them looked edible. Well, there was a rose . . . rose petals were edible, weren't they?

Just as she considered picking the rose apart, her phone began to ring.

'Hello loveliness, how is life in the lap of luxury?' asked Ed, his voice teasing and warm.

'Oh babes, it's hell. Hell on earth. I am so hungry and I don't feel well,' she whined.

'What's the matter?'

'I haven't eaten *anything* – anything solid – for nearly twenty-four hours now.'

She expected sympathy, but instead heard Ed give a loud snort of laughter.

'It's not funny!'

'Yes it is. You've flown all the way to Italy to be starved. Italy? The land of the lasagne, the spaghetti *alla vongole*, the tiramisu . . .'

'Shut up, Ed,' Annie said feeling almost vicious, 'you're not helping.'

He gave another snort.

'Everything's fine here,' he said, perhaps hoping to take her mind off the food situation. 'Dinah has the twins under control. In fact I think she's taken such pity on us that she's going to make us a lovely dinner . . . sorry.'

There was a brisk tap on the door.

'I have to go,' she whispered, hoping that she couldn't be heard.

'Now what? Have you spotted an unattended dessert trolley and you're about to launch an attack?'

'Goodbye,' she hissed and clicked the phone off.

She huddled under the dressing gown and hoped the person who'd just knocked would go away. But the knock came once again.

She held her breath.

The sound of a key being put into the lock. Oh no! Oh help! This was it. A team of them were out there. They were going to pin her down and carry her kicking and screaming to the enema room. Maybe there were laws in Italy, and if you were a certain weight medical people were allowed to seize you for treatment.

She dived onto the floor and rolled under the bed. They wouldn't take her without a fight.

The door opened and Annie saw a small pair of white plimsolled feet pad into the room. A trolley and a vacuum cleaner followed.

Her eyes widened. A vacuum cleaner?! Oh dear God, was that what they used?!

The door closed.

Annie wondered if she could make it to the bathroom and bolt herself in.

But frozen with indecision, she waited. Only when she heard the vacuum cleaner being plugged in and turned on did it dawn on her that it was the maid, come to clean her room.

With a sigh of relief, she popped her head up over the bed.

'Hello!'

The maid gave a scream of surprise.

'Sorry, sorry, I was just down here. I was just . . . hiding, to be honest.'

The maid looked totally shocked.

'I come back,' she stammered at last.

'No, no, it's OK, honestly,' Annie insisted. 'Do you want to sit down?'

'No, I'm fine,' the maid replied in an accent which Annie recognized.

'Are you from the Ukraine?' she asked.

'No. Romania.'

'Hello, I'm Annie.'

'I, Inge,' the maid replied.

'Hello Inge, your English is good.'

'My Italian is better.'

'It's good,' Annie told her.

'I watch some English television,' Inge said.

'What do you watch?'

'Hercule Poirot,' Inge replied with a smile.

'Oh yes, with the little moustache.' Annie twiddled her fingers up at her lip to convey the idea.

'Why you hiding?' Inge asked.

'Oh . . .' Annie wasn't sure if she wanted to admit

to this, 'I . . . erm . . . I didn't want to see the nurse.'

Inge burst out laughing.

'You know about that?'

'Oh yes, we all know about this, the water in the . . .' she pointed to her bottom and laughed again, crinkling the skin around her eyes. She was a little older than Annie had at first thought: maybe mid to late forties. Sometimes it was hard to tell. Life might have taken its toll on a chambermaid from Romania.

'This hotel is very strange,' Annie admitted: 'so expensive and nothing to eat. I am so hungry. I would give anything . . .'

A bubble of hope was forming in her head. Could Inge possibly . . .

The maid smiled but shook her head: 'I cannot help. I cannot give you food. This is lose job. Immediately.'

'No. No, I understand.'

A brisk knock on the door brought their conversation to an abrupt halt.

'Mizzzzzzz Valentina?'

It was the nurse – she was back! She had probably been searching the entire hotel for Annie and this time she wasn't going to take no for an answer.

'Under bed,' Inge hissed.

Annie didn't need to be told twice; she hit the

carpet and rolled under the bed as quickly as she could.

Meanwhile, Inge opened the door. Annie could see the white rubber clogs of the nurse at the door. She gave a little shudder of anxiety.

Some Italian was exchanged, too quickly for Annie to make out. Then, to her vast relief, the door closed and she and Inge were alone in the room.

'Is safe,' Inge told her, 'I say room is empty.'

Annie came out from under the bed. 'You are my new best friend,' she declared. 'Now I know you can't give me food, but you can tell me where to hide when the nurse comes back again tomorrow.'

Chapter Twelve

London

Elena means business:

White blouse (Banana Republic)
Grey pencil skirt (Calvin Klein)
Grey suede high heels (LK Bennett sale)
Tiny diamond pendant (Tiffany's from Seth)
Metallic blue nails (Chanel)
Total est. cost: £460

Elena was sitting in the small basement office of her mother's house, firing out emails from her laptop. She was still seethingly furious with her mother.

How dare she turn all their ideas down without even listening, without even looking properly, without even asking one single informed question!

Svetlana was so stubborn and so pig-headed. Everything had to be done exactly her way, or it couldn't be done at all. Compromise was not a word which had ever entered into Elena's mother's head.

No wonder she'd run into so many divorces. She was a complete tyrant.

She hadn't even wanted to talk to Elena properly again. As soon as Elena's presentation was over, Svetlana had busied herself with her trip to Italy and then, after leaving a great long list of instructions, she'd been driven off to the airport early in the morning.

Elena cared passionately about Perfect Dress. She wanted it to grow and to thrive. She wanted it, one day, to be a leading international label. In Elena's opinion, Svetlana did not care nearly enough about the label. For Svetlana, Perfect Dress was just a hobby, something she'd been happy to create to keep Elena busy.

Was Svetlana really bothered if Perfect Dress survived for another season or not? Elena didn't think so.

Svetlana would still have her mansion, her millions, her London social life, her dazzling jewels, and no doubt she'd be quite happy to give Elena a little allowance and then begin her insatiable quest to marry her off to the richest Eastern European man she could reel in.

Ha.

For a brief moment, Elena stopped raging and thought about the very important man in her life: the non-Eastern-European, non-multimillionaire Seth.

Seth was another reason that Elena needed to make Perfect Dress a success. If she didn't have an office and a business in New York, then she would have to come back to London and say goodbye to Seth – which was impossible to imagine.

Her handsome photographer boyfriend was the best guy she'd ever met; maybe the best guy she would ever meet. He'd been with her since she first moved to New York, in fact he was part of the reason she'd moved. She didn't have any doubts that they were very much in love but a move back to London might ruin everything.

Did Svetlana care?

Did Svetlana even consider her feelings for one moment?

Did Svetlana realize how serious she felt about this business and this guy?

No, no and no.

Fingers slamming against the keys, Elena was back to raging once again. She would show Svetlana. She would have the new dresses made up and she would make them fly!

A timid tap on the office door let Elena know that Maria was on the other side.

'Hi Maria, come in.'

Elena liked and respected Maria and often wondered how Maria had managed to put up with Svetlana and all her demands for so long.

'So sorry to disturb,' Maria began, with an apologetic little bow.

'No don't worry about it. Is everything OK?'

'The tennis coach is here for the boys. He has the right password, I recognize him and the boys know him, but . . .' Maria hesitated.

'What is it?'

'He says the boys are playing in a tournament all day today. I do not know about this. He says he tell Miss Wisneski and maybe she forget to tell me.'

'Well, she was so busy packing and making arrangements for her Italian trip, maybe she did forget to tell you.'

'He say the boys need to bring their passports to register for the tournament. I do not like this. You know there is problem with Mr Igor and taking boys out of the country . . . so I don't know if this is right.'

'Is this the coach they go with all the time?'

'Yes.'

'He knows the password.'

'Yes.'

'He probably just needs the passports to prove their age.'

'Yes, he says he comes back with the boys and their passports at 6 p.m. tonight.'

'I'm sure it's fine,' Elena said, giving her most reassuring smile, 'don't worry about it. Poor Maria, always worrying.'

'But Mr Igor . . . and Miss Wisneski is not here.' Maria frowned. 'I would like to check with her. Is possible to check with her?'

Elena sighed. Ever since Igor had managed to get the boys to Luton airport and within several hundred metres of his private jet, Svetlana had been paranoid. There were all kinds of legal protection around the boys. There was no way Igor could move them near the border without alarm bells ringing all over the country.

Now some poor coach was getting hassled because he couldn't fill in a registration form without everyone jumping into panic mode. It was all completely over the top. But then so was Svetlana.

'It will be fine – but if you like, I will phone her.'

Maria's face broke into a relieved smile.

'Thank you, shall I wait outside?'

'You wait with the boys. I'll come up in a few minutes.'

Elena picked up her mobile and clicked onto Svetlana's number. It went straight through to voicemail.

Svetlana was probably getting her first massage

of the day, being rubbed down and pampered by the minions she liked to surround herself with while poor Maria was worrying herself into a frenzy because as usual Svetlana had forgotten to tell her about the boys' plans for the day.

Elena made her way to the marble-floored splendour of the entrance hall. Maria was hovering anxiously behind Michael and Petrov, while a tanned young man in a tracksuit waited beside them.

'Hi,' Elena greeted them.

'Hello, I'm Yann,' the coach replied. 'Nice to meet you, Miss . . .'

'Elena,' she said. 'Where is the tournament?'

'In Richmond, all day long. We should be back by six.'

'How are you getting there?' she wondered.

'I know the boys sometimes have a driver, but I don't want to put you to any trouble, so I was going to order a taxi.'

'Maria and I didn't know about the tournament, so the driver is having the day off.'

'No problem,' the coach reassured her.

'And you need their passports?'

'Just to prove their dates of birth. It's an official requirement. I'm sorry if there's any inconvenience, I did explain this to Miss Wisneski.'

'Yes.'

'Did you speak with Miss Wisneski?' Maria asked, looking up at Elena hopefully.

Elena hadn't planned on lying. She meant to check out the coach herself and if it all made sense, she'd say she couldn't reach Svetlana but she was sure it was fine.

But now that Maria was looking at her, all troubled and sorrowful eyes, Elena thought a little white lie would be OK. She didn't want poor Maria to worry all day long. It wasn't even 10 a.m. yet: that meant eight full hours of worrying ahead.

'Yes I spoke to her, everything is fine,' Elena said with her most confident smile.

'Ah!'

Maria's face relaxed.

'Are you looking forward to the tournament?' Elena asked the boys, who were dressed in bright, immaculately ironed tennis whites.

Petrov gave an eager smile while Michael shrugged. He was holding a tennis racket in one hand and an iPhone in the other. He didn't bother taking his earplugs out to talk to her.

'I hope you have a really nice day. I bet you'll both do really well.'

'What about food?' Maria asked, looking alarmed all over again. 'If it is all day, I must make more than the drinks and snacks I pack.'

Yann glanced at his watch. 'Please don't worry, I'll take care of that. We should go . . .'

'Are you sure? Really?' Maria asked.

'Maria, they will be fine,' Elena said a little sternly. 'Boys, have a great time. We'll see you later.'

'This is so cool,' Petrov said as he stepped out of the front door behind Yann and his big brother. 'I get to play in a tournament – and I'm not even any good!'

Chapter Thirteen

Milan

Svetlana at ease:

Navy and gold swimsuit (Melissa Odabash)
Gold mules (Manolo Blahnik)
White towelling robe (hotel property)
White towel round head (same)
Black and gold shades (Chanel)
Gold and sapphire earrings (Harry Winston – jeweller)
Marquise-shaped solitaire diamond ring
(Harry Roscoff – husband)
Total est. cost: £36,000

Finally it was lunchtime on day two of Annie's spa
stay. She had staggered to the dining room feeling
barely alive.

Somehow she had survived yesterday: a lunch of vile slimy green vegetable juice, an afternoon of brutal lymphatic drainage massage, and dinner, a measly bowl of vegetable broth. She'd escaped the enema action too – so far.

Her stomach sloshing with the huge jug of water she'd drunk before bed in an attempt to feel slightly fuller, she'd managed to sleep for six hours or so before violent hunger pangs and a pressing need to wee had woken her up early.

From 5.30 a.m. till 7 a.m., she'd made an exhaustive search of her room, trying to find something – anything – to eat. She'd even considered shredding some of the bedding and chewing it down.

She'd made it through the two cups of water with lemon juice labelled 'breakfast' then a torturous two-hour yoga class. Then she'd practically had to crawl half delirious with fatigue and hunger into the dining room where she knew that only an evil vegetable juice awaited her.

She was now halfway down the glass of dismal green goo – she suspected both celery and raw courgette were lurking in there – and was honestly contemplating eating the starched white napkin when Svetlana swanned in, swathed in white towelling, bling jewels and glowing with unbearable smug happiness.

'Look at my stomach,' were Svetlana's words of greeting as a waiter moved forward to pull up a chair for her at Annie's table.

'Your stomach is always as flat as a washboard,' Annie said, trying to keep the resentment out of her voice. Extreme dieting always made her feel like this: vicious, wounded and malevolent.

'I've had two enemas already today. This is the secret,' Svetlana confided. 'This is how to get your colon moving, cleansing, shedding all your debris. I already lose four kilos!'

More than eight pounds. It wasn't possible. How could Svetlana have already lost more than eight pounds?

'Have you had enema yet?' Svetlana asked.

Annie put her lips to her juice straw and avoided eye contact.

'Annah,' Svetlana's tone was stern, 'you cannot come for the programme and not have the enemas. This is the most important part. Everyone is nervous the first time. But after one, is easy.'

'But—'

'No but. The people here are so professional and so caring. You will find it relaxing: the water draining in, the toxins draining out.'

'But—'

'Shhh!' Svetlana shook her head. 'Is no problem. I promise you.'

'I can't! I just can't do it,' Annie blurted out.

'They help you to put everything in place, then they leave you to relax for about forty minutes.'

'Forty minutes!'

It sounded worse than she'd imagined.

'Some litres of coffee need to go up. It takes time.'

Annie's mouth hung open with astonishment.

Litres of coffee had to go up and come back out again ... unbelievable. She looked around the dining room at the other guests swathed in white gowns. They were all doing this? They were all in on it?

'Is interesting,' Svetlana added. 'You get a little sieve, you can examine what horrrrrrible things come out. I will never eat filet mignon again. I have been passing lumps of undigested meat. Unspeakable. By day five, out come little black pellets, as hard as tyre rubber.'

This conversation was making Annie shudder.

'When you leave here, your colon will be as clean as a baby's.'

'I don't think I can do it,' Annie whimpered.

When the knock had come on her hotel room door for her 9 a.m. appointment with the coffee nozzle this morning, she'd sent the woman away, informing her that she wasn't feeling well. But she knew the nurse would come back at 3 p.m. and if Annie still wasn't 'well', she was to be taken to see Dr

Delicioso, who would no doubt prescribe an immediate enema.

'I feel terrible,' she told Svetlana with total honesty, 'my head is pounding, my hands are shaking; I have got to get something proper to eat.'

'Tschaaaaa! This is just the toxins talking,' Svetlana informed her between happy, dainty sips of her juice. Clearly a diet of liquid vegetables in various forms was not causing this dieting disciplinarian the slightest amount of trouble.

Annie's toxins weren't just talking, they were screaming, they were rioting through her system! As she'd walked through the corridor towards the dining room, she'd caught the faintest whiff of coffee and she'd stopped in her tracks like a sniffer dog, wondering how she could beg or bribe her way to a cup of her rich, dark, number one drug of choice.

'If I could just get a sandwich . . . or a cappuccino . . . just one tiny little macchiato, even,' she pleaded, 'I mean, this is a very expensive hotel, surely guests are allowed to order something to eat if they feel as weak and as bad as I do?'

Svetlana shook her head. 'But this is what we pay for: to stick to the programme. If the doctor says you can do the programme then you will do the programme, no matter how much you protest. You can offer the staff as much money as you like – my first time here I took off my diamond necklace and said I would swap it for a pizza – but they are trained not to give in. This is why the programme works, for everyone. When you are desperate, they will bring you a celery and nettle cleanser, to speed up the detox. Maybe this is what you need.'

'I might have to leave,' Annie said weakly.

Once again, Svetlana shook her head. 'They will stop you. Always with tact and charm, but they will persuade you to come back. Please, drink some more water, have your enema, then your massage. At dinner tonight you will eat the soup and feel much, much better.'

Svetlana's juice was finished. She looked happy and satisfied. No sign there of the hammering head, the trembling hands or terrible, killer mood Annie was suffering. Obviously, Svetlana's toxins were leaving her perfect, first class system with barely a murmur of protest.

'I think I lie beside the pool before my programme for the afternoon,' Svetlana said, 'it is beautiful to look out over the lake. Why don't you join me?'

No.

Annie was not going to lie out on a sun lounger in her reinforced, tummy tuck swimsuit waiting to be led like a lamb to the enema.

The enema was the enemy. It had to be outwitted. It had to be avoided at all costs.

Just how hard could it be to escape from an exclusive, ultra-luxurious, six star hotel?

In a bright red swimsuit, flip-flops, Svetlana's Chanel sunglasses and a broad-brimmed sunhat, Annie strode casually out of the front door of the hotel.

It was 2.37 p.m. and she couldn't wait in her room any longer for the knock: the dreaded knock that would mean it was time for either the *procedure* or a trip to Dr Delicious.

Over her shoulder was a large straw bag. The magazine and a hotel towel poking from it were meant to show that she was heading for the pool.

But tucked inside the straw bag was a sundress and her handbag, packed with all the essentials for a break-out: money, cards, her mobile – even her passport, because she was considering running away not just to Milan, but all the way home.

Right, she was going to walk casually across the lawn until she found a nice, quiet spot away from the eyes of the staff but close to the gate at the end of the driveway. There, she would put out her towel and pretend to read her brand new copy of *Vogue Italia*, but as soon as she heard a car approaching, she was going to jump to it and slip out of the open gates before anyone could stop her.

After that, her plan was a little more vague.

Maybe she would find a bus somewhere. All she

142

knew, her guiding principle, was that she had to get to a town and a plateful of food and a glass or six of wine and a huge, steaming, heart-hammering cafetière of coffee very soon, before she started eating grass, or the geraniums in the flowerpots – or began to consider hunting down songbirds.

The electric gates were in sight. Beside them was an elegant pale green painted wooden fence she'd not appreciated before, which probably ran the length of the grounds. It was well over six feet high and obviously designed not to keep intruders out but to keep semi-starved, half-delirious guests in.

She could also see a gardener with a rake in his hand and he seemed to have spotted her. Annie pulled the towel from her bag and began to lay it out across the grass, trying to make it look as if her intentions were entirely innocent.

But he was striding towards her. Maybe he was planning to herd her back towards the pool with several prods of his rake.

She sat down on the towel, opened up her magazine and pretended to read although he was drawing closer now.

'Signorina?' he called over as he approached.

Aw, he'd called her 'Miss', she couldn't help being pleased. Obviously the sunglasses and the hideously expensive swimsuit's superb, curve-minimizing structure were working their magic.

'Ciao,' she offered, 'es una bella giornata.'

'Si, Signora.'

Ah, back to 'Mrs'. Evidently on closer inspection he'd come to a more accurate idea of her age.

Then he said something much more complicated and beyond her grasp of basic Italian, but as it ended with 'piscina', she guessed it was to do with the swimming pool and why wasn't she over there instead of hovering suspiciously beside the gates?

'La pelle inglese,' she said, *English skin*.

This made him laugh.

'Che hai?'

'La pelle Inglese,' she repeated, 'seccato al sole.'

She thought that meant sunburn, but when the gardener looked at her in confusion, she wondered if maybe it meant sun-dried . . . Had she in fact seen it on the side of a jar of tomatoes?

Now she could hear a car in the distance. What if it was driving up to the hotel? What if it was her one and only chance to get through the open gates this afternoon? She had to get rid of the gardener sharpish.

With a flash of inspiration, she decided to play the luxury guest card. Surely in a place like this, even the gardener was trained to do the bidding of the pampered inmates?

'No bevanda,' she told him, hoping that meant

'no drink' and she tried to look a little sad and pleading: 'cosi caldo e no bevanda.'

Hopefully that meant: *so hot and no drink.*

The gardener jumped to attention: 'No problema. Acqua con limone?' he offered, as if there was a choice.

'Si, grazie, grazie multo.'

As he sprinted off in the direction of the hotel to carry out her request, Annie heard the hum, which surely had to indicate that the gates were about to open. Leaving her towel on the lawn, she darted towards the nearest gatepost so that she would be hidden by the gate as it opened.

A taxi! Hallelujah! A real, live, Italian taxi was sweeping up the driveway. Of course she knew what this meant: within a few minutes, an empty taxi in need of a fare would be sweeping back out again.

Tucking her bag under her arm, Annie broke cover and ran for the gap between the gates. They were closing surprisingly quickly and for a hideous moment, when her flip-flop snagged and didn't keep pace with her foot, she thought she was going to be trapped: a chubby Englishwoman in a reinforced swimsuit impaled on the electric gates.

As she tried to wrench the flip-flop free, the thought flashed through her panicked mind that they'd probably keep her there for ever – as a warning to all those who didn't want to complete the programme and tried to get away. But then she was out.

A wide open view of the countryside lay before her: fields of green and gold, hilltop villages shimmering in the afternoon haze and a big blue sky.

She allowed herself a brief moment of elation and considered jogging away from the gates hastily before the gardener or anyone else had time to work out that she was missing.

But she had to wait for the taxi. She could already hear the crunching as it travelled back down the drive. Then came the hum of the gates.

Forgetting that she was dressed only in a swim-suit, she rushed at the car, waving it down and yelling in her Italian for Beginners: 'Buon giorno. A Milano, per favore ! Rapido! Pronto! Presto!'

Only when she was safely in the back seat did she realize that the driver wasn't just smiling from ear to ear because he was a happy man. He was smiling hard because she was dressed in a swimsuit and on the run from Camp Detox.

'Many peoples try to leave,' he began. 'When I here in taxi, always peoples try to leave. But you – first one in a *costume de bagno*.'

Chapter Fourteen

Milan

Annie on the run:

Brown and blue print maxi sundress (Diane von Furstenberg)
Strappy sandals (Hobbs)
Sunglasses (Chanel, via Svetlana)
Total est. cost: £790

'Something else for Madam?'

The waiter raised an eyebrow and Annie knew what he was thinking: that she was the greediest woman who had ever eaten at his restaurant. Well she didn't care.

Had he been locked up in a gilded, frescoed, marbled hell and denied anything but water with bloody lemon juice or celery and courgette cocktails?

'Maybe just one more coffee, please,' she replied.

She was sitting at an outdoor table in the haze of contentment she had promised herself. In front of her were two drained coffee cups, an empty wine bottle, and the bowl, scraped clean, which had once contained a mound of creamy, chocolate-drenched profiteroles.

Before that she'd eaten a dreamy thin-crusted pizza and the portion of garlic-infused, pasta-layered lasagne of her dreams.

Caffeine, alcohol and sugar pumping furiously around her deprived system, she watched as the people in this Milan square went by in the afternoon sunshine.

First of all she was just watching vaguely. But then details began to spring out more clearly. There was a blonde girl with long bright hair in a shiny black leather jacket. Her black ankle-length trousers set off a pair of purple suede pumps and Annie admired her purple tote bag and the white, black and purple silk scarf tied loosely around her neck.

Mmmm . . . a thoughtful outfit all very nicely put together. Only blondes or black-haired people looked truly brilliant in black. She'd suspected that for years.

Now here was an extremely well-dressed Italian

man: white chinos, blue and white striped shirt, then a thick tan belt with a silver buckle around his hips and tan loafers on his feet. That was another great outfit.

Mmmm . . . matching bag and shoes . . . matching shoes and belts. These careful little details got a bad rap for being too matchy-matchy, but really, in the right kind of way, they pulled an outfit together.

She sipped at her third espresso, loaded with a teaspoon of brown sugar, and watched more closely.

Look at those two lovely girls, strolling arm in arm, laughing. One wore a floaty white tunic printed with bright pink flowers, with white leggings and silver gladiator sandals. The other was in the acid shade of yellow that totally complements tanned skin and dark hair. Oooh and she had a miniature bright blue satchel strung across her body. Now that looked good; that really did set the dress off.

Annie smiled. This was fashion-watching and she was enjoying it. She couldn't think when she'd last just sat still, watched people go by and soaked up their inspiration.

A pair of elderly ladies began to cross the square, arm in arm, just like the girls. They were elegantly turned out for their evening stroll, one in a beige linen suit with cream-coloured trim, holding a crocodile clutch, her hair up in a fierce beehive showing off a huge pair of pearl and gold earrings.

Let's hear it for dressed-up old ladies, Annie thought to herself and immediately wondered how her mum was doing.

Annie's mother wasn't quite 70 yet, but she was struggling with a fading memory. That was how Annie liked to think of it. The term 'early-onset dementia' was too poignant. Dementia was too irreversible a word and 'early-onset' sounded as if they had been cheated out of years of Fern's life, which of course they had. So Annie consoled herself with the term 'fading memory' because her mum's memory often came back in fits and starts.

There were flashes of perfect clarity. Annie could visit and find herself talking to her mum just like before, just totally normally. But sometimes when she arrived Fern would be clouded over, still recognizing her of course, but fretting in a circle of concern about all kinds of strange things: snails escaping from the garden ... tins going out of date in the cupboards ... the possibility of moss growing in the bathroom.

Annie looked down at her phone but knew a quick call wouldn't work. Because Fern found phone calls confusing.

Instead, Annie sent a text to Stefano, the student nurse who rented a room very cheaply in her mother's house on the understanding that he kept a watchful eye on Fern along with the home help.

'How's Mum tonight? Thinking of her, just wondered what she was doing. Annie xx'

As she waited for the reply, she watched a family walk past and felt a sharp pang of longing for her own.

'How football and where hv u put laundry?!' she fired over to Owen.

He was the first to reply: 'Washing in machine. Better believe it baby.'

Then came: 'It's Strictly Come Dancing then bed for your Mum before I sneak out later', from Fern's Stefano.

'Good plan', she replied.

For a moment she considered contacting Lana. But Svetlana's instruction had been clear: she was to wait for Lana to come running back to her. She just hoped it would happen soon.

Annie paid the bill, then through the wine and sugar fog tried to decide what to do next. One thing was for sure: she was not going back to Villa Enema. But should she go to the airport? Try and get home?

But she was in Milan on a bright and sunny Saturday. *Milano*, fashion capital: beyond this exquisite square there had to be all kinds of interesting shops and little boutiques, selling unique things.

She could stay here, get a hotel room for the night, have the Villa Verdina send her things. Sooner or later she would have to face Svetlana, though. The thought of that made her want to order another glass of wine.

'I am weak,' she whispered to herself: 'the toxins won.'

Just then, someone she recognized walked into the piazza, not far from her table. It took Annie a moment or two to place the face and recall the name, but then she called out: 'Inge! Hello!'

The chambermaid who had been so helpful turned and looked at her, eyes widening in surprised recognition.

'Hello, have you got an afternoon off?' Annie asked as Inge approached her table.

'Miss Valentine? What you do here?' Inge gestured to the empty bowls, coffee cups and wine bottle with astonishment.

'I ran away,' Annie explained with a grin.

'You run away? Oh no! You can't talk to me. They will think I help you!'

Chapter Fifteen

New York

Potential stoop sale customer:

Purple maxi-dress (Haute Hippie)
Flip-flops (Fitflops)
Sunglasses (vintage Gucci)
Handbag (this season's Coach Hobo)
Bead, pearl and turquoise necklace (vintage costume jewellery)
Total est. cost: $430

'I feel dumb,' Gracie admitted.

'Why?!' Lana exclaimed.

She looked admiringly over the set of stone stairs which led to the tiny apartment that Gracie shared with two other girls in this groovy part of not-so-eyewateringly-expensive Manhattan.

It had taken almost an hour to set everything out on the steps for the stoop sale. On each of the steps were treasures the girls had taken from their own personal collections: unwanted belts, headbands, hair decorations, homemade flower corsages and a large collection of second-hand shop jewellery finds. Bead necklaces, paste brooches, jangly bracelets all vied for attention from passers-by.

Cleverly, the girls had made each step a different price: just $1 per piece on the bottom step, rising to $10 per item on the top step. They needed to make $500 and if they could sell everything on the steps, they estimated they would be at least halfway to their total.

But as they perched on the top step expectantly, people were just walking past without so much as a glance in their direction.

'I feel dumb,' Gracie whispered again. 'We've set all this stuff out but people are just walking past. No one's going to stop and buy anything. We're just going to sit here looking like losers.'

'So . . . we'll just have to get up and sell it,' Lana said, as if it was simple.

She knew it wasn't entirely simple, but she was at a huge advantage. Her mother was a born sales-woman and Lana had seen her in action ever since she was small. Selling outfits in The Store, selling to private clients in the small office she used to run from her home; even on TV to her rapt audience.

Annie was just nice to people, she simply offered, made suggestions, pushed in a happy, enthusiastic way. And that's what Lana and Gracie had to do right now, even if they both felt a little shy and weird about it.

'OK, you pick up the box of $1 items, I'll get the $2 box and we'll get down there and start offering them to the people passing.'

Gracie didn't look thrilled at the thought.

'C'mon, we've gone to all this trouble. We have to make it work now.'

'Suppose—'

Lana took the jug and a small stack of cups and moved down to the sidewalk.

'Hi, we have some great bargains here,' she said to the first person who passed. 'We're raising money to start our own business . . .'

He just shrugged and carried on.

'How about a $1 lapel pin. A very cheap birthday gift,' Gracie offered two teen boys.

They stopped and looked at her: 'How much?'

'You can have three for $2. Half price.'

They paused but finally one shrugged and agreed: 'OK.'

And the first sale was made. Somehow, once

those first two badges had been bought, everything got much easier. The boys came to the steps to look through the other things for sale. Then, because they were at the stoop, other people stopped and looked too.

'Wow, these are pretty. I'll give you $2 for both, if that's OK.'

'Do you have change of $5? I want to take this one – oh, you know what, I'll take that one too, if you'll give me them both for $5.'

Within a few minutes, it was busy. As soon as a small knot of people had stopped, other people stopped too, curious to see what the fuss was about.

Soon the $1 step was almost empty and the Tupperware box already had a thin layer of green bills across the bottom.

Lana's phone, in the back pocket of her jeans, began to buzz. When she saw that Elena was calling, she thought, despite the hustle on the step, she should answer.

'Lana, a change has been made to the company bank account,' Elena began briskly.

'Really?'

'You don't know anything about it? Svetlana didn't phone in or email or anything like that?'

'No, not that I know of. What kind of change?' Lana wondered.

'I can no longer move money on my own. I've just

tried to make a payment and they're telling me everything needs two signatures: hers and mine or hers and yours. This is infuriating. It's going to slow day-to-day transactions right down, and you know why she's done it?'

That struck Lana as slightly obvious.

'She thinks we're up to something,' Elena answered her own question. 'She knows we might do something without her permission; so she's doing all she can to stop us. We go ahead with our own dresses, with our own money and we don't speak to the Mothers unless we have to. OK?'

'OK,' Lana agreed. Well, she and her mum weren't exactly in regular contact anyway. Ever since the day Lana had left London, they hadn't spoken: the odd text just to confirm a safe landing and other details, but no actual conversation.

'Have you made that extra $500 yet? If we're printing up fabric, we're going to need it – it costs a lot,' Elena added.

'We're trying,' Lana said, watching an expensively dressed woman with a beautiful beaded necklace pick something up from the top step and scrutinize it.

'I'll give you $2,' the woman said to Gracie, holding up an elaborate brooch in the shape of a peacock.

'I have to go,' Lana said and quickly shut down the call from Elena.

'No!' Lana interrupted the too cheap sale Gracie looked as if she was about to make: 'that's a really nice piece – we couldn't take anything less than the full $10. In fact, $10 is a steal.'

Without hesitation, the woman opened her bag, brought out her wallet and paid the $10 without a murmur of protest.

'Good going!' Gracie told Lana once the woman had begun to walk away from them.

'I don't know if it was – I think she might clean it up and sell it on uptown for $50.'

'Maybe that's what we should do, if it doesn't work out in the dress business,' Gracie said, eyes widening.

'Who said anything about it not working out in the dress business? Hi!' Lana called out across the sidewalk: 'we've got all sorts of amazing stuff going really cheap over here!'

Several new potential customers began to head over. Once they had been seen to, Gracie caught Lana by surprise by asking out of the blue: 'So, you're still coming tonight, aren't you?'

'Yeah, well, I mean . . . it sounds like a pretty cool party.'

'Yeah! This is one of the hottest tickets in town

tonight. And our names are on the guest list. So – do you like Parker?'

'Well, I don't know him at all, but he seems like a pretty interesting guy . . .'

'You know what I mean. Do you *like* like Parker?'

Lana shrugged. 'I dunno.'

For some reason, she didn't want to talk to Gracie about this. Usually Gracie shared every little twist and turn of Lana's love life. But she just didn't want to discuss her big crush on Parker with Gracie. It didn't feel comfortable.

Lana looked at her friend and suddenly understood: Gracie *liked* Parker. That was the problem, right there. Gracie liked him too.

But that wasn't really fair – Gracie already had a boyfriend.

Was Gracie going to get in Lana's way?

Was Gracie going to stamp on any chance of Lana and Parker getting together because she liked him too?

Chapter Sixteen

Milan

Inge off duty:

Pink vest top (Benetton)
White jeans (H&M)
Pink and white messenger canvas bag (market stall)
Pink leather sandals (same)
Total est. cost: €68

'Honestly, no one is going to think you've helped me. I promise!' Annie insisted, jumping up from her café table to catch up with the chambermaid, who was hurrying away from her.

'But if they see us together!' Inge insisted.

'There's no one to see us and anyway, I've run away from a hotel, not a prison. C'mon, it's OK. This is a beautiful part of town, do you live near here?'

Inge shook her head: 'No ... I've come here to visit a special shop.'

'Really?'

Through the coffee, wine and profiterole haze, Annie could feel a burst of enthusiasm surfacing.

'What kind of shop?'

Inge frowned. 'It sells ... I think it is called ribbons.'

'A ribbon shop?'

'Yes, but beautiful, every kind, every imagining of ribbon,' Inge tried to explain, 'and an old shop. It has been here for many, many years.'

'Can I come and look with you?'

For a moment, Inge hesitated.

'I left the hotel without your help: I will make sure everyone knows that. *Please?*'

Inge smiled. 'OK.'

So Annie and Inge fell into step as they crossed the elegant piazza, Annie asking where Inge lived and what she was doing this weekend and why she was crossing town to visit a ribbon shop.

It turned out that Inge's daughter was graduating from college and for the ceremony Inge wanted to spruce up a trusty linen sundress and jacket.

'I have them in my bag,' Inge explained. 'I cannot afford a new dress, but I would like to make the old things a little new.'

161

'Good idea,' Annie agreed.

They walked from the piazza into a narrow street full of the boutiques Annie had been hoping to find in Milan. There was a shop devoted to perfume, one filled just with candles, one with stationery and fountain pens. Once she'd been to the ribbon shop with Inge, she would come back and browse to her heart's content.

Oh! There was a tiny shop which sold only plaited leather handbags: she really would have to come back. It was just as Dinah had promised – she was in Italy, breathing in colours, cuts and shapes and rekindling her passion for fashion.

For the first time in months, she suddenly *did* feel open to beautiful things, well made, designed to be worn over and over again with love.

'What's your daughter like?' Annie asked her new friend.

'Oh!' Inge turned and gave a beaming smile, 'she's wonderful; a very pretty girl, clever, kind and generous too. I love her. I'm so proud of her, she will be a very good nurse.'

'That's fantastic. And never a cross word?'

Inge frowned at this, as if she did not understand.

'You don't have many arguments?'

Inge shook her head. 'No we are both peaceful people and we agree on most things. It is just the two of us at home now and she only has one serious boyfriend and I like him very much. Do you have a daughter?'

'Yes . . . we've had a very big argument and we haven't really said sorry,' Annie admitted. 'She lives in New York now and we used to be very close. This is our first big disagreement.'

Annie felt a lump building up in her throat.

'She lives in New York?' Inge asked. 'That is far away.'

'Yes.'

'What was the argument about?'

That was a good question. What were they really arguing about? Annie considered what had most upset her about the row. Lana had made her feel out of touch, unwanted, unnecessary and, most definitely, unappreciated.

'She thinks she doesn't need me,' Annie sighed. 'And that's hard . . . she's only nineteen. Every mother needs to feel needed.'

Inge slowed her pace as she considered these words: 'Yes, it's a difficult time because when you are nineteen, you want to be free. You don't want to need your mother.'

Inge patted Annie's arm and for a moment. Annie had to blink back tears.

'But she will grow,' Inge added, 'she will come to understand how important you are. Be patient . . . Here is the shop with the ribbons.'

Inge opened the door and led Annie into a small wood-panelled space that smelled of dust and lemon peel. Inge was right: the rails along the walls were packed with spools of ribbons of every kind.

There were velvet ribbons: from narrow as shoelaces to broad as chokers, in all colours in the spectrum. There were gingham ribbons, conjuring up picnics and plaited hair; gold chiffon ribbons, spotty ribbons, embroidered daisy-chain ribbons . . .

Laid out on small mahogany tables were bunches of silk flowers, silk trims, multi-coloured netting and feathers. Everywhere Annie looked, creative ideas were bursting out at her, desperate to be used.

'What's your plan?' she asked Inge as they browsed carefully through the treasure trove. 'Do you have one? Or are you looking for inspiration?'

'I know what I am looking for,' Inge replied. A moment or two later, she said: 'This one.'

She took one of the spools down from the wall and pulled out a length. It was pink ric rac ribbon; the tightly woven braid which bobbed up and down in miniature waves, crisp and smart.

Inge brought her beige jacket out from her bag and laid the bright pink ric rac over the lapel.

'I sew this round the collar and maybe on the bottom of the sleeves,' she explained. 'I also put some on the front of the dress and around the bottom too.'

'Can I see the dress?'

Inge then brought out a beige sundress with an Empire line bodice and wide shoulder straps. It was as plain as a dress could be and Annie understood just how it would be brought to life with the ribbon trim.

The dress was laid down on a table and Inge placed the ric rac ribbon over the top of the bodice. It wasn't just that it looked good, it was giving Annie the thrilling feeling of a brand new idea: a great idea, an idea she wanted to rush back to London.

Make do and mend, improve don't move – refurbishing your existing clothes so chimed with the times.

'Inge, I have a television programme in Britain.'

Before Inge could register her surprise, Annie went on: 'It's all about making women look better, buying them new clothes. But these days, everyone's saving and paying off their credit card. So making your old clothes new again is brilliant! Getting your nice old comfortable things out of the cupboard and renewing them ... putting a lovely ribbon bias edge onto a blazer, making a crocheted corsage ... plaiting ribbon together for a quirky belt. We could have craft people on, they'll show us how to knit a snood for autumn – how to decorate a hat. Inge! You're a genius!'

The surprised chambermaid was treated to a hug.

'You just can't believe what an amazing favour you've done me. Look at these gorgeous pink velvet roses. Don't you want just one of these stitched onto the jacket? Ric rac and a rose – that will be enough. It wouldn't be good to do too much.'

'No, too much would be . . . too much.'

Annie's phone began to ring and she was immediately transported from the happy bubble of ribbon-based creativity right back to her current, slightly – well – unusual situation.

Svetlana's name flashed at her from the caller display. She could turn the phone off, but wasn't she just putting off the moment when she would have to deal with this?

The ringing went on, as she dithered. Even bolstered by lasagne, wine, coffee and profiteroles, she wasn't ready to have this conversation. She didn't want to be shouted at by Svetlana. She didn't want to be told she was feeble and weak and that the toxins were ruling her life. Or that she was a dreadfully ungrateful friend who had run away from an all expenses paid break at the most exclusive spa in Europe.

But such was the force of Svetlana's personality that Annie found herself answering the phone. Gingerly, she put it to her ear.

'ANNAH?' Svetlana asked at full volume.

'Ye-es . . .' Annie replied reluctantly.

'ANNAH! Where are you?! Annah, I don't care where you are and what you are eating, but you must come back to the hotel – with vodka and Sobranie cigarettes.'

'Really?!'

This was great. Svetlana had obviously cracked too. Sobranie cigarettes?! She didn't even smoke!

'Have you fallen off the celery and courgette wagon?' Annie asked.

'No! Be serious for one minute. My boys have gone. Igor has taken Petrov and Michael!'

Through the happy haze of ribbon shopping and the wonderful meal, not to mention a bottle of Italy's finest, these words took some time to sink in.

'Annah, are you there? Can you hear me? Igor has taken the boys – to Russia! Annah, are you drunk?'

Finally, Annie managed to reply.

'I'm so sorry . . . that's terrible. I—'

'I need you to help me.' Svetlana sounded frantic. 'I'm waiting for more information and I'm going out of my mind because there's nothing I can do yet. All I know from London is they were supposed to be playing tennis all day, but they have not come back – oh!'

The gasp was at once pained and furious.

The pleasant euphoria which had settled around Annie was disappearing rapidly.

'She let them go with the coach for the whole day,' Svetlana wailed. 'But this tournament does not exist. And she let them take their passports. Their passports! I will kill her! I will kill her with my own hands.'

'Maria let them go with their passports?' Annie asked, hardly able to believe it. Maria was always so protective of the two boys.

'Elena!' Svetlana wailed. 'Elena has handed my children over to Igor.'

'Elena? What? Have you been in touch with Igor?' Annie had never sobered up so quickly.

'We cannot contact Igor. Obviously I leave many, many messages and Harry speak to Igor's lawyers, but Igor make no reply. The boys will be in Russia. It is impossible! Oh, I am going to—'

Svetlana burst into a high-pitched, uncontrollable sob.

Annie would not be spending tonight in a hotel room emptying the minibar; she obviously had to go back to Camp Detox and do whatever Svetlana needed her to do.

She took a deep breath and told Svetlana: 'I'm on my way.'

Chapter Seventeen

New York

Parker parties on:

Skinny orange shirt (Gant sale)
Skinny black jeans (Greenwich Village Denim)
Skinny black leather tie (Greenwich Vintage)
Black pork-pie hat (same)
Total est. cost: $180

Lana knew this was the right street, in fact she could already see the retro-neon sign which flashed the words 'Spider's Nest' into the busy street. She was nervous, but trying hard not to act it. So she slowed her breathing down and stepped lightly in her brand new shoes.

It had only taken her two – well maybe two and a

half hours to get ready to go out tonight. Six outfits had been compiled to go with the blue polka-dot shoes and finally she'd made a decision she was almost happy with.

She'd chosen a blue and white patterned blouse, a blue miniskirt and a grey waistcoat enlivened with a flower corsage. She hoped she was saying: cute but hip. Her hair was flowing long and loose down her back and as she stole a glance at her reflection she couldn't help thinking that yes, she looked OK and importantly, she looked totally London.

But would this be a good look for the club? Would Parker be pleased that he'd invited her? There: now her stomach was flipping about, her pulse jumping again. If only she and Gracie were at ease about tonight they'd have been able to meet up and walk into this coolest of parties together.

But instead of peace, there was a polite hostility: both of them pretending everything was fine, but neither really feeling it.

What if Gracie and Parker were already in there together? Lana asked herself. Maybe they'd met up for a drink before. Maybe Bingham was toast. Maybe Parker and Gracie were already an item . . . maybe Parker had invited Lana just so he could get close to Gracie.

Argh! She was going to have to stop this.

Lana was at the entrance now. A long queue

snaked out along the sidewalk and a quick glance told her that she was with the cool people now: distressed leather jackets, funkiest hair, fascinating dresses and everyone sweeping utterly disdainful looks at everyone else.

She was supposed to go up to the doorman and tell him she was on the guest list – but she didn't know if she had the nerve. Still, if she joined the queue she could be stuck there for hours.

C'mon, Lana, she told herself, *if you can get on a plane and cross the Atlantic to work in New York, you can speak to a doorman. C'mon!*

The doorman closest to her looked stressed and busy. He was a heavy-set black guy in a swanky blue suit and purple tie, carrying a clipboard and walkie-talkie. His phone was a silver earpiece with an aerial.

Lana walked over to him, heart in her mouth.

'Hi, I . . .'

'What?' he snapped.

'I think . . . I mean – I was kind of told—'

'Guest list?' he asked, sounding dubious. 'Name?'

'Lana Valentine,' she mumbled.

His finger began to travel down the page. Did Parker even know her last name? She didn't think so. This was nuts. He would never have remembered to add her name. What was she doing here?

'And you're in,' the doorman said. Then the rope was lifted and she was directed to the door.

'Enjoy!' he added as she pointed the polka-dot shoes towards the thumping music.

In the packed throng of bodies she was desperate to find a familiar face. She would make one full circuit, she told herself, and if he wasn't here or if she couldn't find Gracie, she would flee.

Scanning the crowd for faces, Lana couldn't help drinking in the details of this amazing place. It was so cool; dark, but with huge Perspex sculptures in orange and turquoise rising up from the ground and changing colour in the lights. There was a glowing pink and orange neon bar. All around, people were dancing, drinking, slouching with their hip bones out, pretending to talk but really just posing.

This was Manhattan, Lana thought with excitement! She was *here*. She was right here in the heart of it. Never mind feeling nervous about Parker, she was in the coolest place in the coolest town.

The thrill brought a smile to her face and now there was this guy walking up to her.

'Hi, love your shoes, wanna dance?'

This made her smile even more.

'Thanks, but I'm looking for my friends,' she told him. 'Maybe later?'

'Sure.'

They exchanged another smile and she walked on, confidence well and truly boosted.

As soon as Lana saw the yellow dress, she knew she was looking at Gracie. Who else would choose sunshine yellow with frills and a green belt for a night with the cool people?

As Lana approached, a hand slipped around Gracie's waist. Lana followed the arm up from the hand and of course, it led to Parker.

The confident smile froze on Lana's face: she wanted to turn on her heel and head the other way fast but then something made Parker look over his shoulder and he spotted her.

'Hey! Lana!'

He turned, letting his arm fall from Gracie's waist.

Lana, in the same instant that she saw the welcoming smile on Parker's face, saw the smile disappear from Gracie's.

'I'm so glad you could come! Isn't that great?' He turned to ask Gracie, who was trying to cover up the fact that she wasn't so pleased.

'Hi!' she said a little too brightly, 'you made it!'

'Of course she made it,' Parker said. 'This is such a great night – I wanted everyone I know to be here.'

He waved expansively across the area and Lana took this to mean that Parker's friends were all around them.

'What would you like to drink? I'm gonna go fight for a place at the bar.'

Once Parker had left with their orders, Lana and Gracie turned to face each other.

'Wow, what a place,' Lana began.

'Yeah. There are so many famous faces here tonight.'

Lana didn't think she sounded as full of enthusiasm as she usually did.

'So are you getting to know Parker a little better?'

'I guess a little, but he's friendly to everyone. I mean, don't you find him really friendly?'

Gracie was looking straight at her and Lana felt there was a lot in this question. Gracie was really asking how much Parker liked Lana and no doubt wondering if he had made any further moves on her.

'He's really nice,' Lana agreed, 'and he seems to have a lot of friends.'

She and Gracie were on the edge of the big group of people. Lana recognized Fabian, the guy with the green hair and the hat. She gave him a smile.

There was one question Lana wanted to ask. She could pad gently around the edges of it, or she could just take a breath and come right out and say it.

'Does he have a girlfriend?'

'No,' Gracie replied and with that word, her lips

drew into a line and she folded her arms across her chest.

'Right.'

'But there are lots of girls here, so who knows . . . maybe he's planning to pick one.'

'Right.'

Not so consoling. Now that Lana looked at the groups again she saw that Gracie was right: there were a lot of girls. More stylish, groomed, gleaming New York girls than guys. Lana tried to ignore the sinking feeling in her stomach.

She read the same despondent look in Gracie's eyes.

How had this happened? How had Lana managed to fall for the same guy as her New York best friend? Who, by the way, already had a boyfriend.

'Here he is!' Gracie whispered.

Parker came back and handed out the drinks he'd battled through the crowds to buy. 'Please enjoy,' he said, meeting Lana's eyes. 'I just about had to kill to get this for you.'

Was it her imagination or did he hold the look longer than he needed to? She searched his eyes looking for a clue. But then he turned and was offering Gracie a drink with what seemed like the same killer smile and lingering look.

'So are you loving my prints? I've loaned Elena

the $300 she was missing and she's having three of my patterns made up for new sample dresses.' Parker addressed the question to them both.

Gracie and Lana nodded eagerly, then began to talk about how much they loved his fabric ideas and about the NY Perfect Dress line.

'And just before you got here, I was telling Parker that if this first collection goes well, we've got so many ideas, we're going to branch out of dresses into jackets, skirts, maybe even pants and shoes,' Gracie said. Handing her drink to Lana, she asked, 'Can you hold this? I have to skip off to the bathroom for a couple of minutes.'

As soon as Gracie had gone, Parker turned all his attention full-beam on Lana.

'Wanna dance?' he asked. Then he took the drinks from her hand, set them down and pulled her gently towards him. 'Hello Lana from London,' he said, looking right at her.

His hands slid round her waist and he began to walk backward towards the crowded dance space taking her willingly with him. Her hands went up to his arms where she rested them ... unsure ... thrilled. Then they were sort of dancing but she couldn't concentrate on the music, or her steps, or anything except his hands round her waist and his eyes staring into hers.

'Put your hands round my waist too,' Parker said

in his dreamy voice. 'Much more friendly. I like you, Lana from London.'

Lana moved her hands to his lean torso and felt his warmth radiate through her fingers. Now she was looking at his face, at the expressive lips, slightly parted, moving closer to hers.

'Hello,' he murmured, 'this is cool.'

The tingle of nerves, the rush of excitement; there was nothing like it, nothing like it in the world. She couldn't close her eyes; she wanted to take in every detail of this move towards her face.

Her lips parted too and now she felt the warmth of his breath on her face.

Then came a sharp tap on her shoulder.

'Oh there you are,' Gracie broke in.

Chapter Eighteen

Milan

Carlo's middle-of-the-night wear:

Pale blue linen shirt (Benetton)
Dark blue chinos (C&A)
Black leather slippers (a gift from Mama)
Cologne (Acqua di Parma)
Total est. cost: €120

'Annah, look at this!'

The sound of Svetlana's voice jerked Annie from the doze she'd fallen into in one of the sumptuous velvet armchairs in Svetlana's suite.

'Yes?' She sat up and snapped to attention.

Svetlana walked towards her, a mobile in one hand, a drained champagne glass and her eighth pink and gold cigarette in the other. The hotel room with its pale green taffeta curtains, white and gilt furniture and ivy trellis print wallpaper was already in a fog. If Svetlana kept this up, Annie would need a gas mask.

Her friend's usually immaculate blonde hair was wild because she kept frantically running her hands through it. Her eye make-up was smudged with the tears she had shed this long night. Yet she was still elegantly dressed in high-heeled sandals and a summer dress: she wanted to be ready to leave at a moment's notice.

Just as soon as she knew where to go and what to do, Svetlana would be ready. Her handbag and a small holdall were packed.

But in the hours Annie had spent trying to help and console Svetlana there had been little news. Harry had been on the phone regularly, but had nothing to report. There was no word from Igor's camp. Border police could not confirm that the boys' passports had been used to take them out of the country.

'Maybe they are taken through Dover, in the back of a car,' Svetlana had wailed. Several times she had issued dire threats about Elena, who had apparently handed the boys over to their tennis coach with their passports. The coach must have been paid by Igor to deliver the boys to him.

Now Svetlana was standing over Annie, pushing the mobile phone in front of her face: 'Look at this!' she repeated.

Annie gave her dry, weary eyes a rub and peered at the short email on the screen. The words seemed to jump and blur in front of her exhausted eyes.

'It's very small print,' she said, turning to Svetlana, who she saw now was wearing a pair of heavy, black-framed glasses which looked comically out of place on her chiselled features.

'You need reading glasses,' Svetlana snapped.

'No, I'm just tired,' Annie hissed.

'Denial. Take these. They are Harry's. I don't need glasses either.'

Annie might have laughed at this if the look on Svetlana's face hadn't been so serious. The email was obviously urgent.

She put the clunky glasses on the end of her nose and the words came into focus:

Dear Mama, we are in a car. We have been on the boat and then we sleeped somewhere. One of the men said we would drive to Vienna and sleep there. I don't know if I want to go to school in Rushia. Petrov does not want to go. He keeps crying. I remembered I have email on this. The men think I'm playing on a game. Can you get us home? Michael.

'Oh my goodness!' Annie exclaimed, 'Your clever boy has email. He's been able to tell you where they're going.'

'Yes, is good news,' Svetlana agreed in a whisper.

'It's a breakthrough! You can tell the police. You can get them back.'

'Yes. We try with police, of course, but the important thing is to follow the boys, try and get them back quickly.'

'Follow the boys to Vienna? Good idea,' Annie agreed. 'Who's going to do that?'

With eyebrows raised, Svetlana looked at Annie as if the answer was blatantly obvious.

'Who?' Annie repeated.

'Me,' she replied. 'I am going to Vienna right now. I will find them.'

'But it's—' Annie looked at her watch – '4 a.m. There probably won't be any planes till . . .'

Svetlana was looking at her phone, scanning through pages, searching for the information.

'Nothing till 9.50,' she said, 'so we go by car.'

'Car? *We?*' Annie repeated.

Both of these words were worrying.

'We are in Milan, Annah, is not so far away from Vienna. We find my boys and bring them home.'

Annie swallowed.

'If we take a car, is perfect. We can follow them, wherever they go.'

'But we can't drive to Vienna! It's thousands of miles away,' Annie protested.

Svetlana looked at her phone once more.

'Is 628 kilometres. We leave now, we can be there before the plane from Milan even takes off.'

'Where are we going to get a car?'

'We take a hotel car,' Svetlana replied, unruffled. 'This is a very good hotel, they do everything for their guests they do every tiny little thing . . .'

'Except feed us,' Annie said under her breath.

'They will find us a car. They will lend us a car if they have to.'

Annie remembered seeing a little white Fiat parked round the back of the hotel. She tried to imagine Svetlana driving 628 kilometres in a car the size of a roller skate. It couldn't be done. Svetlana would never be able to fit her handbag, let alone her hair and her heels into a car as small as that.

'We get car and we drive to Vienna,' Svetlana insisted.

'No, we cannot give you one of the hotel's cars,' Carlo repeated for the fifth time, 'it is out of the question.'

In other circumstances, Annie might have found Carlo quite thrillingly attractive. The shirt he'd flung on when the night porter had woken him up with this outlandish request was loosely tucked into his trousers and only half buttoned up, revealing a deeply tanned chest. His inky hair was ruffled and falling over his dark brown eyes, but wrenched from his bed by Svetlana and her, the evil British escapee, he was very definitely not amused.

He kept shooting Annie deeply hostile glares.

'My children have been kidnapped!' Svetlana declared once again, 'I know where they are going and I am going to follow them in a car. I do not care how much it will cost. I must have a car!'

Carlo's eyes met Svetlana's. Working here he must have had many dealings with über-wealthy women who were used to getting exactly what they wanted all the time.

He must have realized he could only go on refusing for so long. The moment when Svetlana was going to insist on waking the chief executive was surely approaching.

Carlo glared at Annie again, as if it was all her fault, but then finally said with barely suppressed irritation, 'The hotel has two cars: a Fiat 500 and a small Fiat van. You could take one of these to drive to Vienna and back. The cost is 200 euro per day.'

'A van? A Fiat 500? Just who do you think you are talking to?' Svetlana demanded imperiously. 'A *van*? Never. And I wouldn't go anywhere in a Fiat 500 if it was the last car on the face of the earth.'

'Aren't your boys getting closer to Russia with

every minute you waste, Ms Wisneski?' Carlo risked.

'How dare you! I will have you dismissed.'

But then Svetlana's furious face cleared, as if inspiration had suddenly come to her.

'You will take my card –' she whisked her charge card (Svetlana never needed credit) from the depths of her discreetly logoed lambskin treasure and handed it to Carlo, 'you will deduct 2,000 euros for three days' hire and full insurance for the hotel's Bentley—'

The Bentley! The hotel's beautiful, liveried Bentley! Annie's head reeled. But what had Carlo been thinking? Of course Svetlana could not possibly travel in anything less.

'And you will bring me the keys. Now!' Svetlana added.

'But . . . I will need to check this . . .'

'No, you will not. You will tell your boss that I will more than compensate him for his trouble. Now bring me the keys.'

Carlo stepped into a small room behind the reception desk and when he returned, he had car keys in his hand. In silence, he led them out of the hotel and across the gravel to where the majestic car was parked, polished to perfection and gleaming in the moonlight.

'This is an expensive car,' Carlo began.

'Yes. The best. This is the car I have, much better than Rolls-Royce. We can look after it, Carlo, it will be returned before you even know it's gone,' Svetlana assured him. 'If there are any problems, I can pay.'

Svetlana, handbag and overnight case in one hand, stood expectantly beside the rear passenger door as if waiting for her chauffeur to take her belongings, open the door and drive her around the streets of Mayfair.

'But you're not going in the back,' Annie reminded her.

'No . . . you are right, I could come and sit in the front beside you.' With those words she walked towards the front passenger's door.

'But . . . but aren't *you* going to drive?' Annie asked.

Svetlana looked at Annie with astonishment.

'No,' she replied, 'I have no idea how to drive this car. This is why you have to come with me, Annah.'

Chapter Nineteen

New York

Gracie's party outfit:

Bright yellow sundress (Domseys Warehouse Outlet)
Red sparkly shoes (theatrical suppliers sale)
White hand-held basket (Alice's Toy Store)
Gold hoop earrings (hand-me-down from big sister)
Red lipstick (Elizabeth Arden)
Total est. cost: $55

'So we're dancing? Fabulous, I love to dance.'

Gracie sidled onto the dance floor and somehow managed to get between Lana and Parker. She was smiling hard and Lana couldn't tell whether this was genuine Gracie or if she had spotted Parker leaning in to kiss her and was now flat out trying to stop them.

The music kicked up a notch, Gracie's arms moved out to the side and she began the kind of sophisticated, complicated dance that Lana might have expected from a girl who almost always wore dance shoes.

As Parker turned to face Gracie and tried to join in with her dance, Lana let a sigh of annoyed disappointment escape. They had been been about to kiss! Now Gracie had stolen the show.

'I'll be right back,' she called in their direction, but neither head even turned to acknowledge her.

'Or maybe not,' she said to herself and swallowed hard.

Lana turned the key, opened the apartment door and tiptoed in expecting to find darkness and quiet waiting for her.

'You're back early.'

The sound of Elena's voice startled her.

'Oh, I thought you'd be in bed,' Lana said, entering the small but all-white and calmly organized living space. Her boss and flatmate Elena was curled up on the small sofa with her laptop.

'Too much to organize, plus jet lag,' Elena said: 'short trips to London mess you up. Seth recommends watching sunsets and sunrises "so that your body understands", but it doesn't work for me.'

Elena was wrapped in a fluffy white dressing

gown with a takeaway coffee beside her, which probably wasn't helping to make her feel sleepy.

'How was your evening? It's only midnight – for Manhattan that's very early home.'

Lana shrugged: 'OK, nothing special.'

'But weren't you at the opening of that new place, the Spider's Nest? It's already famous, apparently Blake Lively was there.'

'Really? I didn't see her.'

Elena gave a little smile: 'No? But maybe this is because you were so busy trying to get the attention of the sexy Mr Parker Bain, am I right?'

Lana shrugged again, set her bag down on the white tiled floor and kicked off the polka-dot shoes.

'Don't pretend,' Elena teased. 'When he came into the office, I noticed you. You couldn't take your eyes from him. No wonder, he is a very nice boy. Cute looking.'

'He's OK,' Lana said, stepping into the kitchenette so that Elena couldn't read anything too obvious from her face.

'Ah . . . but do you know what else I saw?' Elena went on. 'I saw that Gracie likes him very much too.'

Lana made no reply to this. She poured herself a glass of water and gulped it down, then came back into the room with a second glass in her hand. She tried to brush away the memory of Parker on the dance floor. When he'd held her waist and leaned in towards her, she'd felt her heart leap with happiness, but when he'd turned away to dance with Gracie, it had sunk like a stone.

'This is a problem,' Elena persisted: 'you and Gracie are good friends and now you both like the same boy.'

Lana might have made a scornful reply – along the lines of: '*If we're all so easy to read, maybe you could just tell me which one of us Parker likes best? It would save a lot of trouble*' – but Elena's mobile, on the heart-shaped pink rug beside her coffee cup began to buzz for attention. She picked it up, checked the screen, then put it down again.

'My mother,' she said, sounding exasperated. 'I already have five missed calls from her and six messages. I don't even listen to them, I hit delete. Ever since she refused to listen about the dresses, I refuse to listen to her.'

'But she does own the company,' Lana pointed out, 'I mean, if we're not careful, she could wind the whole thing up – or sack us.'

'Yes, but I don't think so,' Elena replied. 'We have a plan and we have to carry it out. We all must stop worrying about the Mothers and focus on NY Perfect Dress. I already have the first dresses ready to collect tomorrow and they are going to be good. Really good. There is no possibility of this not working. No possibility.'

'Tomorrow? But it's Sunday tomorrow,' Lana pointed out.

Elena shrugged: 'I ask for special treatment, for favours and everyone is working extra to help us out. The first dresses could be unpacked and for sale by Tuesday. I want to be big success in London first. I want Svetlana to walk past shops with our beautiful dresses in the window and understand just how wrong she was.'

'Wow, that would be great,' Lana agreed, imagining the scene. 'I hope my mum is with her when it happens. I hope they're both walking arm in arm feeling completely smug when our amazing dress stops them in their tracks. That is definitely the aim.'

Chapter Twenty

Italy

Annie behind the wheel:

Trusty brown linen wrap dress (Hobbs)
Tan heels low enough to drive in (LK Bennett)
Trusty Daria Hobo, well-worn, scuffed and squished
(Mulberry)
Wristwatch (Prada)
Lipstick (Mac)
Squirt of morale-boosting perfume (Chanel No. 19)
Total est. cost: £1,200

Annie was used to big cars. Before the practical seven-seater familymobile had come into her life, complete with its baby-barf-stained seats, side doors stuffed with rotting banana skins, used baby wipes and empty crisp packets, she'd driven a huge, indestructible gas-guzzler Jeep all over London.

But the vintage Bentley was big on a whole new scale. The driver's seat was as wide and leathery as an armchair. The steering wheel was a huge, carved wooden affair and now, as she aimed the bonnet of the car at the hotel's opening gates, she felt as if she was steering a barge towards a mouse hole.

Help, I can't do this! I can't drive this thing! How have I got myself into this?! her inner voice protested as she tried to maintain outer calm.

'The engine is roaring, you are still in first gear, you need to move up,' Svetlana instructed from the passenger's seat.

Annie was tempted to reply: '*Darlin', if you want to drive, be my guest,*' but instead she managed: 'I'm going slowly until I know what I'm doing. I'll speed up once I've got my bearings.'

Unfortunately, her foot, clad in the lowest shoes she could find, slipped from the heavy metal brake pedal as she reached the gate, so she turned into the road with much more speed than she might have liked.

A brief but ugly scraping sound meant Bentley had met gatepost, but she carried on regardless.

'Annah! Annah! We said we would look after the car,' Svetlana protested.

'I'm trying,' Annie replied through gritted teeth,

her knuckles already white on the steering wheel.

'Left? Is this the way we should go? We need map!'

'We have a map,' Annie reminded her, still trying to sound calm. 'Carlo put a map into your car door. Now take it out and look it up. Left leads to the main road. I remember that from my trip in the taxi.'

'Oh yes, your escape,' Svetlana said darkly. 'I am still angry that you run away from my all-expenses-paid spa visit.'

'In my defence, I was delirious with hunger, I hardly knew what I was doing.'

Svetlana brought out a thick map book and immediately complained: 'This is just for Italy.'

'Well, find the motorway which will take us from here to the border and we'll pick up another map on the way.'

'The border,' Svetlana repeated. She opened the book and began to look for the relevant pages: 'we need the computer in the front of the car ... the satnav.'

'This is a vintage Bentley, I don't think it does satnav. Have you heard anything more from Michael?'

Svetlana looked at her phone, held at the ready in her hand.

'Nothing,' she replied. 'I'm frightened that when I sent him my reply it bleeped and the men guessed what he was doing. I'm frightened we won't hear anything more.'

'OK, you need to calm down, sweetheart. And I need to calm down.'

Annie took a deep breath in, let it out slowly then added: 'Let's try to trust in luck and good fortune and everyone doing all they can to find your boys. Let's not freak out . . .'

Let's not freak out, she repeated to herself as she tried not to think about what she would do if she met another car on this tiny, twisty road. The Bentley seemed to take up every inch of available space.

Svetlana switched on the reading light and shone it into her lap because although the first palest hint of dawn was emerging on the horizon, it was still dark. After several minutes of study, she told Annie: 'Is a long way to the border and we have to go over the mountains.'

Annie's hands tightened on the steering wheel.

'Mountains?!' she repeated.

Mountains . . . *mountains*?! Who said anything about mountains? She was expecting a nice, wide-laned motorway between Italy and Austria. She was barely managing to keep control of this beast on a B-road.

'Just drive, Annah, you are good driver, you will get used to this car.'

The little country road came to an end and as Annie nosed the Bentley along a wider, smoother main road, her tense shoulders began to lower from her ears. With each gear change she grew a little more in confidence, until at last she began to feel in control of the great purring luxurymobile.

Svetlana seemed more relaxed too. Ever since they'd been on the road, heading somewhere, doing something, her face had lost its terrible haunted look. It was obviously helping her enormously to know that each mile they drove was bringing her closer to her beloved boys.

'Michael's very clever to think of emailing you,' Annie said. She knew that Svetlana's relationship with her older son was a little prickly so she always did what she could to try and remedy that.

'Yes.'

'And he's obviously brave. I mean, he's been bundled into a car by strangers and he's got the nerve to send an email he knows could get him into loads of trouble.'

'He is afraid of no one – just like his father.'

'Just like his mother,' Annie said, with a sidelong glance at her friend.

'Ha . . . maybe,' Svetlana admitted.

She didn't add anything else and for many miles there was a companionable silence between the two, broken only by map directions from Svetlana.

The early morning sky, pale apricot, dotted with dark blue-grey clouds, spread out before them as they roared along the motorway towards the border. The dark blue Italian Alps rose ahead of them, snow-capped, in the distance.

The mountain range separating them from where they wanted to be looked vast and Annie had a growing suspicion that the roads would be twisting and demanding. But she tried not to worry about the hours of difficult driving ahead.

'I've never been to Austria, have you?' she asked, when the silence in the car seemed to have been going on for too long.

'Yes, many times,' Svetlana replied: 'the opera, the concert halls, always with Russians making deals – so many Russians in Vienna and in the big houses in the mountains all around. Is interesting country. Very formal. Very old-fashioned. Is one of last places left in civilized world where you can smoke in a café.'

'I've known you for – how many years? – and I didn't know you smoked.'

'I don't smoke any more.'

Annie was about to remind her about the box of gold-tipped, multi-coloured cigarettes inhaled just a few hours ago, but then, people did all kinds of strange things in a crisis.

'Smoking terrrrrrrrible for the skin,' Svetlana added. 'My first Botox was my last cigarette. Last night, a ... a...' she waved her hand as she struggled for the right word.

'One-off?'

'Yes. One-off. Never again, no matter how bad things get. My throat feels like is missing one layer of skin.'

'It probably is.'

'You never smoke?'

Annie shook her head: 'I tried. When I was at art school all the cool people smoked. But I could never get the hang of it.'

'I loved to smoke. I begin when I train to be army nurse.' Svetlana gave a throaty laugh: 'all the army nurses smoke because is stressful life. Army drills, living in tents in the cold, nursing very injured people. I leave as soon as I can and become model. In fashion everyone smoke, smoke, smoke, never eat. Want to be as thin as a greyhound ...'

'On a diet,' Annie added, with a smile.

'Thin as a greyhound on a diet, yes. I like this. Then I enter the Miss World competition – and then so many bad boyfriends who also smoke. You must worry about your daughter and the bad boyfriends. I wish Elena and Lana never meet even one boyfriend as bad as my many bad boyfriends. Elena's father – tschaaaa – he was one of worst. I was so young, but determined, Annah, determined not to let him ruin my life.'

'Is that when you left the Ukraine?'

'Yes, I have to run away. I hide baby Elena with my aunty, deep in the countryside, and then I run away from this bad man and his bad friends. Ugly old politicians and pretty young girls . . . it was no good: drugs, abuse. I don't like to talk about it.'

But then after a moment's pause, Svetlana added: 'The most important thing is that I get away. I did not let him ruin my life or my daughter's life. But I don't go back to Ukraine for long, long time. This is why I don't see her until she has grown up and comes to find me.'

'Where did you run to?' Annie asked, longing to hear just a little more about Svetlana's colourful past.

'I hitch-hike to Paris and get job as model,' Svetlana replied, matter-of-fact, 'then comes cat-walks and smoking, smoking, modelling and meeting rich men. Always I have my eye on a rich man because I think: I am no one. I have nothing. I know nothing except army nursing. But I have this idea that if I can marry rich man, I can be rich wife and maybe make something of my life.'

'Your face really was your fortune.'

'And figure,' Svetlana reminded her, 'but you know how hard I work for these things. People always think: is easy for her, she is born beautiful. Pah! I have first nose job, age twenty-four. I still do gymnastics for two hours every day. I will never look old and I will never be fat. This is my promise to myself. These are the things every woman needs to conquer, then she will make a much more interesting life for herself.'

'Really . . . do you think . . . ?' Annie began dubiously.

'I don't think. I know. If you exercise and eat well, the energy will come. Then you must make more money to spend on yourself. The better you look, the more money you make. You are on television, Annah, you must know this. People want to look at beautiful women on television.'

'But viewers like me!' Annie protested. 'They relate. They think I'm just like them. I make normal women look and feel better. There are lots of TV people who look normal.'

Svetlana was shaking her head. 'Looking fat and ugly and learning to love yourself is almost an obsession in Britain. When I am sixty, I am going to look like forty.'

Annie couldn't help laughing at this: 'You're admirable, babes, truly admirable. When I'm sixty, I'm probably going to look like a burst couch.'

'No, Annah,' Svetlana shook her head, 'I will not let this happen. Now, service station in 15 kilometres. We need to stop, go to toilets, buy water, buy petrol and maybe satnav too.'

Annie looked at the Bentley's fuel gauge. It was registering completely full. It hadn't moved at all although they were now almost 200 kilometres from Villa Verdina. Either this was the most fuel-efficient limousine ever invented or the gauge was faulty. The Bentley was probably over twenty years old, it was bound to have developed a fault or two. It was probably carefully nursed along by its loving driver, who only ever took it from Villa Verdina to Milan airport and back at a sedate 50 m.p.h.

So she could start worrying right now about how long the Beast would hold out in the mountains, or she could do as she'd told Svetlana: try to trust in luck and good fortune.

Chapter Twenty-One

New York

Elena's brunch outfit:

White broderie anglaise dress (Perfect Dress free sample)
Natural leather gladiator sandals (Brooklyn Leather)
Orange tote bag (Coach sale)
Tiny gold hoop earrings (gift from Seth)
Total est. cost: $130

As the waiter set Lana's latte in front of her on the outdoor café table, she looked down the street for any sign of Gracie. It was early on Sunday morning, but Gracie had already texted, desperate to meet up for breakfast and discuss last night.

Lana had agreed and arranged a meeting place just round the corner from her apartment, but her stomach was clenched at the thought of the news Gracie might bring. Surely the only reason to meet up so urgently was that Gracie wanted to talk about how amazingly her night had gone with Parker?

Lana looked down at her coffee cup and admired the way the beige and white foam swirled together. For a moment, she was distracted enough to take a quick photo, ping it to the Perfect Dress ideas blog and write underneath: 'A silky beige dress with cream coloured swirls? A beige dress printed with white and brown coffee cups?' That would be cute: she smiled at the thought. She was happy to do anything to take her mind off Gracie and Parker and the death of hope on the dance floor.

'Hi! You're already here! But I'm not late, am I?'

And there was Gracie, practically skipping towards her table in a bright green and pink dress with her hair curled jauntily out, rosy pink blusher and lip gloss already in place.

'Hi Gracie, no it's fine, I just got here.'

Gracie pulled up the chair beside Lana's and gushed: 'Wasn't it awesome?! Wasn't it the best night out ever?! Immense! Did you see all those cool people? And famous people too: Blake Lively was there! I didn't even see her until like way late on. I stayed till four in the morning, but I'm so wired, I woke up early and just had to see you.'

'It was a great night,' Lana agreed, but she felt a

growing sense of dread at Gracie's happiness, 'it was so nice of Parker to invite us . . . and you guys were . . . well . . . really getting to know each other, weren't you?'

Lana didn't want to know. But yet she totally did. It was like pulling off a plaster or waiting for the injection at the dentist: it would be best to get the pain over with quickly.

Gracie set her basket, yes straw basket, complete with appliqué flowers, down on the table, then folded her hands under her chin and gazed off into the distance, in the style of the truly smitten.

'He is great, isn't he?' she said. 'I mean, he's funny, he's smart *and* he's into fabric design! We talked for the longest time about our favourite vintage stores. I mean, how many guys would do that? He likes vintage leather jackets; ones so beat up you know they've lived. He says leather only starts to get interesting when it's five years old. You know his leather bag? It's a proper English satchel and he's been carrying it since Grade School, since he was nine! How many guys are like him? I'm just thrilled to have him as my brand new best friend.'

Lana smiled, agreed, did everything she could to make out she was delighted for her friend. But inside, she sagged with unhappiness. This was not good. Gracie would ditch Bingham, then she would go out with Parker. And for how long?! Would

Lana have to watch from the sidelines for months?

Maybe Gracie and Parker would be together for ever and Lana's life would be ruined. She'd have to move out of New York with her broken heart to get away from them.

And he had asked her out first, she reminded herself, with a rush of injustice.

'So when are you going to see him again?' Lana asked, trying to fill the question with encouragement, 'Have you guys already got plans?'

'Ummm . . . well . . .' Gracie turned to her basket, searched about, brought out her phone and checked the screen.

Lana sort of didn't like herself for feeling a little burst of hope at this hesitation.

'He said there was an art show opening next weekend,' Gracie went on, 'and maybe I'd like to come along. So he said he would let me know: send me a message.'

'Sounds really interesting. So new best *friends*?'

Gracie looked at Lana, with a sweet little frown between her two pale, perfectly tweezed eyebrows.

'Friends, yeah, just friends,' she said airily, with a little shrug.

'OK . . .'

Lana hoped this hadn't come out wrong. But Gracie saying 'friends' . . . and not mentioning any other plans, despite the weekend art show, gave her a flicker of hope. Gracie already had a boyfriend, she reminded herself, and hadn't she and Parker almost kissed? Hadn't he asked her to be his girl tonight? Cheesy, but he'd made it very sexy too.

Not that she wanted to hurt Gracie. Not in any way at all. But she felt a little comforted by 'friends'.

'Hey girls, I hope you're talking about work!'

They both turned in the direction of the familiar voice and saw Elena strolling along the sidewalk hand in hand with her very handsome boyfriend, Seth.

All four said hello to one another.

'Do you want to stop and have coffee with us?' Lana asked.

Seth ran a hand through his dark blond hair and gave them a big grin. 'I would, but she won't let me,' he joked: 'work, work, work. We're walking to this little park I know because I thought it might make a good place to shoot the new dresses.' He pointed to the camera bag slung over his shoulder.

'But you always carry that,' Lana said. 'Didn't you tell me a photographer has to be prepared?'

'Yup. A dress designer always has to be prepared too; inspiration could strike at any time.'

'Yeah, I already saw your blog post with the coffee cup dress idea, Lana, and I liked it,' Elena added.

'Thanks.'

'We've all got so many fantastic ideas—'

'That you're going to be a huge success,' Seth finished Elena's sentence and landed a proud kiss on her cheek.

'OK, enjoy some time off, because I am going to be working you so hard tomorrow and for the rest of the week, month – year!' Elena joked.

As the two strode off down the pavement, Gracie and Lana couldn't help watching with a touch of jealousy.

'He is so nice and so good-looking,' Gracie said.

'I know . . . and he is so in love with her,' Lana added. 'You can just tell; he's always so nice about her.'

'Oh sigh for a lovely boyfriend just like Seth.'

'Yeah well, but you have a lovely boyfriend.'

'Yes, but . . . well,' Gracie seemed to stumble a little. 'We're not Seth and Elena though,' she said.

'No? But I thought . . .' Lana fished for more information, but Gracie headed her off with a change of subject.

'Oh, you must see this,' she said, picking up her phone. 'Is this not just perfect? Genius, in fact?'

The screen was filled with a print, vibrant swirling pink, green and yellow designs against a dark blue background.

'Apparently it's a modern homage to paisley.'

'Wow,' was Lana's reaction. 'Did Parker do this?'

206

'Yeah. It's going to be on some of the next NY Perfect Dresses to come in. *His* fabric on *our* dresses. Isn't that going to be amazing?'

'Wow,' Lana repeated, trying hard not to let Gracie know how annoyed she was that Parker had texted this to her friend and not to her.

An urgent buzz let Lana know that there was a new message on her phone. She picked it up, puzzled. The most frequent texter was her mum, but communication between Lana and her mum had not exactly been regular since she'd stormed back to New York after the row.

Bsssssssst, her mobile buzzed insistently.

Lana reached down to her handbag, slid the phone out and clicked through to the message. She had to read the text several times before she could fully take in its meaning. But finally it made some sort of sense.

'Still sad u left early. Meet me tmrw? Pls say yes. Parker ☺'

'What's up?' Gracie asked, 'You look like you've had big news.'

Chapter Twenty-Two

Italy

Passenger Svetlana:

Multi-coloured wrap dress (Missoni)
Suede and linen summer shoe boots (Manolo)
Python clutch bag (Lanvin)
'Low key' diamonds on fingers and wrists (Cartier)
Total est. cost: £37,000

Annie steered the Bentley with concentration through the service station car park. She was looking for an enormous parking space, because 'easy to manoeuvre' was obviously not one of the boxes ticked when the Beast had been designed.

The Bentley was a car built for splendour, built for valet parking and peak-capped chauffeurs who pulled up right outside a grand entrance. It was not a car for squeezing into spaces designed for Fiat 500s in an Italian service station car park.

Had the Bentley – or indeed Svetlana – ever had to endure the horrors of a service station before?

Annie finally found a double space, pulled in, cut the engine and turned to her passenger.

'Here we are then: a refuel, a toilet break, a quick coffee and maybe a croissant to keep us going.'

Svetlana pulled a face. 'Coffee? A croissant?! But I am not ready to break my juice fast. I haven't lost my 10 kilos. All those enemas, they will have been for nothing.'

'Svet, my lovely, last night you hoovered up an entire box of fags and a bottle of champagne. I think the juice fast is well and truly over.'

There was a pause. Svetlana's lips tightened and Annie wondered if she was going to be told off. But then Svetlana shrugged and admitted: 'Coffee sounds good.'

The service station, although Italian, was not one tiny bit more chic, glamorous or stylish than anything to be found off the M6. There was garish lighting, horrible plastic seating, plastic-looking food and toilets which could have done with a good clean.

Nevertheless, in the Ladies Svetlana clicked open her crocodile clutch at the mirror and made repairs to her face. She was tired and she was deeply upset, so today she only looked ten years younger than her real age, rather than the usual incredible twenty.

Annie checked herself over in the mirror too.

She hadn't thought to bring any make-up with her from the hotel, except for a stub of lipstick; in fact she hadn't even had time to wash her face after she'd woken up from her doze in Svetlana's hotel room, so to her horror she saw now that she was all smudged mascara and the very faded remains of creased foundation.

Annie had always believed in the morale-boosting qualities of make-up and now here she was marooned in a bad situation without a smidge of Chanel or Estée Lauder.

Svetlana glanced at her and after a moment or two of obvious hesitation, decided to intervene.

'Here,' she said, handing over her Hermès embossed make-up bag.

'No, no really, I'm fine. I couldn't use your things,' Annie insisted.

'Please,' Svetlana said, 'it will make me feel better if you look better too.'

'Oh.'

Annie looked inside the little bag.

'First you must cleanse,' Svetlana suggested.

Annie delved in and brought out a sachet of ultra-high-end 'jet-set refreshers'. She pulled one from the packet and ran it over her face.

It was creamy, dewy, refreshing and re-moisturizing all at the same time.

'Very nice,' she said, looking at her bare features.

'Now begin again,' Svetlana suggested.

After several minutes spent applying Svetlana's luxury cosmetics, Annie looked in the mirror and saw her best self reflected back once more. As a finishing touch, she wound up the deep red lipstick and dabbed it on her lips with a clean pinkie.

'We're all set to face the world again and bring your boys back home,' she said brightly, but it didn't have a cheering effect on Svetlana.

Instead, despite the heavy Botox use, Svetlana's eyes crumpled at the corners. For a moment, it looked as if she was going to cry.

'I can't let him take the boys away. I have always, *always* stopped him from taking the boys away,' she whispered.

'And you'll stop him again,' Annie insisted.

'Annah, I have to get my boys back . . . My mother made a mess of everything, I make a mess of being Elena's mother . . . The boys – the only good thing I do in my life is be a good mother to my boys.'

At this, Svetlana put her hands to the corners of her eyes and pressed hard in an effort to stem the tears.

'We'll get them,' Annie insisted, although she far from believed it. 'We will get the boys, no matter what. And you are a good mother to them all. C'mon –' she linked her arm through Svetlana's – 'let's grab a coffee and get to the border.'

On the mountain roads, the Bentley was as much hard work as Annie had feared. She had to steer hard at every corner and slow to a pace far too snail-like for the impatient Italian drivers building up behind her. There was horn honking and horribly impatient, risky overtaking.

'I'm not enjoying this,' she admitted with gritted teeth, as another tiny red car sped past, the driver turning to glare at her furiously.

'You will get used to the road and you will be able to drive more quickly soon,' Svetlana said, trying to be reassuring.

'Do you think?' Annie said, hauling the steering wheel round as they went into another terrifying hairpin bend, the mountainside falling away dizzyingly at the side of the road. The tiny metal barrier between them and disaster didn't stand a chance if the Bentley set a wheel wrong.

The driving was so physical now that Annie was beginning to sweat with effort: 'Let's hear it for power steering,' she panted: 'your chauffeur must have arms of steel.'

'I not make him drive in mountains often.'

'No. Is it . . . do we have . . . ?' Annie hesitated. She wasn't sure she really wanted to know how much further she had to twist and turn the Beast up and down these hair-raising roads.

'There is still some way to go,' Svetlana answered but then folded her arms and carried on gazing straight ahead.

Probably best not to know exactly. Just slow into the bend, steer, steer, steer, straighten out and enjoy the little bit of straight road before the next one.

'Do you think you should try emailing Michael again?' Annie asked once another ten bends were under the bonnet.

Svetlana looked for a long time at the phone and then suddenly began to tap out a message at speed.

'Now we wait,' she said as soon as she'd hit send.

'Are you sure? Are you *sure* this is right?'

For the past twenty minutes they'd been travelling along a tiny road; a road so small it had potholes, loose gravel and even the odd goat. They were high up in the mountains with bare rocky terrain all around and a panoramic view of . . . more mountains, making Annie wonder just how many they would have to cross.

'We've seen no one else – not one other car since we got on to it,' Annie said anxiously.

'This is the right road,' Svetlana insisted. 'I read the map. This will take us into Austria.'

If we don't ground the Bentley on one of those craters first, Annie couldn't help thinking.

There was another pressing problem.

The coffee stop at the service station had been hours ago. Annie double-checked the clock face on the dashboard. Could that be right? Could it really be nearly one o'clock? Weren't they supposed to be near Vienna by now?

In short, Annie needed to pee. Badly. Badly, badly, badly. So badly that just thinking about how much she needed to pee was causing cramp.

'What are our chances of finding a toilet out here?' she said out loud.

Svetlana turned her head: 'If you need to go, you must go. Is bad for the kidneys to hold on too long.'

'Well, what about you? You've been holding on as long as me.'

Svetlana considered.

Annie whacked into another pothole and the Bentley groaned.

'You are right we must go,' Svetlana replied.

'But where?'

'Au naturel.'

For a multimillionairess with a Mayfair mansion, bespoke Hermès luggage and several hundred thousand pounds of diamonds scattered across her fingers, Svetlana could be practical and surprisingly earthy. Maybe it was her army nurse training.

Annie didn't really want to bare her bottom on the top of an Italian mountain, but the growing pain in the pit of her stomach told her that she must. She slowed the car down to a stop. The road was so small and so deserted she didn't see any point in steering the Bentley to the side.

Then she was squatting between two opened Bentley doors, while a shaggy grey goat watched from a safe distance.

'*Come to Milano*,' she whispered to herself, imitating Svetlana's accent. '*A luxury break, totally pampering, all expenses paid. This is what you need to recharge the batteries.*'

Ha! And now where was she? She was squatting with a goat audience, on the remote and deserted peak of an Italian mountain, trying not to let a puddle of wee creep into her sandals while she wondered how to manhandle a vintage Bentley beast safely down to the other side.

'Annah! Annah! Get back into the car. Quickly!'

Annie did not like the note of urgency in Svetlana's voice.

'What's the matter?' she called over to the other side of the car where Svetlana was relieving herself.

'Quick!'

Annie finished, snapped her knickers back into place and jumped into the driving seat. Svetlana was already in the passenger's seat with the door closed and locked, her face upset.

'What's wrong?'

'Drive! Just drive – *hurry*!'

Annie fired up the engine and set the car going over the lethal potholes once again.

'What is it? Have you had news?' she asked.

'You have to go faster, I think they are coming.'

'Who?!'

Annie, anxious herself now, risked a move up to third gear.

'I see these men; a group of men – in the distance still, but when they see car, they start jogging towards us.'

'A group of men?'

Annie considered. A group of men could mean anything. Hillwalkers, goatherds – it didn't have to be a threat.

'Maybe they're in trouble?' she suggested. 'Maybe they need help. Maybe their car broke down, or they're climbing and someone's been hurt.'

Svetlana gave a snort at this.

'You are too nice. No! These men are not in trouble. These men *are* trouble. I can tell. I have seen this kind of man before. They are always Serb.'

'Svetlana, you can't say that! If you don't like the look of someone, you can't say they're bad and they must be a Serb.'

216

'But I know this kind of man. Bad. Very bad.' She glanced over her shoulder: 'Can you see anyone?'

Annie's anxiety kicked up a level, even though she didn't want it to. She glanced in the rear-view mirror.

'No. There's no one there. Maybe you imagined it.'

'Imagine it? No way. Maybe they wait for us further down. You must drive on, Annah, even if someone jump out in front of us.'

'What?! Run someone over?'

'Annah, I know this kind of man,' she repeated urgently. 'Hungry, dirty, desperate, very far away from home and looking for anything. We have to get away. This is a bad situation. I *know*.'

Annie felt her heart begin to thump in her chest. She clicked the door lock button and pressed on the accelerator, pushing the Bentley to 40 miles an hour, sending it thudding and thumping over the rough road.

As the first tight bend approached, Svetlana sucked in her breath: 'Try not to slow down, they could be here. They could be hiding, waiting for us.'

'Please Svetlana, try not to get carried awaaaaa—'

A man leapt to his feet at the side of the road and ran towards the car.

'Drive!' Svetlana shouted, sounding panicked. 'Don't stop! DRIVE!'

Chapter Twenty-Three

New York

Lana channelling Gracie-style:

Floral sundress (Century 21)
Cropped cotton cardigan (Old Navy)
Wooden soled clogs (thrift store)
Cloth messenger bag (craft stall)
Total est. cost: $55

After breakfast at the café, Lana had turned down Gracie's invitation to wander round a favourite flea market, which sprang up in a vacant lot on Sunday. Instead she'd gone back to the apartment, holed up on the sofa and looked again and again at the message from Parker on her phone.

When she'd read and reread it about one hundred

times, she still hadn't worked out how to reply to it.

A fresh, new, horrible thought flew into her mind – what if Parker had sent it to the wrong girl? What if he'd meant to send this message to Gracie? What if it was Gracie he wanted to see?

But no, wait a minute . . . he'd said: 'sorry you left early,' hadn't he? And she'd been the one to leave first – but then maybe Gracie had left earlier than lots of other people there.

Lana chewed at the skin around her nail and tried to make a decision. Could she say yes and meet Parker? *Should* she meet Parker? She knew she might die of disappointment if she didn't.

Impulsively, before she could change her mind, she hit the button to call him back. This was super-cool, super-confident New York Lana, she told herself, the kind of girl who called boys back, just to get things straight.

The dial tone purred in her ear. Just as she became convinced this was the worst idea she'd ever had, Parker picked up.

'Hi, Parker here.'

'Hi Parker, I got your message.'

Lana tried to channel: sexy, casual, seductive.

'Hey, did you enjoy the club?'

'Of course I did.'

'So why did you run out on me?'

'I didn't think you were paying me enough attention,' Lana dared.

'Whooo, sorry!'

'So are you going to make it up tomorrow?'

'I think so, Miss Lana from London.'

When he finally said her name, she felt she could relax. So it was her he wanted to be with.

'What's your plan?' Lana asked.

After he'd outlined his suggestion, she managed her coolest ever: 'Hmmm . . . I guess I might like to do that. Sounds kinda cool.'

As soon as the call had finished and Lana, cheeks blazing with excitement, had jotted down the details of where and when they were to meet, she heard a key turning in the lock and within moments, Elena was in the apartment.

Setting a bag of groceries down on the floor, Elena asked: 'Why are you inside? It's a beautiful day. Outside is Manhattan, everything is going on out there. And I warned you, you must enjoy your day off before I work you to the bone tomorrow and for the rest of the week.'

Lana smiled and shrugged.

'You're not worrying about something, are you?' Elena asked with a look of concern.

'No, nothing. Really.'

'You are not allowed to worry about the Mothers, OK? We will solve these problems in time, I promise.'

'I hope so. You do really think NY Perfect Dress is going to work, don't you?'

'I can't promise you yet,' Elena admitted, 'we take a big risk. We could upset everyone, including the Mothers. But we have to do something. By the end of this year, if we do nothing, the business might die anyway and our careers in fashion would be finished, before they'd even begun. I hope that the Mothers will get over this.'

'I don't know . . . you've not known your mother for as long as I've known my mother,' Lana warned.

'Shhhh. I think it will work. Sometimes . . . you just have to do things,' Elena added with a little smile, 'and worry about the consequences later.'

Ha. Lana thought about her date with Parker tomorrow night, despite the fact that her New York best friend had a huge crush on him too. Yes: sometimes you did just have to do things and worry about the consequences later.

Just then, the apartment phone began to ring. Elena and Lana looked at each other with surprise because this was so unusual.

'Maybe the landlord?' Elena asked with a shrug.

'On a Sunday?'

Elena picked up: 'Hello?'

For a few moments Lana watched as Elena's face went through a range of emotions. First surprised, then confused, shocked . . . even angry.

'Yes, it's me ... hello ... oh. I'm sorry, I've not answered calls from Svetlana, we are having big argument about the dress company,' Elena told the receiver.

Then came a gasped: 'WHAT?! Oh no. NO!'

Followed by: 'No! This is all wrong ... Igor has ... OH! Harry, you know me. You know that I would never, ever ...'

Elena fell into the metal chair beside the tiny café table, grabbed for a pen and a scrap of paper. She was listening intently and firing off questions too.

'So when did this happen?'

'Oh my goodness ... oh my goodness ... why did no one tell—? Messages? No, I didn't listen to my messages. Oh no!' Harry ... of course I did not know. Please, you must believe this.'

As Elena pushed the hair from her face, the anxiety written across her features was plain to see.

'This is terrible. The poor boys ... poor Svetlana ...'

The boys? Svetlana? This was the first inkling Lana had of what the call was about. Now she grew anxious.

'Please, Harry, just tell me what can I do to help you?' Elena asked. 'There must be something. We need to think. There must be something we can do.'

When at last the call was over, she put the receiver

down and turned to Lana, a shocked expression on her face.

'What on earth has happened?' Lana asked. 'Is everyone OK?'

'That was Harry, Svetlana's husband,' Elena began, her voice unsteady. 'The boys, Michael and Petrov, they've been kidnapped.'

Lana was so startled by this news, she couldn't think of an appropriate reply.

'Almost certainly by Igor,' Elena added. 'Harry believes Igor has taken them out of the country, although he's not allowed to, and they think he's going to put them in some military school in Russia.'

'What?!' Lana exclaimed. 'But can't the police stop him? Can't they do something?'

'The boys are out of Britain now and as soon as they are out of Europe, it becomes much more complicated. But, of course, the police and the lawyers are all involved. Harry didn't have time to go into all the details, but the worst thing, the reason he was phoning me . . .' Elena rubbed her fingers over her eyes, 'is that they thought I knew.'

'What do you mean?'

'They thought I might be in on it. The day the boys went missing was my last day in London. The person who handed them over to their tennis coach – with their passports – was me!'

Elena hid her face in her hands.

'But, you told him, didn't you? You told him it was nothing to do with you? They wouldn't really think that?' Lana insisted.

'Oh, the poor boys! I can't imagine how terrible this must be for them.' Elena now began to cry: 'Of course, I tell Harry I would never . . . but Svetlana is furious with me. She says she will never forgive me.'

Chapter Twenty-Four

Italy

Randall on the road:

Tropical print board shorts (O'Neill)
Surf-bleached pink T-shirt (gift from a kindred spirit)
Rubber flip-flops (beach shop)
Full-sized surfboard (Pete's Surf Shack)
Total est. cost: $580

Annie rammed her foot down on the Bentley's accelerator to get away from the man who had leapt up at them. He was waving his arm, shouting at them.

She threw him a glance but drove on.

'Go! Go!' Svetlana urged her. 'There will be more, they will be waiting round the next corner. This could be a big trick.'

A look in the rear-view mirror told Annie that the man was running after the car. She accelerated harder. But a second glance told her that he didn't look hungry or desperate, or in any way evil.

This man had shoulder-length wavy blond hair, a deep tan and a big white-toothed, friendly grin on his face. He was wearing board shorts, a faded T-shirt and a backpack. And on top of a mountain, hundreds of miles from the ocean, he was waving with one arm and carrying a surfboard under the other.

Svetlana urged Annie on. But Annie caught the guy's smile and instantly thought of Owen and his teenage friends. They would soon be old enough to backpack on adventures, hike through Europe, dare to thumb lifts from strangers. Her heart was already softening.

When the guy changed his frantic wave to a hands-together pleading gesture, she was lost. She began to brake and he ran to catch up with the car.

'Annah!' Svetlana shrieked. 'Don't stop! I will not allow you to stop. If you stop and let this man in I will never, ever be your friend. Lana will be sent home from New York.'

Annie turned to her friend.

'What?!'

'Drive!' Svetlana said, sounding frightened. 'It's a trap.'

The guy had already jogged up to the driver's window and now grinned a wide, toothy smile at Annie. She slowed almost to a stop and wound the window down.

'Hello, look, I am sorry, but my friend doesn't want me to let anyone into the car. She's very nervous about strangers.'

'Hey, but I'm Randall . . . I come in peace,' he said and stuck his tanned hand through the window, ready to shake. 'See, I'm Randall, no longer a stranger to you. Peace, *paix, mir, shalom* – I know the word in 131 different languages.'

His accent was broad, sunny American.

'Where are you going?' Randall asked, leaning down to the car window. 'Wherever you're headed, I feel I should ride with you. You're in a car, on a mountain, one of you goes in fear. I know I should ride with you. Think of me as a man of calm in the back of your car. A lucky charm. Your travel guardian.'

Annie shook his hand and held his bright blue eyes. He was making her smile. In fact, she could even feel her heart flutter a little because he was so handsome, so muscular and such a big presence.

'No, we must drive on!' Svetlana insisted, looking over her shoulder anxiously, obviously expecting the bad Serbs to appear at any moment.

'I'm sorry, is there anything else we can do?'

Annie asked. 'Apart from a lift. Could we phone someone?'

Randall smiled. 'No. I need a lift and the karmic forces have brought you in your awesome car right up to the top of my mountain. So I think you should accept that I should travel in your car. I have bungee springs, the surfboard will attach to your roof in a moment. You are the first car that has come by in hours.'

'In hours?' Annie repeated. 'But I thought we were heading to Austria?'

In all honesty, her hope that this was the main road to Austria had evaporated with every mile they'd travelled along this rutted, deserted mountain road.

'No, I don't think so. I think you've taken one serious detour. What did I tell you about the karmic forces? Do you have a map?'

'Yes, we have a map,' Annie looked at Svetlana pointedly.

'We are on wrong road?' Svetlana asked, even more anxious now. 'But how far are we from Austria? We have to get to Vienna, and very quickly!'

'It must be written in the stars. Our paths are meant to cross. You need me because I can read maps and I am fated to guide you to Vienna.'

With that he pulled two elasticated ropes with

clips from his pockets, attached them deftly to the car roof, slid his surfboard in under them, then popped open the rear passenger's door and got in.

'Wow! Look at this car,' he said, settling back, hands behind his head, in the luxurious leather seat. 'I've never been in anything like it. This is truly fit for a prince.'

Annie and Svetlana looked at one another.

'Go on,' Annie said: 'he's a little bit bonkers, but otherwise, he seems fine. Think of him as protection.'

Finally Svetlana shrugged. 'If this is a trap,' she said darkly, 'don't say I did not warn you.'

'OK, map reader.'

'Tschaaaa . . .' Svetlana turned to look out of the window and did not say another word as Annie passed Randall the map, listened to his road directions and, starting up the car once again, drove on.

Annie peered at him in the mirror. She was finding Randall a calming presence, plus he looked reassuringly strong. If they came across the bad men of Svetlana's imagination or if they punctured a tyre – which was slightly more likely – Randall would be able to help. In fact, Annie even wondered if they could persuade him to come to Vienna and help fight off Igor's henchmen.

'We're going to Vienna to get Svetlana's boys back

from their father,' she explained, then filled in further details of the story.

'So I'm in a limousine with two ladies from London who are on the tail of their missing children? Man, I have been on some wild adventures in Europe, but this . . . this could be my best one yet.'

A big grin appeared on Randall's face.

'Vienna: cool. I might stay for the ride, or I might get off before then – I'm kind of looking for a beach, but I like to obey the call of the karmic forces,' Randall said.

'Get off? This is not a bus service. You will leave when we ask you to leave,' Svetlana said coldly.

'Yes ma'am, I certainly don't wish to outstay my welcome.'

His reply softened Annie's heart even more. *Yes ma'am?* He was obviously such a well brought up boy.

'Where are you from?' she asked. 'And why are you on top of an Italian mountain with a surfboard?'

'Now that is a long story,' Randall replied.

'Fine,' she said, nudging the Bentley, with increasing expertise now, round another tight corner. 'We have plenty of time so why don't you tell us all about it?'

Svetlana looked down at her phone, which had been silent for at least an hour and complained: 'Out of signal! I could be missing the most important message.'

'I'm sure we'll get to civilization very soon,' Annie reassured her.

'You, American boy, open up the cupboard in front of you,' Svetlana commanded. 'Is there anything to drink in there?'

'Svetlana, my love, are you sure that's a good idea?' Annie asked. 'You've been awake all night, you've only eaten a croissant today. Are you sure you want to have a drink?'

'Wow! There are three bottles of champagne in here!' came Randall's astonished reply. 'They're even chilled. It's some kind of icebox compartment. Man, that is cool. Are you like multimillionaires on the run from the law or something? It's OK, you can tell me, I come in peace.'

'No! We are not on the run,' Annie protested. 'We borrowed this car from the hotel we were staying in when we got the news about the boys.'

'The boys . . .' Svetlana repeated sadly. 'Open the champagne, quickly.'

'Your wish is my command, ma'am.'

There was a dull pop then the fizzing, gluggity-glug sound of a glass being filled. Moments later, Randall passed a tall champagne flute, filled to the brim, to Svetlana, who drank half of it in one go.

'Would you like a glass, Miss Annie?' Randall asked.

'No thanks. I don't like to mix huge old cars with hairpin bends and champagne. And please, Annie is fine, Miss Annie makes me sound like some Southern spinster. Are you from the South?'

'No, I'm from Bridgeport, New England.'

Svetlana finished her glass and passed it back to Randall with the words: 'I would like some more.'

Despite Annie's warnings, Svetlana swigged back the second glass with two pills which she had taken from her handbag.

'Have you got a headache?' Annie asked.

'No, I take sleeping pills,' Svetlana replied, when she'd swallowed them down, 'I need to have a rest.'

'Sleeping pills?! Sweetheart, you are definitely not meant to wash sleeping pills down with champagne.'

Svetlana shrugged. 'I'm a strong woman,' she said. 'One more glass.' She passed the flute back to Randall who paused, looking at Annie for advice.

'Svetlana, I really don't think that's a good idea,' Annie said.

'Do not tell me what to do,' Svetlana insisted.

Randall filled the glass three-quarters full and as Svetlana took it Annie warned: 'Sip very slowly.'

For the next half an hour or so, the car wound down the mountainside. Looking ahead, they could see that the road was finally heading away from the mountains, towards a great green land mass ahead.

'There's a sign!' Annie exclaimed.

A small metal road sign with an Austrian flag welcomed them over the border in several languages.

'You're joking!' she exclaimed with a laugh. 'You're a genius, Randall. We're in! We've made it to Austria!'

Chapter Twenty-Five

Austria

Annie in her art school days:

Pink silk blouse (Oxfam)
Cream beaded cardigan (market stall find)
Levi 501s splattered with paint (borrowed from Roddy)
Sparkly silver belt (Miss Selfridge)
Pink Mary Janes with heels (Office)
Pink lip gloss (Rimmel)
Lashings of eye kohl (same)
Total est. cost: £45

Annie looked over at her passenger, but Svetlana, head on her shoulder, was in the deep, dreamless sleep of her knockout cocktail.

'OK Randall, concentrate on the map and tell me

where we are and where we're supposed to be going.'

'Yes ma'am, I'll try. So tell me all about London.'

This simple instruction began a long and involved conversation as Annie, prompted by further questions, told Randall all about herself and her life. Maybe because she was driving with her eyes on the road, maybe because he was a good listener, she found Randall easy to talk to.

'You're on television!' he exclaimed. 'Oh my, I am hitching with the rich and famous!'

'It's a makeover show – I'm not that famous, believe me.'

'Wow. Can I look you up on YouTube? Are you in fact Britain's Oprah?'

Annie laughed.

'I'm definitely on YouTube,' she said, thinking back to the toe-curling live event. That was bound to be there, courtesy of someone's mobile. It had probably already scored one million hits and a thousand nasty comments.

'But I'm not Oprah,' she added. ' I mean . . . must be nice to be as famous as Oprah.'

'I don't think so,' Randall said, 'I think it must be bad for the soul to be as famous as Oprah. She can never be free. She can't walk down the road, or hitch-hike . . .'

Annie laughed at the thought.

'She can't even pick her nose without guards, assistants, somebody somewhere watching her. Can you imagine what totally bad karma that must be?'

Annie considered the pros and cons of being Oprah. Maybe Randall had a point but . . .

'I'd be willing to trade up to the Oprah lifestyle for a bit,' she admitted, 'just to try it out. Just to make sure it's hell.'

'But you must be very happy with your life: you have a husband, four kids, a beautiful house, a great job. That sounds pretty good.'

It did.

It did sound really good. So why was she so frazzled with it all that she'd bailed out and run away to Italy for a break?

And then Annie found herself telling Randall about the punishingly long hours, the disastrous live event, the feeling that she'd lost the one thing she'd always been good at, and finally: the row with Lana which still hadn't been resolved.

'Whoa,' he sighed when she had finished, 'you've got it sussed. You've got it made but you feel miserable, like . . . just about every single grown-up I know.'

'Ha.'

A light shower of rain was misting the windscreen, so she searched amongst the levers and the knobs for the windscreen wiper control.

'Too much stuff in your life, I'm guessing. You're weighed down. You need to clear out, give away and travel light. I'm just a guy with a backpack and a surfboard and I've never been happier.'

'Ha!' she repeated. How did anyone travel light through life with four children, a husband, a TV career and a dog?

'What do you do?' she wondered. 'Or what do you plan to do?'

'I surf,' Randall answered simply. 'I used to study. I had all sorts of plans, or certainly my parents did. But right now, I surf therefore I am.' He paused to let that one wash over her. 'I'm travelling through Europe in search of the perfect wave.'

'Are you being serious?'

'Yes and no,' he answered. 'I don't think you should be too serious about anything. That's the problem with grown-ups: way too serious. Remember when you were my age? You probably didn't give a damn.'

Annie cast her mind back to her late teen, early twenties self.

The art student. Then the film costume designer. Then the girl – not much older than Lana was now – wildly in love with charming, handsome actor, Roddy, who had been her first husband: father of Lana and Owen.

'You grow up, you have children, you have to get serious,' she told Randall.

'You don't have to,' he reminded her.

'My first husband died and I had to get very serious.'

She hadn't meant to mention it, but the heart-to-heart atmosphere had drawn it out of her.

'Oh, Miss Annie, I am very sorry.'

For several minutes there was quiet in the car as Randall considered her words and Annie wondered how to steer the conversation away from them.

'I was an art student when I was your age,' she offered, hoping this would move their conversation on.

'Really? Painting and everything?'

'Yup, painting and everything – abstract oils, mysterious sculptures – then I went into costume design.'

His face seemed to lighten with understanding.

'I get it now, you're an artist!' he said, 'you're a creative person all snarled up with TV shows and making a living and trying to get people to buy things that designers tell you to wear every season, no matter how crazy they are.'

He leaned forward and looked at her earnestly: 'You need to get back to your roots. Be creative and arty again. Reconnect. Then you'll feel happy. And you'll probably be a better friend to your daughter too.'

Annie wanted to laugh it off.

She wanted to make fun of his hippie-kid ideas: set herself free . . . be creative . . . reconnect . . .

Hadn't Lana said the same thing? *'You were really arty and creative.'* She wanted to laugh at Randall and tell him: *'Yeah, right and what is Tamsin, my producer, going to feel about this?'*

But instead, Annie couldn't say anything because all she could feel was the hard lump in her throat that meant tears were threatening.

'It's easy to say this stuff,' she blurted out, 'but it's not so easy to do.'

'But you need to do it, Miss Annie, otherwise you're just one more unhappy grown-up troubling the cosmos.'

It was beginning to grow dark. Annie was still driving and Svetlana was still sleeping. Although Annie had looked the map over carefully with Randall and had tried to convince herself they were travelling in the right direction, she was not entirely sure.

How on earth could it already be nearly 7p.m.? They were supposed to have arrived in Vienna hours and hours ago. But they were still on small, quiet roads, passing forests, farms and the occasional village. They were in the deepest countryside, miles from any kind of city.

'Langenstein?' she asked, looking at a forlorn

239

little white signpost: 'haven't we already passed a signpost for Langenstein?'

Randall just shrugged.

'We have to stop. We've got to find someone, we need to ask directions.' Annie was beginning to feel panicky. If Svetlana woke up and found they were still nowhere near the capital and her boys, she would freak out.

Annie had to get them to Vienna – and fast. The sleeping pills couldn't last for ever.

She pressed hard on the accelerator and tried to build up speed. But the reverse happened: the car slowed. She pressed harder, but it slowed right down. Finally, it crawled to a complete stop.

'Oh no, now what?'

'Well, I'm no expert . . .' Randall's voice sounded infuriatingly relaxed and sleepy: 'but I think the universe could be trying to tell you that you've run out of gas.'

'What?!' Annie exclaimed. 'And shut up about karma, the cosmos and the blinking universe!'

She turned the key in the car's ignition, but nothing happened. Obviously the broken fuel gauge had continued to register full, but she'd thought that last fill-up would keep them going to Vienna. She should have guessed that the Beast would find going up and down a mountain range very thirsty work.

'And just what are we supposed to do now?' she

asked, wondering, not for the first time, how she had managed to get herself into this hideous mess.

For a horrible moment, Svetlana's head jerked forward and Annie thought she would have to deal with an enraged Ukrainian tantrum, on top of everything else. But the head went back down and Svetlana's sleep continued.

'What now?' Annie asked her hitch-hiker.

Randall leaned over and whispered back: 'You give me some money and I'll find us some gas or someone who can tow us to a garage.'

'But I've hardly got any money – I always use a card.'

Randall pointed to the luxurious clutch bag lying in Svetlana's lap. 'I have a feeling that there might be some cash in there.'

'I can't just give you Svetlana's money!'

'You should really learn to be more trusting,' Randall told her, with a hint of disappointment. 'But I'll leave you my surfboard as insurance.'

Annie didn't have much choice; well, her choices were not appealing. Either sit tight in a fuel-less car and wait for Svetlana to wake up and *kill* her. Or try to prise Svetlana's clutch from her drugged hands and hand over cash to the surfer dude she'd only known for a few hours ... in the hope that he'd come back with petrol.

Right.

She'd have to go with option two here because there was less chance of death.

She leaned over and gently, very, very gently took hold of one corner of Svetlana's clutch. Thinking about all the times she had eased a blanket, soggy biscuit or toy from her babies' sleeping hands, she wiggled it free.

Although Svetlana moved slightly in her sleep, she did not waken.

With the clutch in her lap, Annie unclasped the substantial brass lock and looked into the pigskin-lined interior. Alongside a phone and a selection of Chanel cosmetics was a purse, probably Hermès, which was absolutely bulging with euro notes. Seriously – thousands of euros' worth.

She repressed the desire to gasp; after all, it wasn't good to let a virtual stranger (albeit one she'd poured her heart out to just an hour or so ago) know how much was in the bag.

This stash could probably fund Randall's surfer bum lifestyle for quite some time to come.

'Right, well . . . I think there might be something in here,' she fibbed, then pulled out a 100 euro note and held it out to him. 'Can I trust you?' she asked.

'Of course you can trust me. Look, my board cost like five of those. I am not about to leave it on your car.'

'Do you promise?'

'Yes, I promise. Besides, you're too lovely to abandon in a car overnight. Trust me.'

With a gentle clunk of the back door, Randall was gone.

Annie leaned back in the driver's seat and waited. She listened to Svetlana's breathing and she waited. It grew dark but she didn't dare to turn on any of the car's cabin lights in case she drained the battery.

Much time passed.

Time for Annie's thoughts about Randall to move from: *Lovely? He thinks I'm lovely. Why did he say that? Why am I even wondering about why he said that? I really shouldn't even be spending one second thinking about this . . .'*

To: *'He's gone. He's definitely gone. He's left us. He's taken 100 euros – from Svetlana! And I gave it to him! And he's left some useless beaten up old surfboard on the roof. Maybe he plays this trick all the time. Maybe he unscrewed the petrol cap . . . maybe that's why he had a surfboard up a mountain in the first place . . .*

She decided to stretch her legs and get some fresh air. She'd been sitting in the Bentley for far too long.

Closing the door quietly behind her, she walked a short distance along the deserted road and back. Only one car had gone past in all the time Randall had been gone. It was far too quiet. The blooming countryside! She'd always been suspicious of it; that was why she lived in London, where the chances of being abandoned on a deserted road, miles and miles from a takeaway, a toilet or a coffee kiosk were very small.

She sat down on a grassy slope, which led towards some very dense and creepy looking woods, and gave a long, heartfelt and dejected sigh.

Out loud, in the immortal words of Owen, she said: 'PANTS! This is just totally, unbelievably PANTS!'

Chapter Twenty-Six

New York

The stallholder:

Bright blue T-shirt (Old Navy)
Faded jeans (Lee)
Red suede sneakers (Adidas)
Vintage bead and turquoise necklace (craft fair)
Total est. cost: $260

'So, any plans for tonight, now that Elena's finally allowed us out of the office?'

'No . . . ummm . . . not really.'

It was nearly evening, Lana and Gracie were walking through one of the little markets on the way back to their neighbourhood from work, eating frozen yoghurts and browsing occasional items for sale.

Lana was sorry she'd come, as she'd known she would be, but Gracie had insisted. Lana hadn't wanted to tell her the reason why she needed to go home and scrub up because she knew Gracie wouldn't like it at all.

As they wandered from stall to stall, looking at the offerings and flirting with the stallholders, Gracie peppered their chat with Parker questions.

'He still hasn't left any kind of message yet. Do you think he will?'

'Do you think he really wanted me to come to this art show on Saturday, remember, or do you think he just said it but didn't really mean it?'

'I think he must have changed his mind. What d'you think?'

'I don't know, Gracie!' Lana said with a touch of exasperation, as she picked up a beaded necklace and examined it carefully.

'Oh yes, that would so suit you,' the stallholder, a young guy not much older than them, insisted. 'Look up at me, Miss? Yes, blue eyes, you have beautiful blue eyes. This is the necklace for you. It's antique, you know, turquoise and genuine silver. Navaho.'

'Thanks,' Lana said, smiling at him, 'I'm kinda looking around, I might come back . . .'

'It'll be gone and you're gonna regret it. It's a special necklace, very lucky.'

246

'Thanks.' She waved and backed away from the stall before he could talk her into it.

Gracie linked arms with Lana: 'You know it's just friends, it's just about making a new friend. It's really not anything else.'

'What is?'

'Me and Parker, of course. But it's just amazing to make a new friend, isn't it? I'd forgotten how exciting the whole thing is, like a crush,' Gracie gushed, 'but in a small way, of course.'

'Are you going to stop?' Lana asked, slightly shocked at how abrupt this sounded.

'Huh?' Gracie asked, letting her arm fall from Lana's.

'Well, you just have to stop now. You already have a boyfriend. A really nice, really sweet boyfriend called Bingham. Have you forgotten? Parker is just this guy,' then with barely checked irritation, Lana added: 'All Parker said to you was: there's an art show next Saturday, see you there, maybe? No. Big. Deal.'

'What's got into you?' Gracie demanded, all hurt now.

'Well, you're just acting like he's the most important thing in the world – and he's not. He's so totally not. The most important thing in the world right now is that we've spent $4,000 of our own money making new dresses and we have to make sure they fly off the rails. That's the only thing we ought to be thinking about. Not some dumb guy who might or might not ask us out.'

'*Us?*'

Gracie wheeled round to stare at Lana; there was no ignoring the iciness in her voice.

'Has Parker asked you out?'

Lana didn't say anything, but she could feel a telltale blush radiating across her face.

'You better tell me, Lana,' Gracie went on, 'otherwise I'm going to call him right now, right this second, and find out.'

'He asked me out. I'm meeting Parker tonight,' Lana blurted out.

Gracie's expression went from angry to stunned in a heartbeat. Now Lana could feel blood pounding in her cheeks and in her ears. Did she really just say that out loud? Had she just told Gracie? Even though, deep down, she knew how Gracie was going to feel.

'What?!' Gracie asked, her voice squeaky with astonishment.

'He asked me out yesterday,' Lana began, 'and I said yes because you have a boyfriend and I don't. I thought it would be OK.'

'I can't believe you!' Gracie exclaimed. 'I met him first. I introduced him to you. You've never said you liked him like that. I can't believe you . . .'

Gracie's face was creasing: it was clear that she was on the verge of tears.

'Well, I'm sorry—' Lana began.

'You're sorry?! Oh please, don't even bother pretending to apologize. How can you say you're sorry? All I've been saying for days is how much I liked him and you . . .' Gracie paused, her voice all tight and choked, 'you never said a single word.'

'Gracie, I didn't mean . . . I didn't know . . . not really,' Lana tried.

'You didn't mean what? You didn't mean to snatch Parker from right under my nose? Oh and I suppose you didn't mean to exactly copy my bangs? You didn't mean to start dressing in exactly the same way as me? What are you doing? Are you trying to be me?! Are you some weird stalker person who is planning to take over my entire life?'

'Gracie!' Lana exclaimed, but she felt properly stung now, 'I didn't . . . I haven't . . .'

'Yes you have!' Gracie chipped in. 'You've done all of those things. You've totally copied me and now you are stealing the guy who is supposed to be mine.'

Her voice was loud and passers-by were stopping to stare.

'Please be quiet,' Lana asked.

'I hope you have a lovely evening. I hope you have a truly wonderful time and make a brand new

best friend, because you're going to need one!'
Gracie exclaimed. Then she turned on her heel and
began to walk away quickly.

Lana just stood there, feeling her cheeks burn.
This was horrible and she felt awful.

She *had* copied Gracie's bangs – and she had
bought vintage dresses and little bags and pinned
brooches to her lapels all in the Gracie style . . . and
now she was going on a date with the guy Gracie
liked best of all. Gracie hadn't needed to say it, Lana
had guessed. Lana should have known it was the
wrong thing to do.

In fact, it was a horrible thing to do.

'Ooooh, you should have bought the lucky
necklace,' the stallholder with the turquoise
jewellery told her.

The humiliation brought tears to Lana's eyes. She
trudged out of the market and back to her apartment, her mobile phone clutched tightly in her
hand.

She was a tiny speck of person alone and lonely in
New York. There was only one person she wanted to
call. But she didn't know if she could. How did she
get over the awkward beginning and have a proper
conversation with her mum?

Chapter Twenty-Seven

Austria

Ed on the line:

Denim shirt (used to be Owen's)
Pink woolly tank-top (no idea)
Baggy beige chinos (John Lewis sale)
Old squash shoes (school lost property sale)
Total est. cost: £25

'PANTS,' Annie repeated to herself.

She was still stuck in the woods with the empty Bentley and the sleeping tigress. The surfer was still missing in action.

'And now what?' she asked herself. 'If you think you're so clever, girl, just how are we supposed to get out of this?'

She took her mobile out of her handbag, saw that the battery was already two-thirds spent and wondered who she could phone. Maybe she should try and get through to the British AA? Maybe they had a European branch, which would bring petrol to Bentley-driving damsels in distress.

Before she could make a decision, the phone in her hand sprang to life and seeing at once whose number it was, she burst into a very welcome hello to her husband, Ed.

'Oh darlin', how nice to hear from you. I can't tell you how good it is to get a phone call. Oh babes, I'm in such a fix, it's lovely to hear from you. How are you? What is happening at home?'

'We're fine, Annie. All quiet on the home front,' Ed told her. 'What do you mean you're in a fix? What's happened now?'

'Oh, you know, nothing much,' she replied, not really wanting to worry him.

'Well what? Why don't you just tell me? Is it serious? Or just the imaginings of a dessert-starved dieter?'

'Oh sweetheart, I am stuck in a wood in Austria with a clapped-out Bentley and a sleeping millionairess, waiting for the return of an escaped surfer.'

'What?!'

Annie decided it was safe enough to give her

husband, thousands of miles away, a quick summary of the situation.

'WHAT?!' Ed repeated when Annie reached the end of the update.

'That's my story so far,' she added, 'so now it's your turn.'

'But what are you going to do?' Ed asked.

'Don't worry about me . . . something will turn up.'

'But I do worry about you. I constantly worry about you. Now I'm going to worry about you all night long. You need the police. You need to dial 999 or whatever it is in Austria and get help.'

'Probably. That's probably what any normal person would do. I don't know, my love, the police, the lawyers, they're all on the case somewhere. We're just out on a limb, on a detour . . . but we're safe.'

'Are you? Are you sure?' Ed sounded a little frantic.

'I am sure we are safe. We can always lock ourselves into the Bentley until the morning . . .'

'Annie!'

'Svetlana wants to get the boys back herself. I think it's something about standing up to Igor on her own. I think she wants to show him she's a totally worthy opponent. That he can't crush her.'

'Annie, you need to get help. Are you sure you shouldn't phone the police?'

'Look, babes, if the surfer hasn't come back in an hour, I promise, I promise you that's what we'll do.'

'OK . . .'

There was a hint of relief in Ed's voice.

'Have you heard from Lana?' she asked.

'No. Have you?'

'No.'

Annie took in the dark woodland around her and the little road, empty apart from the Bentley.

'I miss Lana,' Annie admitted, 'it's like a bad break-up. I feel sad and I keep hearing songs that remind me of her. I want to sit in her bedroom and sniff things, hoping to get a little whiff of her.'

'Just give her a phone,' Ed suggested.

'Svetlana said she would run back to me.'

Ed snorted. 'And since when has Svetlana been an expert on teenage behaviour?'

'She won't be our teenager soon,' Annie said, feeling almost choked at the thought. 'She'll turn twenty and then she'll be fully grown up. I have to go,' she remembered: 'save my battery for phoning the police if I need to.'

'Right. You take care, let me know what's happening. I love you and I'm going to worry about you.'

'Love you too.'

Reluctantly, Annie clicked off the call and put the phone back into her handbag. Right. It was time. Time to go back to the Bentley, wake up Svetlana, endure the Ukrainian tantrum and try to decide what to do next.

But just as she reached the car she heard footsteps behind her and a jaunty whistling. She turned to look and the sight of Randall strolling along with a huge plastic container bumping against his legs made her grin with relief, with happiness ... with all sorts of slightly over the top feelings. She was just so pleased to see him.

'You came back!' she called out to him.

'Of course! Were you thinking I was going to run out on you? Why did you not trust in the cosmic forces?'

'Oh good grief. What's the difference between a cosmic and a karmic force, by the way?' she asked, heading towards him, intending to help him get the container to the car.

'No, I've got it,' he insisted, 'and I can't answer your question ... well, not in one sentence. Not even in one evening.'

'Never mind. Has this got petrol in it?'

'What do you think?' he smiled: 'That I've walked back with a water urn so we can have a long drink?'

The muscles under his smooth brown skin flexed as he manoeuvred the container towards the car. Now that Annie was standing beside him, he towered above her, well over six foot tall.

'I'll bet you missed me?' he asked playfully.

'It's been very quiet without you,' she admitted. 'Svetlana is still asleep: thank goodness.'

'Well, my fellow traveller, I have good news for you and I have bad news.'

'I'm not sure I want to hear any more bad news at the moment,' Annie replied, which was putting it mildly.

Randall went to the Bentley and unscrewed the petrol cap. He began to pour in petrol a little too messily for Annie's liking, as splashes kept escaping and sliding down the side of the car.

'OK, the good news: we're just a mile or so from a good road with a big service station,' he told her. 'So once I've put this in we can drive down there and fill up properly. From there, the motorway is only like seven kilometres away – that's not far, is it?'

'Four miles or so,' Annie said.

'And then you're only 15 kilometres from Vienna.'

'We're 15 kilometres from Vienna? Is that all?' Annie could hardly believe it. 'But we've not seen a single town.'

'We've come in on a strange route.'

'You were the map reader,' she reminded him.

'European maps,' Randall said, as if that explained it, 'I'm obviously not used to them. But have faith. This was the path we were meant to take. The reason for the detour may not be obvious now, but its meaning will be revealed in time.'

'You might have to stop with that, before I smack you.'

He had emptied the container and now turned to her with a smile: one of his cool, make that super-chilled, saintly, surfer smiles.

It was impossible not to smile back.

'OK, so what's the bad news?' Annie asked. 'And am I going to be able to cope with it?'

'I'm not going to Vienna with you. I'm going to the other side of the motorway to hitch a lift to Spain. I met a fellow traveller at the service station and he's waiting for me. Spain is where the world-class breakers can be found.'

Annie gave a little 'oh' and suddenly found herself in a bear hug, her face squashed against the kind of taut muscular chest she associated with perfume ads.

'We feel close right now, don't we?' Randall said, which was sort of stating the obvious.

She could feel his massive chest vibrating as he said the words. His arms were holding her tightly and his heart was beating just beside her ear.

She nodded.

'That's being on the road. People meet and share their stories and suddenly they're best friends in a day. Or closer . . .'

Annie breathed in his salty, sweaty smell and let

her arms hug him back, feeling solid muscle beneath her touch.

Whoa . . .

She had to pull right back here. She might have been through a lot of stress lately, but there was no need to do anything crazy. His handsome face hovered for a moment a little too closely over hers.

'Thanks, Randall,' she said with forced cheeriness, pulling her face safely out of his way, 'thanks for getting the petrol. That was very kind.'

She let her arms drop from his sides, so he let go too, then she turned quickly away. As she did, he landed a cheeky slap on her bum.

'Randall!' she said in her best bossy mum voice.

'I'd have kissed you, just to be nice,' he said, shooting her another lazy grin.

'Well, that's . . . um . . .' Annie realized she was blushing and feeling properly flustered: 'nice to know.'

The Bentley's passenger door flew open and a loud, unmistakable voice exclaimed: 'Annah? Where are we? This is not Vienna!'

Chapter Twenty-Eight

New York

Lana ready to go:

Skinny logoed sweater (Markus Lupfer, via The Outnet)
Denim pencil skirt (Banana Republic)
Black footless tights (Gap)
The blue polka-dot shoes (Chie Mihara, but on sale)
Total est. cost: $220

Lana checked herself over carefully in the bathroom mirror as she applied a final dab of lip gloss. She was almost satisfied. The dark eye make-up was edgy enough and although she'd fiddled with her hair for ages, it didn't look too done and it hadn't gone crazy with static.

She looked good. Face and hair: gold star. Outfit:

could do better. But she'd already ransacked her wardrobe, tried on five different outfits and she'd decided this was the best she could do. So there was no point torturing herself about it.

Her best outfit was the one she'd worn to the club opening and she couldn't wear it again. Not for a date with the same guy. Especially Parker. He designed fabric, for goodness' sake! He would notice.

So she was going to chill about the top and the skirt she was wearing. They weren't the most rocking combination in the known universe, but they'd do. She was going to chill right out . . . and wear the polka-dot shoes again – because she couldn't help thinking of them as her lucky shoes.

She was going on this date. She'd made that decision as she'd walked home, blazing with anger about the row with Gracie. Yes, Gracie had met Parker first. But they were supposed to be just friends. Had Parker done anything to suggest otherwise? Lana pushed earrings into the tiny holes in her lobes and glared at the mirror with defiance.

A buzz on the apartment's intercom made her jump. The buzzer never rang, except occasionally in the morning when the mailman was making a delivery. *Mailman*, she checked herself with a smile. How could she be calling the postman the mailman?

She couldn't do that if she was to milk the whole Londoner-abroad image.

She picked up the intercom handset with a brisk 'Hello.'

'Delivery,' came the abrupt reply.

'OK, come on up, 14th floor.'

She hit the unlock button.

Lana was glad that Elena wasn't at home this evening. Elena would of course ask why she was taking so much trouble with her look. Elena would want to know everything about her date and Elena would totally guess that Parker was the cause of all the effort.

Truthfully, Lana couldn't resist meeting Parker. She couldn't help wanting to know what he thought. Did he really like her? Could they get together? Could she ever be super-cool Parker's girlfriend? She would just die of regret if she didn't at least try to find out.

She heard footsteps heading down the hallway towards the apartment door, so she slid out the bolt and opened the door a little. This was New York City, you were supposed to be ultra-careful.

She peeked out, expecting someone weighed down with a parcel and a clipboard, but was astonished, not to mention nervous, to see Gracie striding down the hallway towards her.

Lana would have slammed shut the door and slid

the bolt back into place before she could listen to another angry word, but Gracie had already seen her.

And then Gracie smiled. What did *that* mean?

'Hi . . .' Lana began nervously.

'Hi,' Gracie said . . . too cheerfully.

'You look really nice,' were Gracie's next words as she came towards the door.

Lana just stood there, frozen.

'Aren't you going to let me in?'

'I don't . . . I mean, aren't you still really annoyed with me? Or has something changed?'

'Yes, something has changed.'

Lana held her breath and realized she was waiting for terrible news. Parker had cancelled . . . Parker had invited Gracie too, Gracie instead. Yes, Gracie was going on this date and not her.

'I'm not angry with you any more,' Gracie said simply.

Lana waited anxiously for the reason.

'You're just doing what I would have done if he'd asked me out first.'

Lana felt a small sense of relief. *If* – Gracie had said 'if', and that could only mean one thing: Parker hadn't asked Gracie out.

Gracie was looking at her expectantly. It was obviously Lana's turn to talk.

'I'm sorry. I didn't even tell you that I liked him,

so it must have been a surprise. A nasty surprise,' she offered, apologetically.

'It was, kinda,' Gracie said, but gave a shrug, 'but I guess I'll get over it.'

Lana looked at her, eyes wide with surprise. 'Really?' she couldn't help asking. 'Do you really think so?'

Gracie shrugged again and smiled: 'Yeah, well . . . You need to find out all about him, so that when you guys break up I can decide whether I want to go after him or not,' she said in a teasing voice.

'Gracie! I can't break up with him because I'm not even going out with him,' Lana protested. 'This is just a go-see – who knows what will happen?'

'He'll like you, I'm sure. Who wouldn't?'

'That is too nice of you. Way too nice. Do you want to come in? I've got to go in like ten, but come in till then, help me pick out my shoes,' Lana said, even though she'd already decided.

'That will be too easy,' Gracie said, following Lana into the hallway of her apartment. 'You have to wear the polka-dot shoes! Like, so totally obvious.'

'Is my outfit OK?' Lana asked a little anxiously. 'I mean it's not the best, but I wore my best one last time – so is this OK?'

'Well, that's the other reason I'm here,' Gracie began. She unhooked her straw basket from her shoulder and brought out a plastic bag.

'I think you should wear this.'

Lana took the bag, opened it up and peered inside. She knew at once what she was looking at.

'You are joking! Where did you get this? How did you get this? And you brought it to me!'

Lana put her hands into the bag and brought out a soft, slouchy tunic dress: it was gorgeous, drapy, funky and – all importantly – made from the blue and yellow print that Parker had designed.

'I absolutely love it! It's amazing!' Lana gushed. 'Oh my goodness. This is an NY Perfect Dress and it's unbelievably good!'

'Yeah. I stormed back to the office after I left you and Elena was still there with this whole rail of new NY Perfect Dress dresses and they are way, way better than I could ever have imagined.'

'Look,' Lana said, holding the dress up in front of her. It was a great cut and made of supple, fluid fabric which she knew would hang and cling in just the right kind of way. The neckline was a simple scoop and the three-quarter-length sleeves were wide with a gathered button detail at the ends.

'Oh,' she held the sleeve button in her fingers, 'that's just right, just enough detail to give it a lovely finish, but nothing fussy to detract from the pattern.'

'Try it on! Try it on!' Gracie insisted.

'What should I wear underneath?'

'Tight trousers, the polka-dot shoes and I

might allow you to wear a belt if it's too baggy.'

Lana rushed to her room to change. When she came back out into the living space she and Gracie did a little victory dance together, because the dress was so good.

'Imagine what he'll say when he sees you wearing his fabric and rocking it!'

'It's definitely his fabric?' Lana asked. 'It just . . . I dunno . . . It looks a little familiar to me.'

'No, it's definitely his – a Parker Bain original. He's going to go crazy for you.'

Lana reached for her friend and flung her arms around her.

'Gracie, I hope you know you're the best. Only the best kind of friend would do something as nice as this. I am not the one rocking tonight. You totally rock.'

Gracie hugged her back.

'Go knock him out,' she said, 'and I'm sorry I yelled at you.'

'I'm just really sorry there aren't two Parkers. Do you think we could clone him?'

'Maybe he has a brother? Please ask.'

'Do you really like him so much?' Lana looked at her friend in total seriousness.

'Yeah. I just finished with Bingham, because you have to be honest. If I'm thinking this much about Parker, well, I had to let Bingham go.'

'Gracie, I can't go. I can't go on this date. This is obviously your guy.'

'Don't be crazy. Go. Check him out. We'll worry about cloning him when you're sure he's a good one.'

'Are you sure? Are you really, really sure?'

Chapter Twenty-Nine

Austria

> *The garage customer:*
>
> *Inter-Milan football top (gift from son)*
> *Jeans (Lee)*
> *Leather man bag (Steffl department store)*
> *Trainers (Adidas)*
> *Total est. cost: €220*

'Annah?' Svetlana repeated, 'What is going on? Why are we here? It is dark already, why are we not in Vienna?'

After such a long, pill-induced nap, Svetlana's blonde beehive was tufty and askew and she wobbled a little on her heels as she walked, but she still looked a formidable sight. The way she was glaring was making Annie feel horribly nervous.

'We ran out of petrol. But Randall has been to the station and filled the car up again. We're all ready to go: only 15 kilometres from Vienna,' Annie added quickly.

Thankfully, instead of having the tantrum Annie was still expecting, Svetlana nodded curtly. Then she licked at her parched lips and asked, 'Is there any water?'

'Maybe in the minibar,' Annie remembered. 'Come on, we'll get back into the car.'

As Svetlana downed the glass of mineral water Randall had poured for her, Annie started up the Bentley and followed directions to the service station. As soon as they reached it, they all piled out of the car once again: Annie and Svetlana planned on using the bathroom, stocking up with fuel, more mineral water and Austrian chocolate bars; Randall was to meet up with the fellow traveller headed for Spain on the other side of the motorway.

He released his surfboard and bungee ropes from the top of the car, then squared up to Annie to say goodbye.

'I think we have to hug,' he said with his arms already wide open.

'A hug would be nice,' she told him, 'but nothing else. Don't be getting any ideas.'

She found herself crushed up against his chest

again, trying not to focus on the outline of a rock-solid pec right in front of her eyes.

'I hope Spain is cosmically good,' she told him.

'It will be. Good luck in Vienna and make sure you have a really nice life. Make sure to get back in touch with your inner artist . . . or you'll always be sorry.'

'Right.'

Svetlana looked on icily as Randall said his good-byes. He didn't even dare to try and shake her hand, just gave her a friendly wave.

'It was an adventure meeting you, ma'am. Hope you get your boys back.'

Svetlana scowled and stalked off in the direction of the illuminated petrol station.

'What time is it?' Annie wondered.

'Aha!' Randall cracked another grin. 'Time for our paths to uncross and for the rest of your life to begin.'

A plastic cup of coffee in her hand, Svetlana stared at the motorway ahead and watched as the road signs counted down the distance to Vienna.

'What are we going to do when we get there?' she asked, not taking her eyes from the road.

'You'll need to get some more information for us. Try Harry, try Michael again, or maybe you should finally talk to Igor so he realizes you're totally serious about getting the boys back no matter what.'

Svetlana spent several minutes firing out messages with her phone and dialling numbers.

'Harry has no more news on where the boys are,' she said, staring at the text which had just come in. She punched in another number.

'Hello, I wish to speak with Igor please. Tell him it's Svetlana.'

She obviously got short shrift because she took the phone from her ear and exclaimed: 'Oh! Igor!'

She tossed the remains of the coffee down her throat.

'I will never get Igor out of my life. So long as I am the mother of his children, the boys who will inherit his empire, then I will always have to deal with his bullying.'

Annie suspected this was true. Men like Igor – well, there weren't in fact many men like Igor. How many mighty, all-powerful billionaires could there be? Moguls who flitted between London, Moscow, the Middle East and the USA the way most people flitted between home, the office and the supermarket.

What advice could she possibly give on how to deal with an ex-husband like Igor? It wasn't as if she could refer Svetlana to a self-help manual: 'How to Cope with your Billionaire Ex-Husband.'

But then again, when Svetlana had worked out how to control him, she should probably write the book. There was bound to be some demand, although it was undoubtedly a niche market.

'Just keep standing up to Igor,' Annie advised: 'that's the only thing he respects. Never show weakness, just stand your ground and fight for your rights. It's like dealing with a Rottweiler or an angry bull . . . probably.'

She'd be the first to admit she'd never had to face down either of these horrors.

Before Svetlana could reply, the phone she was holding tightly in her hand began to buzz.

'It could be a message!' she exclaimed, fumbling the handset and almost dropping it in her agitation.

'We are in Vienna, staying here tonight,' she read out, *'Michael.'*

'Fantastic news!' Annie said. 'But where in Vienna? Ask him quickly, while he's still got the phone in his hands.'

Svetlana tapped out a message and together they waited for the reply, Svetlana in a state of almost unbearable tension. For several minutes there was silence, apart from the hum of the Bentley engine, probably thrashing its way through one litre of fuel per second.

Then the phone buzzed again.

'I don't believe it!' Svetlana whispered.

Holding the screen up she read out: '*Near a big church, in a square, saw sign for Konig something.*'

She turned to Annie, asking anxiously, 'Do you think that could be enough? It doesn't sound like enough . . . will we be able to find them?'

Chapter Thirty

New York

Parker's date wear:

Skinny cut navy shirt (PS By Paul Smith – gift from Mom)
Black skinny jeans (Old Navy)
Brown leather sneakers (Converse)
Black pork-pie hat (The Brooklyn Hat Store)
Total est. cost: $195

Lana and Parker had first of all done coffee in a place so urban cool she'd panicked about what to order. 'Caramel latte' just didn't look as if it would cut it in a hangout with jagged metal sculptures rearing from the walls and moody waitresses with cropped hair and chunky boots.

Then they'd gone on to a live art event where the

artists had splattered the crowd with paint while wailing at them about the destruction of the individual in a sea of corporate clones.

So far, this was Lana's most exciting night out in New York ever. She'd hung onto every word Parker said and everywhere they'd gone, she'd been introduced to his friends and he'd explained about her tunic.

'Look at this, look at this dress she's wearing,' he kept telling people. 'This is my work. This is my print. Doesn't it look cool? Lana works for this independent label and they are making up some really cool designs with my prints.'

One thing Lana had picked up in the course of the whirlwind evening was that Parker knew a lot of people.

He knew waitresses and doormen. He knew artists and gallery types. He knew students and designers, shop owners and barmen. On this evening alone, he seemed to have made seven new friends. He'd added everyone to his Facebook page and Twitter feed. He had 13,870 followers, he'd told her, twice.

And everyone who'd met her had been just a tiny little bit uninterested; well, that's how Lana had read it.

No one had gushed: 'Hi, how are you? How did you meet Parker?' in that sort of you-must-be-Parker's-new-love-interest kind of way.

In fact people had been very: 'Hi . . .' and then straight back into conversation with Parker. Was this because he was so charming and interesting and out-there and she, by comparison, just wasn't?

And although it was a really fascinating evening and she'd loved being right beside him as he toured her through it, they'd hardly had any time to talk.

These were the niggles, the little considerations she thought about as they made the long walk to her apartment. He'd insisted on walking her home and told her off when she'd suggested a cab.

'But it's such a great evening. And New York at night is the best, plus walking is the most environmentally friendly way. You've got to remember that.'

They were walking past a huge gallery window with an oversized, multi-coloured cube in the window.

'This is such a great piece, isn't it?' Parker said, slowing down and turning to face it.

'Ummm . . . very colourful . . . very imposing,' Lana said, hoping she didn't sound like a complete twerp.

'I have always wanted to kiss someone right here, right in front of this window. Right in front of the Vronsky cube.'

Lana felt a weird little shudder pass all the way down to her toes when he said this.

Kiss . . .

She had been thinking about kissing all evening: the if, the when, the where of kissing – and now it sounded as if there was about to be an important development on the kissing front.

'You've always wanted to?' she asked, then couldn't help adding a little cynically, 'but that cube's probably only been there for a few weeks.'

Parker shrugged: 'You know what I mean.'

'You've always wanted to kiss *someone*,' Lana repeated. 'That doesn't sound so good. That sounds as if anyone would do.'

She was standing very close to him now, close enough to see the stubble on his upper lip, close enough to smell the soap-meets-coffee smell he was giving off. Definitely close enough to kiss.

Here she was right at the moment she had been thinking about for days: right beside him, right beside the Vronsky cube. A kiss was imminent. His lips parted slightly, he leaned just a little closer, towards her.

And suddenly she just wasn't quite sure.

She did very much want to see what it would be like to kiss Parker. But then the thought of having to tell Gracie was unbearable. Gracie had just about been able to forgive her for going on a date with Parker . . . but kissing . . . Lana did not know if Gracie would ever forgive kissing.

Now his lips were right in front of hers. Wouldn't she like to find out . . . ?

She moved forward, just to the point where she could feel Parker's warm breath on her upper lip.

But no – Gracie, what about Gracie? Lana pulled her head away.

'What's the matter?' Parker asked, his pupils wide and his voice a little husky.

Lana blurted out the first thing she could think of: 'Look at the cube! It's changed colour!'

Parker glanced through the gallery window then back at her. He put his hand under her chin and held it so she had to look into his face once again.

'Lana from London?' he asked. 'Are we going to kiss . . . or what?'

Chapter Thirty-One

Austria

Lady of the night:

Short black fake fur coat (an admirer)
Black lace babydoll (C&A)
Black lace underwear (same)
Black stockings (same)
Dangly diamanté earrings (market stall)
Comfortable patent black heels (Prada – real)
Black and gold handbag (Prada – fake)
Total est. cost: €570

'Vienna North? Or Vienna South? What do you think?' Annie asked as the motorway began to divide up into exits and options.

She was not exactly thrilled at the prospect of

having to haul the great, clunking Bentley around city streets that she didn't know. But now was not the time to dwell on minor inconveniences.

Svetlana was poring over the street map of Vienna she'd found in the back of the Austrian map book.

'There are so many, many, many places with Konig at the start of their name. Too many.'

'Don't panic.' Annie saw a sign above the next lane which indicated 'Vienna Centrum', made a late lane change and earned herself a severe honking from the car behind.

'No need to panic,' she added, although her heart was now racing: 'I thought we would drive around the places you and Igor used to visit. Men are creatures of habit, if they've been somewhere once and liked it, they usually go back. Is he like that?'

'Yes!' Svetlana exclaimed and suddenly looked much more hopeful. 'He has two favourite hotels in Vienna, this is where we need to try first. Genius Annah, I would not have thought of this.'

'Right. Get out your phone, look those hotels up, find the addresses and see if you can download some basic sort of satnav that will get us there. It's only eleven o'clock . . . we've got hours of time to find them.'

'We will find them,' Svetlana said, but her voice didn't have its usual ring of confidence. 'OK,' she said, 'The Hotel Brunswick. We try there first. Keep following signs for town centre and I will try to direct you.'

At least the roads were quiet, Annie kept telling herself as she navigated the Beast up streets and along avenues, trying to negotiate traffic lights, tramlines and all the other hazards of a foreign city.

She clipped the high kerb of a roundabout once and dragged the bottom of the car over several vicious speed bumps. These injuries to the Bentley made her cringe because one day, hopefully soon, the car would have to be returned to the Villa Verdina and she did not want to be around when Carlo and the chauffeur took a look at it.

Thunk.

As she pulled up for a red traffic light, she clipped the wing mirror against a railing.

'Be careful,' Svetlana warned.

'I'm trying.'

'This is the opera and the Hotel Brunswick is not far from here.'

After a missed turning, a slightly heated debate and a U-turn across four lanes, the Bentley rattled to a halt outside exactly the kind of hotel Annie could have guessed Igor would frequent: an ornate, classical building with liveried doormen in top hats and tails.

'I will go in and ask. You wait here,' Svetlana instructed.

'You'll go in and ask?' Annie repeated incredulously. 'Do you think they're just going to tell you at reception: yes, no problem, Igor the billionaire and his two kidnapped children are staying here?'

Svetlana reapplied her lipstick, smoothed down her hair-do, then pushed open the car door and stepped out, clasping her clutch bag firmly.

'I know all of Igor's aliases and I know how to make hotel staff talk,' she said firmly.

Annie felt a wave of relief. Svetlana was back in action. With that kind of attitude and an alligator purse full of huge denomination euro notes, she was very likely to succeed.

As Svetlana strode towards the hotel lobby, Annie reverse parked gingerly in a space she hoped would be big enough. A nasty scraping sound suggested that hubcap and solid Viennese kerb had suffered another bruising encounter.

She leaned back in the seat and rested her eyelids briefly. Tired? Tired didn't even come close, plus her shoulders and arms were locked solid after an entire day and night spent manoeuvring the Beast up and down the mountains.

A luxury spa break?! Pah! She would need one to recover from this trip.

When she opened her eyes again, she saw a woman a little way off leaning against a railing and looking at the car. She was in the highest heels, sheerest black 10 deniers and what looked like a very short black fur coat over a very short dress.

'No, I'm not your taxi and I hope it turns up soon,' Annie said to herself.

Moments later, Svetlana's high heels could be heard clacking down the pavement towards her. Annie reached over to open the door and Svetlana flung herself into the seat.

'I have never been so insulted in my life!' she declared. 'They think I am some hotel hooker, like this one over here.'

With that she pointed at the woman in the short fur coat.

'Oh, is that what she's doing? I thought she was waiting for a taxi.'

Svetlana snorted.

'I check all his names, they say no to every one of them. Then they look at me and say women like me are not welcome at the Hotel Brunswick. Can you believe this? I mean – I have stayed there! In the presidential suite! I show him my necklace and say what kind of woman do you think I am? Do women like this buy their jewellery in Cartier? He replies: "I believe so, ma'am." Oh my God, I am so angry I just about kill him.'

'Right. So Igor's not there. What do we do now?' Annie asked, trying to get Svetlana to refocus on their mission.

'No. He's not here. So we have to try the Hotel Mercure Centrum. But I don't know, Annah, maybe this is too obvious. He have so many friends with homes in Vienna. Why would he not just go to private address?'

'Plus, I was just thinking, there's no church here,' Annie added, 'no square and no Konig-anything nearby. I've just checked the map. We have to trust Michael. He sent you those details because he was sure they would help. If they'd been at a hotel, he'd have sent you the name of the hotel, wouldn't he?'

'You're right,' Svetlana said quietly, 'we must listen to Michael's advice. Get out the map, we will study all the street names with Konig which coincide with churches and squares.'

Annie didn't like to tell her how long that might take. Instead, she brought out the map, turned on the interior light and smoothed the pages out between them.

Just then Svetlana's phone began to ring. Immediately, she snatched it up.

'Is it Igor's number?' Annie asked.

'No, it's Elena,' Svetlana said, sounding severe. To Annie's knowledge, Svetlana and Elena hadn't spoken since the boys had gone missing.

'Maybe she has some news,' Annie suggested. 'Try and hear her out before you launch in with your tirade.'

'All I want to do is kill her!' Svetlana said, repeating the threat she'd made many hours ago.

'Please just try and listen to her,' Annie urged.

Svetlana put the phone to her ear and barked out: 'How can you have the nerve to phone me? How can you do this?'

A little pause followed while Svetlana obviously waited to hear Elena's response, but the next moment she was shrieking: 'This is all your fault. Do you think Igor would have those boys if you hadn't handed them over? And with their passports! I just can't believe how stupid you have been.'

A stream of very ugly sounding Ukrainian came next, then Svetlana clicked off the phone, letting out a sigh of fury and exasperation.

Annie looked across at her friend: 'So . . . that went well?'

'I *kill* her,' Svetlana repeated, with full melodrama.

'Why was she phoning? To say sorry?'

'She try saying sorry, but I cut her off. I don't want to hear from her now. Is too soon. Maybe when I have the boys back. Maybe I can face talking to her then. You think Maria would have given anyone the boys' passports?'

Annie decided to leave the argument there. She looked back down at her map and said, 'There's a square not far from here with a church and a street called Konig Allee leading from it. We could try there first.'

'Yes. Let's go,' Svetlana agreed.

They parked in a side street, then walked into the heart of the pedestrianized square. It was elegant and stately even in the dark, maybe especially in the dark with the grey buildings asleep and the central fountain trickling quietly.

'It's a lovely city,' Annie told Svetlana. 'I wish I was here for a good reason and could enjoy it a little.'

'As beautiful as Paris, but full of Austrians,' Svetlana replied.

The buildings on the square were four storeys high, divided up into countless flats. As Annie and Svetlana looked around, they wondered just how on earth they could find two small, sleeping boys here.

'What do we do now?' Svetlana asked.

Annie wasn't sure how to reply. She couldn't suggest that they just sit on a bench and watch the comings and goings out of the flat entrances. That was too feeble for words.

Svetlana reached into her clutch bag and brought out her embossed box of Sobranie cigarettes, so now Annie knew just how rattled she was.

In her long raincoat, with her blonde hair up in a

chignon, walking through this timeless Viennese square in the lamplight, smoking a cigarette, Svetlana looked like a heroine from a war movie.

'We could start with the cars,' she began. 'We must see if we can find a car that Igor owns. If not, then we try the next square on the list with a church and a Konig-something.'

'Do you know all the cars that Igor owns?'

Svetlana thought for a moment and sucked on her gold-tipped cigarette. Exhaling smoke, she shook her head and admitted: 'He loves cars. He owns many cars. But they are always the biggest, the most expensive and German. He would never own a French car – or a British car.'

Annie pointed to the nearest side street and the long row of BMWs, Mercedes and Audis parked bumper to bumper.

'So we're looking for a top of the range German car . . . The problem will be working out which one is Igor's.'

Svetlana threw her cigarette to the ground and stamped on it, letting out a gasp of pure frustration.

'I thought we would work out what to do. I thought we would get some more news . . . I thought we would *win*!' she exclaimed. 'Someone must know something. Why is no one telling me?!'

'Maybe we should go back to the car. You could try phoning everyone again: Harry, Igor . . . Is there anyone else you can think of? Anyone who might have a connection?'

'I think Elena maybe wanted to tell me an idea . . .' Svetlana began.

'Elena? What do you mean?'

'Well, she said there was someone she'd spoken to. But I was so angry, I didn't listen to her. It's probably nothing. What does she know? She was just saying this to make me feel better.'

'But you cut her off,' Annie reminded her. 'Maybe she did have something important. And now she's so annoyed with you she hasn't phoned back.'

'Tschaaaa,' Svetlana said and shrugged her shoulders.

'Look, I know it's hard to make up with your children when you've fallen out with them –' Annie was speaking the truth here: 'But sometimes, you just have to swallow your pride and get on with it. We aren't always right, you know. Elena did not know the tennis coach was part of the kidnap plan, she must feel terrible about what's happened.'

Svetlana just shrugged again. But she did look slightly shamefaced now.

'Why don't you call her?'

'I don't know. I'm not ready.'

'Right, I'll phone her,' Annie said briskly. Really, there wasn't time for mind games. If Elena had information, then they needed it immediately.

The phone against Annie's ear rang with an unmistakable transatlantic tone. She realized that she was feeling well and truly rattled. She wanted to help Svetlana, of course she did. Would she have got behind the wheel of the Bentley and driven all this way if she didn't want to help Svetlana?

But sometimes Svetlana was virtually impossible to help. Unless you rolled over and did everything Svetlana's way, there were times when you couldn't get anywhere with her at all.

'Hello?'

She recognized Elena's voice.

'Hi, it's Annie, I'm in Vienna with your mother.'

'Hello, Annie.'

'She's just told me there might have been something you wanted to say. We're lost, babes. We're in the centre of Vienna without a clue. I don't think we've got a hope of finding your brothers unless we can get more information. Michael's managed to send us a couple of emails, but it's not been enough to go on. So ... if you have anything you think might help in any way at all, my love, just never mind the old dragon, cough it out and I might be able to use it. No one wants to see those little boys forced into military academy.'

Elena's voice sounded strained as she replied: 'I never meant anything to happen to them.'

'No, no,' Annie assured her, 'of course you didn't. Everyone knows that.'

'Svetlana does not know.'

'Your mother is very stressed right now. Please don't take anything she says too seriously because I'm sure she's going to take it all back later.'

'OK . . .' Elena paused, but then came straight out with her information: 'I know one of Igor's men and I have an address in Vienna for you to try.'

Annie almost dropped her phone with surprise.

'You have an address!' she exclaimed. 'You know where they're staying?'

'I have an address in Vienna which Igor uses. I don't know if that is where he has taken the boys.'

'But it's got to be. Does this man want something for this information?'

'If Igor finds out and he loses his job . . . or worse . . .' she added ominously, 'I have promised that Svetlana will help him.'

'That seems reasonable.'

Annie glanced further along the square to where Svetlana was still striding along fiercely. Where was she heading? What was her plan now? Maybe she was too out of her head with worry to even know.

'Thank you so much,' Annie told Elena, 'I'll let you know if we have any luck. Is this man in London? Could he find out any more for us, if we needed it?'

'I don't know.'

Annie called out to Svetlana: 'I need a pen and paper, or for you to type this address into your phone.'

Svetlana swivelled on her heel.

'Address?' she repeated.

'Yes, Elena has an address – that's what she was trying to tell you.'

'Then why did she not tell me?' Svetlana asked so savagely that Elena must have heard.

'I text it to *you*, Annie,' Elena said and hung up.

'You have got to stop!' Annie shouted, glaring at her friend.

'Stop what?'

'Being at war with her! She made an honest mistake and she's trying to put things right. You have to stop pushing her away and frightening her off.'

Annie's phone buzzed and she quickly looked at the message.

'OK, here we go, look this up,' she instructed. 'Hopefully, it won't be too far away.'

Svetlana fumbled with her phone keypad, her fingers betraying her nerves. But within moments, she had a map on her screen.

'It doesn't look far away. We drive the car there and ... we should be there very soon ... and then ...'

It was far from obvious what they would do when they got there.

It was close to two o'clock in the morning. Knocking on the door and asking Igor's men to hand over Michael and Petrov; well, that wasn't going to work.

'What if they have guns?' Annie asked, suddenly anxious.

She was all for doing everything she could to help Svetlana, but she wasn't prepared to take a bullet for her.

Chapter Thirty-Two

New York

The waitress:

Black short-sleeved mini shift dress (Banana Republic)
White moccasins (Nine West)
Dangly brass and semi-precious stone earrings (vintage)
Total est. cost: $150

Now that they were in a booth in a gaudy Chinese restaurant, eating duck dumplings and drinking little cups of green tea, it seemed totally obvious to Lana that she honestly didn't like Parker nearly as much as she'd thought she did.

It had just been part of the whole: 'Why can't I be more like Gracie?' thing.

The same reason she'd bought a cute little yellow

sun-dress, even though it made her look like the living dead. The same reason she now had *four* swing skirts and looked all wrong in every single one of them. She would give the sundress and the four skirts to Gracie.

She would also try and give Parker to Gracie too.

Gracie was Gracie. Inimitable. And if Lana couldn't be Gracie, she would just have to try and be . . . much more Lana-like.

'So . . .' Parker began, munching his dumpling, 'why don't you tell me a bit more about Gracie? I think she's cool. Do you know her well?'

The bubble had burst. When she looked at Parker now, he looked like a friend, like a real person – even just a little bit like her brother, Owen. The whole gorgeous, dreamy, romantic hero bubble had absolutely popped. Whatever magical chemistry was required to make someone amazing to you, it was missing between her and Parker.

'Gracie is a fantastic person,' Lana gushed: 'she's my New York best friend because she's just so fascinating. She's like a fashion and design geek, she knows everything. I bet she could have named the Vronsky cube and told you all sorts of things about it that you didn't even know. She's cool.'

'You're really interesting too,' Parker told her, dipping his next chopsticked morsel into soy sauce. 'Well, OK, maybe I was a little dazzled by the whole

293

"from-London" thing . . . I am obsessed with London. I already love everything about London and I haven't even been there, so when you said you were from London, well, like I say, I guess I was dazzled.'

'I was a little dazzled myself,' Lana admitted with a shy smile.

Parker landed the food in his mouth.

'I think now that we're going to be good friends,' she added, 'but maybe you should call Gracie. I mean, she hasn't said anything to me, I have no idea what she thinks of you, but you two might find yourselves on the same wavelength.'

'Do you think?'

Parker was definitely looking interested.

'Yeah – why not? You've both got that whole arty-quirky-creative vibe going on. I think you'll find each other really cool.'

'Arty-quirky-creative . . . You could be starting a whole new movement there.'

Now it was Lana's turn to laugh.

'I thought she was seeing someone?' Parker asked, his brown eyes fixing on Lana's with a serious look.

Lana realized she couldn't lay it on too thick here. She couldn't let Parker think Gracie was going to be a total pushover, he obviously had to believe he would have to do plenty of work to win her affection.

'Well, to be honest, I think that ended recently. So you might find she'd like someone to take her to galleries. She loves, LOVES your designs. She really thinks you have a very special talent. So I think you two might find you have a lot to talk about.'

'Really?'

It was working. A sort of glowing look was coming over Parker's face.

'Did she know we were meeting tonight?' he asked, sounding a little anxious.

'Well . . .'

Lana thought quickly. What was the right answer here? She had a feeling it was one of those moments when a white lie was called for. If it all unravelled later on, everyone would see she had been trying to do her best at the time.

'Well no,' she replied. 'I was a bit confused about seeing you . . . I wasn't sure if I wanted a friend or a date, so I kind of didn't mention it. I mean, I was going to tell her all about it tomorrow, you know if things had gone . . . you know, differently. But now, I could say I bumped into you and we got talking and I said maybe you should give her a call.'

'Yeah, well I asked her along to this art show.'

'I kind of knew about that.'

Lana smiled at him and now it was Parker's turn to look awkward. 'That doesn't look so good now,' he admitted: 'kind of like I was checking you out but I had her as a back-up plan.'

'Yeah! That is *exactly* what it looks like, maybe because that's what it is!'

Lana flicked a little piece of dumpling at him.

'Rat!' she added.

'I'm sorry, really, it was kind of dumb of me.'

Lana flicked another crumb of dumpling in his direction.

'In future maybe you should try and make your mind up. OK, to be honest, I came because I thought it would be fun,' she began, 'and – well, since we're being totally honest, aren't we? – this is fun. Friends is fun too. I've not been in town long, I need all the friends I can get.'

Parker grinned. Then he reached his hand across the narrow table and held it out, palm open, for Lana to shake.

'Friends,' he said: 'friends who aren't going to rat each other out. Agreed?'

Lana took his hand in hers and shook it, a big smile breaking over her face.

'Agreed!'

'OK, so now you just have to tell me everything I need to know to totally impress Gracie on Saturday.'

Chapter Thirty-Three

Vienna

The lookout:

Black leather jacket (via a contact in St Petersburg)
White T-shirt (Gap)
Blue jeans (Levi's)
Red trainers (Adidas)
Fluffy white cotton socks (Aldi)
Collapsible switchblade (military supply store)
Total est. cost: £180

Annie nosed the Bentley into a narrow street of tall, elegant houses.

'Number 22 . . . number 32 . . . there it is, number 36,' Svetlana whispered. 'Park in this space here so we can see the house. We must not take our eyes from the house.'

Annie pushed the gearstick into reverse and began to manoeuvre the Bentley into the tight space. The inevitable scrape of hubcap against viciously high Viennese kerb followed. Ouch.

'You walk past the house, Annah,' was Svetlana's next instruction, 'and see if any lights are on or if there is any sign of anyone. Also look for a very expensive car. Tell me everything about the cars you can see closest to the house.'

'Why can't you go and look?' Annie whispered back.

Now that they were at the address Elena had given them, Annie wasn't feeling quite so gung-ho about the whole snatch-the-boys-back plan. In fact, she was growing increasingly terrified about it.

'Because they know me,' Svetlana replied, 'there might be someone on guard and they will see me.'

There was no denying she had a perfectly reasonable point there. So with a deep sigh, Annie stepped out of the Bentley and closed the heavy door as quietly as she could.

She tiptoed to the pavement, then pushed her hands into her jacket pockets and tried to walk slowly, but casually along the road.

Glancing left, she took in the huge four-storey house which was number 36. Up on the second floor, one of the windows was faintly lit, suggesting a light on in a room beyond it, the hallway maybe. Otherwise, the house was in darkness.

Directly outside was an impressively vast black four-by-four car. She didn't know the model, but could see that it was a BMW and expensive. As she walked past, she clocked the creamy leather interior.

She kept on walking for 20 yards or so, then turned around, eyes peeled for a second swoop. This time she slowed down to take a look at the car's registration plate. She had to bend down to see it properly. Her heart leapt when she saw the letters which formed the first part of the plate: GAS.

This had to be Igor! Wasn't Igor's billion pound fortune built on Russian gas fields? Wasn't Svetlana always referring to him as the gas baron?

Annie straightened up and began to speed towards the Bentley, casting another long look at the house. What she saw in the garden made her heart beat even more quickly.

A man was standing there watching her.

The tall, heavy-set man, with short dark hair and a hip-length leather overcoat paused in the action of lighting a cigarette, his eyes fixed on her.

Annie gave him a brief flick of a smile and realized she would have to carry on walking, loudly, clip-clopping her heels all the way to the end of the street and beyond, to shake off any suspicions he might have. So she pulled her jacket tightly against her and walked on.

As she approached the Bentley, she desperately signalled to Svetlana that something was up. She tried all kinds of hand gestures meant to tell her: I'm walking on – you stay here.

But Svetlana just stared at her in utter confusion.

'NO!' Annie mouthed as it looked as if Svetlana was about to get out of the car. She signalled frantically for Svetlana to stay in her seat and finally she seemed to get the message and sank right down, pulling her jacket collar up over her face.

Annie walked to the end of the street, then turned the corner. She waited, listening to the thump, thump, thump of her heart.

What were they to do now?

How had they even begun to imagine that they could get the boys away from a group of Igor's solid, muscular bodyguards? Those men were probably graduates of the military academy. Guys who could crush your skull with their bare hands . . . snap your neck like a carrot . . .

She peered back around the corner. The street was empty. The man hadn't followed her. She waited for a few more minutes, just to be sure, then crossed the street and began to tiptoe back towards the Bentley.

When she was just across the road from it, she double-checked that no one was around, even risked a quick glance at the garden. The man had gone. She tiptoed to the car, opened the door quietly and got in.

'What happen?!' Svetlana demanded in a fierce whisper.

'There was a man in the garden of the house . . . he was smoking . . . he looked at me . . . he was a huge, dark-haired man and I panicked. I thought he was going to chase after me,' Annie blurted out.

'You do the right thing.'

'Do Igor's number plates have GAS in the title?'

'Ya,' Svetlana nodded vigorously, 'almost all. This is his favourite for plates. GAS 1, GAS 2 and so on.'

'Just outside the house there's a huge BMW with GAS in the number plate and it's a British plate.'

'This is it! This must be it! I also check against the map when you are gone. There is a square two streets away, a church and a street named Konigsweg.'

'But what can we do?' Annie asked. 'There is only one light on, and there's a huge man hanging around. How are we going to find out if they are in there? And how will we get them out?'

'I don't know yet,' Svetlana admitted, 'but I'm thinking. You must think too. We have to come up with an idea.'

Chapter Thirty-Four

New York

Gracie at home:

Vintage cotton embroidered nightdress (Marie's Lost and Found Store)
Silky antique kimono (same)
Sponge toe separators (Duane Reade)
Sponge hair rollers (same)
Bright green nail polish (Mac)
Total est. cost: $78

'How ws ur date? U hv to call me asap. G x'

Now that she was back in her apartment, Lana could make this call with a happy heart. In fact, she was going to love making this call. She settled down on the sofa, hit Gracie's number and listened to the ringtone for only a moment. Gracie picked up almost immediately.

'Lana, hi, so tell all!'

'Gracie, you just so will not believe how it went tonight—'

'Oh no!' Gracie interrupted with a wail, 'I don't know if I can bear it. Please don't tell me you've realized you're long-lost soulmates who met before in a brief, but never forgotten encounter at a foreign airport when you were seven.'

'Very elaborate but totally wrong. Guess again,' Lana said, almost enjoying this little bit of friend torture.

'The only thing that's going to be good for me to hear is if you actually discovered you're his long-lost sister who was given away for adoption and therefore can never date.'

'Yes, that would be good!' Lana agreed, 'but in fact, this is waaaaaaay better, because there's no major family drama or personal crisis involved.'

'So – well, just tell me. What?!!' Gracie urged, desperate to know.

'OK, we had a great evening, we went to all these amazing gallery places where scary girls with scary hair all seemed to know Parker. In fact, the entire world seems to know Parker. Then he insists on walking me home.'

'Ohmigod,' Gracie whispered.

'And we're standing at this gallery window beside this amazing multi-coloured cube—'

'The Vronsky cube, I know it, oh that is just the perfect setting for what I know you're about to tell me. Oh I can't listen . . .'

'Gracie, will you shut up and let me talk?! You know the cube? Oh you two are just perfect. Anyway, so we're leaning in, we are just about to kiss . . .'

Gracie gave a little whimper.

'When we realize, practically at the exact same second, that we just don't like each other in that kind of way.'

'Huh?!!' Gracie gasped.

'Yeah!'

'But how? What do you mean? At the exact same moment? You *both* realized? What happened? You both had bad breath or something? Had you been eating garlic sausage? And did you kiss? Did you kiss and then realize? Or did you not kiss?'

'No, we did not kiss and no, we had not been eating garlic sausage! I think it was maybe me first. I pulled away and then I told him that I just didn't think this was going to work for me.'

'What?! Excuse me, Parker Bain was about to kiss you and you backed out? Are you serious? You backed out? Are you sure you don't mean you *blacked* out? Because I know that's what I would have done.'

'No, I did not black out. But after that happened, we went and got something to eat and then we got on great and we were much more relaxed than we had been for the whole evening. We are totally friends. There is nothing romantic or date-y between us: we are friends. I think we'll be good friends. But that means the coast is clear – you can totally go for him.'

Gracie gave another dramatic gasp. Then there was silence for a moment before she blurted out in a voice close to tearful, 'Really? Do you really mean that?'

'Yeah, I really mean that. He's not the one for me. But he is definitely the guy for you. I mean, the cube – no one but you two have heard of that cube.'

'Oh. My. Goshhh!'

'Yeah, and we talked about you and I promise, I didn't say anything totally obvious. But I said you were looking forward to seeing him on Saturday and he was definitely asking a lot about you.'

'Really?'

'Really.'

'Lana, I think you could be like my best friend ever.'

'I'm honoured. Somehow I've managed to go from zero to hero in one evening.'

This made Gracie laugh.

'I'm sorry about earlier.' Gracie was the first to say it.

'No, I'm sorry about earlier. Really, I am very, very sorry. You saw him first. I should never have gone there. And as for the clothes and the bangs—'

'Oh, *please* don't go there. I shouldn't have said any of those things,' Gracie interrupted her.

'No, but I shouldn't have copied you like that. I didn't mean to, Gracie, I love the way you look and I was inspired by it and I wanted to try some vintage things and I swear I did not mean to turn into your evil twin.'

'It's OK. Really. Now that you're not dating Parker Bain, you can wear everything in my closet, honestly, knock yourself out.'

'Yeah, but . . . you know what, I've actually come to the conclusion that I don't rock a floral-print dress the way you do. It's time for me to hand my puffy skirts and sundresses over to you and find out what I do rock.'

'You look much meaner in a pencil skirt or skinny jean than I ever will.'

'Thanks.'

'I still cannot believe you didn't kiss Parker Bain, I mean didn't you at least want to see what it was like?'

'Gracie, I was looking at Parker's lips and all I could think about was how furious you were going to be with me.'

'I've been home all evening figuring out how I'd

306

be able to talk to you in the office tomorrow,' Gracie admitted.

'You know, I think we would have worked it out.'

Lana looked across the small room and noticed for the first time that one corner was stacked all the way to the ceiling with big brown boxes.

'There are so many parcels in this apartment. Elena must have the latest dresses and she's obviously spent all evening packing them up to send to the boutiques.'

'Every dress I've seen so far looks awesome,' Gracie replied.

'Oh man. I really, really hope they sell like crazy – or you can forget all about boyfriend troubles,' Lana added. 'If those dresses don't sell, the only thing we'll have to worry about is the Mothers, because they are going to KILL us.'

Chapter Thirty-Five

Austria

Petrov:

Grubby white tennis top (Babolat)
Grubby white tennis shorts (same)
Grubby white tennis shoes (Nike)
Man-sized anorak (borrowed from kidnapper)
Total est. cost: £67

There was total concentration in the Bentley. Svetlana drummed her fingernails on her clutch bag, deep in thought. Annie twisted and re-twisted a strand of hair, which had worked itself loose from her ponytail.

All sorts of crazy scenarios from films were running through Annie's mind: she would go up to the house and ring the doorbell, then Svetlana would hit the man on the head with . . . with . . . a broom handle? A shovel? Whatever might happen to be lying around the garden?

It was just so implausible.

'We do have an empty champagne bottle,' she said out loud.

'So what?' Svetlana responded.

'It could be a weapon.'

Svetlana shrugged and said, 'They might have a gun. I did not want to say this, to make you frightened, but it is a possibility.'

'A gun?!'

Annie shrank down in her seat. She didn't want to be here any more. Helping Svetlana out was one thing, but Annie did not want to be shot in Vienna by the henchman of a billionaire while her beautiful children thought she was hundreds of miles away in Italy sipping vegetable cocktails and being massaged by a hunky Italian stallion in a vest.

How would they ever understand what had happened?

'Maybe we should leave this all to Harry, and to the courts,' Annie began: 'we can't take the law into our own hands. I mean – bodyguards! *Guns?* I'm not Angelina bloomin' Jolie, you know.'

'Annah, shut up,' Svetlana ordered. 'You are here and you are going to help me.'

Lights went on in the big front windows on the first floor of the house.

'Something's happening,' Annie whispered.

The window on the ground floor lit up as well.

'Maybe they are going to move ... maybe the boys will come out of the house.' Svetlana leaned forward and strained to see.

A movement on the other side of the road caught Annie's attention.

'A policeman!' she said, with relief. Svetlana looked over too and they both saw a small middle-aged man with a peaked cap on his head and a notebook in his hand.

'No ... Postman, I think,' Svetlana said.

All the relief that had built up in Annie's chest vanished. Now she felt even more scared than she had a few minutes ago. She was about to be shot in a Viennese street in front of a postman.

The postman crossed the road and knocked on the window of the car. Annie wound it down and wondered if she could cobble together the German for: 'We're about to be shot at by some Russian bodyguards.'

'Guten Morgen,' the postman said.

'Guten Morgen,' Annie replied, almost tearful at the thought of Owen and all the times she'd told him not to speak German round the house. She would do anything to be in her kitchen listening to Owen's botched German right now.

'Sie können hier nicht parken. Ich muss Sie eine Strafzettel geben,' the postman said and began to scribble in his notepad.

'What?'

Annie turned to Svetlana hoping she might have understood this.

'This postman is a traffic warden and he is giving us a parking ticket.'

'Small mercies,' Annie muttered. 'At least if we're dead we won't have to pay the parking ticket.'

The front door of the house opened.

'I think they're coming out!' Svetlana said, reaching for the handle and flinging open the passenger door.

'Svetlana!' Annie warned, trying to catch hold of her and pull her back in. But too late.

'Excuse me,' she said as politely as she could to the traffic warden and opened her own door.

The warden protested, but stepped aside.

'Oh God, oh God, oh God, oh God,' Annie chanted, panicking properly now. She opened the back door and lunged for the champagne bottle: she couldn't face guns with nothing in her hands.

The man in the leather jacket emerged from the house. Behind him, Annie could see Petrov and Michael! There they were, still in their adorable little tennis outfits, their faces pale and tense. Her heart went out to them. All thoughts of ducking

311

down behind the car and hiding until this was over went out of her mind. Despite the size of a second man who was following the boys, Annie knew she had to help them.

With a roar of maternal rage, Svetlana charged down the pavement towards them and Annie began to run behind her.

'Michael! Petrov!' Svetlana shouted.

Everyone turned, expressions of astonishment on the faces of the men, pure happiness on the faces of the boys.

'Mama!'

'Mama! You came!'

The joy in those voices spurred Annie on.

The boys raced towards Svetlana, before the men could stop them. Svetlana grabbed hold of them and with a bloodcurdling shriek ordered the men: 'Leave us alone! Leave us alone or I will kill you both. I will kill you!'

Then she turned and ran with her sons, straight past Annie, back to the car.

'IN! IN!' she ordered the boys.

The men were rooted to the spot with sheer surprise – but just for a moment. Now they began to run too.

Annie found herself alone on the pavement between the men and the car. Holding an empty champagne bottle.

Oh God.

She knew she had to delay the men just long enough for Svetlana to get the car started. So she put her head down, her arms out and charged, roaring at the top of her voice.

Whump.

She collided hard with one of the men and they both fell sprawling and winded to the ground.

Owwwww.

The champagne bottle at the end of her outstretched arm somehow landed a direct hit on the other man's ankle and for a moment he was hobbled.

Oh God, oh God, oh God.

She heard the Bentley engine start up.

The traffic warden was shouting in German. Maybe he'd not had time to put the parking ticket on the windscreen.

As the man she'd run into picked himself up, something clattered to the ground. At once Annie knew she was looking at some sort of weapon – a knife or maybe worse. She instinctively kicked at it, sending it flying towards the gutter and causing the man to shout at her.

Now she was in serious, possibly even deadly, trouble. But at least she could hear the Bentley pull away, the engine revving wildly. Svetlana was trying to find the bite point, get into gear and away.

The traffic warden was still shouting furiously.

Maybe Svetlana had run over his foot ... The Bentley, its engine roaring and jumping, began to move up the street.

The men were shouting and cursing in a language Annie suspected was Russian. They ignored her in her winded and undignified heap on the pavement and ran to the big black car right in front of her. They leapt in, slamming the doors shut and sparking up the engine.

Annie picked herself up. The BMW was parked facing the other way and this street was too narrow to turn in. Svetlana had a chance, she really could get away from them if she kept the Bentley going at speed.

The champagne bottle was miraculously still in Annie's hand.

What could she do to stop this car leaving with just a champagne bottle in her hand?

Should she throw it?

The engine roaring, the car was about to pull off and chase after Svetlana and her boys.

Then, in one of the bravest, most foolish moves Annie had ever made, and hoped she would ever have to make, she ducked down and placed the bottle in the gutter right in front of the BMW's rear tyre. Then she backed away as quickly as she could.

There was a terrifying, exploding sound followed by a tinkling shower of sharp, stinging pieces of glass. Annie turned on her heel and ran blindly.

Chapter Thirty-Six

Austria

The volunteer

Corduroy car coat (charity shop)
Red T-shirt (market stall)
Jeans (Lidl)
Black trainers (Nike)
Total est. cost: €40

Annie had been crouching behind the bins at the back of a block of flats for some time now; about thirteen minutes, according to her watch. She wondered how much longer she should wait here to be sure she was totally safe. It was dirty and smelled of cat wee.

In fact, *she* was dirty and smelled of cat wee and

when she lifted her head from her knees she could see small blood marks on her skirt. She put her fingers to her face and realized that there were four or five small cuts which were bleeding.

Now what?

She didn't know where Igor's men were . . . she didn't know if it was safe to come out . . . she didn't know where Svetlana was. In fact – what was she supposed to do now?

She was in Vienna without a map, she'd left her handbag in the car, so she didn't have a penny or one single bank card, and she looked as if she'd been in a fight. She imagined that her chances of getting arrested for vagrancy were probably quite high.

She patted the pocket of her jacket, hoping against hope – oh, hallelujah! There it was: her mobile phone! She took it out and looked at the screen. She had one bar of battery charge left, probably just enough for a couple of texts, and maybe even one short call.

'Where you?' she texted Svetlana.

'We hv boys,' she texted Harry.

Harry would do something. He would leap into action. Annie always thought of Harry as a sort of pinstripe-suited, bowler-hatted, ultra-posh, middle-aged legal Batman. He came to the rescue with the kind of heavyweight backing every girl needed once in a while: the force of an expert lawyer.

It was time to leave the bins. Slowly she stood up and brushed herself down, then she walked towards the gate and stepped out into the street.

It was still very early and hardly anyone was around. But, desperate not to bump into the Igor mafia again, Annie walked quickly away in the opposite direction to the house. She needed a main street. As soon as she was somewhere with cars and cafes opening up for the morning breakfast trade, she would feel safer.

At the thought of a cafe and breakfast, her stomach gave a theatrical rumble.

Shut up! she willed it. Now is not the time.

Several streets later and she was on a busier road. Although everyone she passed gave her a strange look, she walked on, feeling a little safer with every step.

Harry or Svetlana would call her. Someone would help her out, she was sure of it.

'Ein Kaffee?' a voice called out.

Cafe? Coffee? Could this mean coffee?

She turned her head and saw a little stall set up with a coffee machine and a plateful of bread rolls.

A young man with curly hair and a cheerful smile was holding up a paper cup.

'I have no money,' she said slowly, hoping he would understand.

He shrugged.

'You don't need money,' he replied in English.

What kind of heavenly city was this? They set up booths and gave people their morning drug of choice for free?

'Really?' she asked, approaching the stall.

'Do you need some help?' the man asked with a sincere and sympathetic smile.

Annie took the paper cup he was holding and took a long, warm mouthful. It was weak, milky, instant coffee, but it tasted like the best ever premium blended, hand-roasted, lovingly crafted, bijou coffee house cup.

It tasted gorgeous.

She took another sip and another, then looked properly around. There was a bench on either side of the booth and on each bench two or three men were sitting, cradling their paper cups. Some chewed on the bread rolls.

The men had the matted hair and dirty, worn-out clothes you only saw on beggars.

This was a soup kitchen; well, a coffee kitchen.

Oh good grief, had the man behind the breakfast counter honestly assumed she was a homeless person?

She looked down at her outfit. Two days in a car had not done her stretchy, patterned go-anywhere dress many favours. The dress had gone every-where, including behind the cat wee bins.

Her denim jacket was filthy from her encounter with the pavement and her refuge behind the bins. She knew her skin and hair must be a complete mess. Mascara last applied almost twenty-four hours ago. Well, who knew where it was now? Probably heading towards her chin. Plus she was covered in small bleeding cuts.

No wonder he'd offered her a free coffee.

'Do you need help?' he asked again in his charming, accented English. 'We have someone who comes every morning from the ... erm ... government?'

Annie couldn't help backing away from him. The thought of having to explain why she was here to someone from the government was terrifying.

'To help,' the man emphasized.

'No, I'm fine ... I'm really fine. I'm just waiting for a friend.'

But really? Things were far from fine.

She had one bar left on her phone. Svetlana was obviously focused on trying to get her boys out of Igor's clutches. It was quite possible she would forget about Annie altogether. In fact, knowing Svetlana, it was *completely* possible she would forget about Annie altogether.

So what was she realistically going to do if Svetlana didn't come back for her? Annie would have given anything to be able to call Ed. But she needed to save the precious little bar on her phone. If she lost that, she would have nothing. It was the modern equivalent of a tiny flame in the hearth. She couldn't let it go out.

'Are you a visitor to Vienna?'

'Oh . . .'

'Are you sure you would not like our doctor to look at your face? I can take you there.'

This was so kind, so sympathetic that Annie could detect a prickly, snuffly feeling at the back of her throat.

'No, no, I'm fine. I'm a tourist, a visitor. Is there a bus to the airport?'

'Yes, and a tram.'

'Where do they leave from?'

He gave her the simple instructions, then reminded her of her obvious predicament: 'But you said you have no money.'

'No.'

What was she to do? Barter her way on with an empty coffee cup?

'You buy a ticket in a shop, you validate it on the machine, but most tourists do not understand the system and do not pay. It is not so serious for tourists.'

'Really?'

Annie had a feeling that getting to the airport would be good. At airports, they understood about

320

lost handbags and lost passports and tourists stranded abroad. They would have the systems in place. She would go to the police and maybe she could get her phone charged, then she'd be able to call Ed – even if he was in school. He could wire money to her, pay her airfare with a credit card. This could all be sorted out and she would be home very, very soon.

All she had to do was get to the airport without paying.

Chapter Thirty-Seven

Austria

Tram passenger:

White, green and pink floral dress (Peek & Cloppenburg)
White trench coat (Gap)
Green sandals (Schuh-Welt)
White-strapped watch (Swatch)
Total est. cost: €340

Annie was the first to jump off the tram at the terminal. She couldn't stand the guilt for one more second. For the entire journey, she'd kept her head down and avoided the many disapproving glances she imagined were being directed at her.

Because she'd jumped on without stamping her ticket, like she'd seen every single other passenger do. Because she didn't have any luggage, not even a handbag. Because her clothes were grubby and her face was smeared with dried blood.

She was a sight. A fright!

Imagine if a fan of *How To Be Fabulous* spotted her now? In the best-case scenario, she'd be the subject of an emergency intervention makeover; in the worst case, she'd be fired.

As she walked through the automated glass doors, the sight of trolleys full of luggage and rows and rows of check-in desks was a relief. She would find the airport police and explain her predicament to them. Surely, they would be used to tourists without passports turning up to ask for help.

As she passed under the huge departure boards, she thought she might as well check to see when the next flight was departing to London. Her eyes scanned down the list of cities: Berlin, Zurich, Warsaw ... Gatwick. The next flight was at 9.50 am., in 55 minutes with British Airways. Maybe if she got really lucky, she could make it onto the flight.

She could be home by lunchtime. She could be soaking in a long, long hot bath within a few hours. This whole nightmare could be over by then. No, she reminded herself, not with no money and no passport: that would take some time to sort out.

She looked above the row of check-in desks in search of the British Airways logo. There it was –

there were the people who could take her home.

And there *she* was!!

A tall blonde woman, back towards Annie, with two boys, one on either side of her. Both with jet black hair, wearing tennis whites.

It was Svetlana!

Svetlana was queuing to get onto the British Airways plane. Svetlana was going to head back to London without even a thought as to where Annie was or how she would get back home!

Annie began to run towards her.

'Svetlana!' she called out as soon as she was within range, 'SvetLANA!'

The blonde head swivelled round.

'Annah!'

Svetlana's look of relieved surprise quickly turned to dismay.

'Oh! Annah! What has happened?'

Annie hurried towards her: 'Are you all OK?'

'You got away from them? No one's following?'

'Are you going to get on a plane all right?'

They started talking at once, firing questions at each other.

'Harry sort everything,' Svetlana said.

'Mama came to get us. Just like she said she would and she's very proud of me using my phone,' Michael said, holding the gadget up for Annie to examine.

He looked more happy and relaxed than Annie had ever seen him look before.

'Mama came,' Petrov added, smiling, his hand attached firmly to Svetlana's coat. As if he was determined not to ever let go of her.

'My boys are fine. Both fine. I'm so proud of them both,' Svetlana said, putting her arms protectively round their shoulders and squeezing them in tightly.

'We are getting back to London just as soon as we can,' she added, 'where I will meet Igor. We must sort this out once and for all.'

'So I managed to stop the men in the car?'

'I think so. They didn't follow. But Annah, what happened to you? What happened to your face? I couldn't stop to find you. I had to get away.'

Annie shrugged. She would probably have done the same . . . wouldn't she? But as far as she knew Svetlana hadn't even texted – hadn't even sent the words: 'meet me at the airport.'

'I put the champagne bottle under their car wheel and it exploded,' Annie admitted. 'Hopefully, it ripped their tyre apart, but I didn't stay to find out.'

'Annah! You are amazing.'

'So . . .'

There was an expectant lull. Annie wondered what was coming next. She hoped Svetlana was going to offer Harry's help to her too. She wanted to be boarding the next BA flight and arriving back in sane and sensible London in a few hours.

'Annah, I would really like you to come with us . . .'

'Yes? That's what I'd like too.'

'But, I . . . well, Annah, I need you to drive the Bentley back to the hotel.'

Hotel? Which hotel? Surely Svetlana couldn't mean the Villa Verdina? *What!*

'I know. I know is a very, very big favour to ask,' Svetlana went on, 'but I have message from the Villa, if they do not get the Bentley back today, they will declare it stolen and even go to the police. So the Bentley must go back and we still have luggage at the hotel. I think is easiest solution if you take the car back and get the luggage.'

'You want me to drive all the way back to Italy?' Annie asked, feeling completely winded.

'I have money, plenty of money for your journey.'

Svetlana opened her clutch bag and Annie knew she was about to be handed a wodge of euro notes. It was always Svetlana's solution: fistfuls of money.

'But I want to go home,' Annie protested. 'I'm exhausted. I've about had enough of all of this.'

'I'm so sorry, Annah. You will go home. You will fly home first class from Milano, just as soon as it can be arranged, maybe even later today, if you can get there quickly enough.'

'But I want to go home now. I don't want to drive all the way back to Italy. I have a concert to go to and the twins' birthday party . . .'

She'd lost track of time. When were those things even happening? Tomorrow? Could it already be the day before the twins' birthday?

'Annah, please . . . I know you have done so much for me, too much. I really am so very thankful. But I have to take the boys to London and you are the only person I can ask to do this one more thing. I know it is too much. But still I ask you, as my friend.'

Svetlana was actually doing gratitude, real heart-felt gratitude. Annie had seen it just a handful of times before and it always moved her. Svetlana was a proud and fiercely independent woman who thanked people rarely but always sincerely.

'Madam, can I see your tickets please?' the agent behind the check-in desk asked.

Annie was left looking at the boys.

They were totally worn out and not nearly as neat, tidy and groomed as usual. Their tennis outfits were stained and grubby. Maria would have a fit when she got them safely back.

'How are you?' she asked, kneeling down to be on their level.

'OK,' Michael replied, while Petrov shrugged.

'We would never have been able to find you

without the emails, Michael. You were really brave. Your mum is incredibly proud of you. Don't forget that.'

'I know,' Michael said, his chest swelling.

'We never have to go to the school in Russia,' Petrov added. 'Mama promised.'

'No. I'm sure your dad will have to say a really big sorry for all this.'

Michael giggled at the thought.

'Did Michael look after you?' she asked Petrov.

'Yes.'

'Yes,' Michael agreed. 'Petrov was brave too.'

'I think you're going to be much better friends now you've had this adventure together.'

'Yes,' Michael said, then he reached over and ruffled his little brother's hair: 'you weren't a baby hardly at all.'

Svetlana finished checking in and turned back to them: 'Annah, if you take the car back to Italy I promise Harry will help you sort everything out. New plane tickets, everything.'

'Where is my handbag by the way?'

'Oh ... I have locked it into the car's glove compartment. Here is the key, and this will be enough for petrol and any other problems,' Svetlana said, handing over a thick wad of euros.

'Svetlana, you can't pay me to do this,' Annie protested. 'I'm not accepting payment. Everything

328

not used for expenses is coming straight back to you.'

'Fine,' Svetlana said, pushing the money and the Bentley keys into Annie's hand.

'But you will owe me one very big favour,' Annie said.

'Of course, just say what it is.' Svetlana looked at her expectantly.

'I don't know yet,' Annie replied, 'but I'm going to think about it and when I ask for this favour, you will grant it. No questions asked.'

Svetlana's eyes met hers and Annie saw the look of concern on her face. But still Svetlana said 'OK', so seriously that Annie knew she had a deal.

'The car is in the car park on level four. Here is the ticket,' Svetlana added and the ticket materialized in Annie's hand, just as if Svetlana had planned for her to show up at exactly this moment to take over all the troublesome details.

'Maybe you should wash your face first,' was Svetlana's next suggestion.

'Yeah . . .'

The alligator clutch began to ring so Svetlana turned away from Annie to answer the call.

'The glass bottle burst under the men's car tyre and blew it up?' Michael asked Annie.

'And the glass bits went into your face?'

Annie nodded. 'Don't worry, it's nothing serious.'

'But that was very brave,' Michael told her.

'Or stupid,' Annie admitted. 'I always think brave is very close to stupid.'

This made Petrov laugh.

'What is happening with Perfect Dress?' Svetlana turned to ask Annie, once her call was over.

'Well, I've not exactly heard much,' Annie said, which was putting it mildly. 'They're just getting the designs together for the new season, I think.'

Svetlana shook her head vigorously.

'No. Something is going on. I just speak to Elena, I leave her message about the boys and she just call me back.'

'I hope you were very nice to her, I hope you said sorry properly.'

'Yes. I said sorry.'

'Really? *Properly?*'

'Yes! I say sorry to her and she say: "not bad, Mother, I know this is the hardest word for you".'

'She's right.'

'But I just get a feeling from her when we speak about the business that she is not telling me everything,' Svetlana added.

'Oh no . . .' Annie was getting the first inkling of an idea, 'you don't think those silly, stubborn girls have just gone ahead and made up the new dresses on their own, do you?'

Chapter Thirty-Eight

Austria

The perfume counter girl:

White blouse (Aldi)
Bright silk scarf (once grandmother's)
Pencil skirt (Peek & Cloppenburg)
Wearable shoes (Ecco)
Too much make-up (Estée Lauder Christmas Gift Set)
Total est. cost: €160

Once Annie had waved Svetlana and her boys through the departure gate, she decided that first of all – before she did anything else – some of Svetlana's expenses money would have to be spent on several key rescue products.

The horrifying sight of her reflection in the

bathroom mirror galvanized her into action: panda eyes, those small but bloodied cuts, dirt, grease, even a dark smudge or two. It was desperate. She rushed from the mirror to the airport pharmacy where she grabbed toothpaste and a toothbrush to deal with her actually furry teeth.

At the cosmetics counter she bought the make-up fundamentals: eyeliner, mascara and lipstick, and persuaded the startled sales assistant to hand over tester sizes of face wash, moisturizer and foundation.

'This is an emergency,' Annie assured her, 'I really honestly do not look like this usually.'

After a ten-minute stint in the Ladies applying her haul, and a pass of the Chanel counter where she doused herself liberally in No. 19, Annie began to feel less like a bag lady and much closer to her usual self.

Her next purchase was a phone charger for the car and a hands-free kit. Just as soon as she'd revived the phone battery, she had a lot of calls to make and explaining to do.

Finally, she stocked up on provisions for the trip: a vast mug of coffee, two Viennese pastries, a huge bottle of water, three chocolate bars and – in honour of Dr Delicioso – one small green apple, which she sort of already knew she wouldn't eat. She was going to be the first person to come back from a spa break five pounds heavier.

Bag of goodies over her shoulder, she made for the car park. Up on level four, after a short walk about, she found the Bentley, but as she drew closer, she couldn't help gasping with shock.

The Bentley was trashed! No other word for it. At the back of the car there was an alarming dent and the metal bumper was hanging askew. Svetlana must have reversed into a bollard, maybe even a lamp-post.

She walked round to the side of the car and found it peppered with dents, scrapes and a long, ominous white scratch. On the other side, it was a similar sad story. In fact it was slightly worse, as the front wheel arch had obviously been crunched against something hard.

In her short but frantic drive to the airport, Svetlana must have got into even more trouble than Annie had in her journey all the way over the Alps.

Carlo was going to freak out. Whatever relief he might feel at the sight of the Bentley rolling back up the drive of the Villa Verdina would be short-lived.

Annie unlocked the door, dumped her bags on the passenger's seat and climbed in. She put the phone in to charge and rigged up the hands-free system. She would phone Ed and let him know everything was OK, just as soon as she had some power. Then she fired up the engine.

It sounded throaty, but fine. Hands on the

steering wheel, she prepared to seriously haul the car around into reverse and felt almost pleased to be back in the the Beast again.

'Don't even think about letting me down now, old boy,' she said out loud, 'because we're going home.'

Annie had been driving for several hours and recrossed the Italian border via a perfectly straight-forward motorway, which somehow she and Svetlana had missed on the way in, before she got a reply on Lana's phone.

'It's 5.50 a.m.,' Lana croaked into the Bentley's cab, thanks to the hands-free kit.

'Elena has been up all night worrying about her brothers, I thought you might have been up too,' Annie said, not exactly in an apologetic mood.

'Have they been found?' Lana asked, already sounding more awake.

'Yes, we've got them. They're safely on a flight back to London with their mum, while I get the honour of driving the Bentley back to Italy. But never mind that, I'll tell you the whole story when I'm on a much cheaper phone line. Lana, right now I need you to tell me all about the new Perfect Dresses. Just what is going on?'

She delivered this in her best *I'm-your-mother-and-don't-even-think-about-messing-with-me* voice.

'Oh . . . do you know? Did Elena—?'

'Not yet,' Annie interrupted. 'I haven't heard the full story, but I think it would be a good idea for you to start coughing.'

'We haven't spent any company money,' Lana said quickly.

'Well, that's a good thing. But what have you done?'

'We've made up a prototype line for NY Perfect Dress and we've sent it out to a selection of buyers to see what they think,' Lana blurted out.

'To see what they think ... *really*? Or are those dresses in fact on sale, with OUR label on them?'

'They are ... ummm ... probably ... for sale by now,' Lana admitted.

'Well that's just great. And so when were you planning on breaking this news to us, exactly?'

'When the feedback came in amazingly positive.'

'And what if it doesn't, Lana?' Annie demanded. 'That is some risk, some unbelievable risk you are taking – and how have you paid for it all?'

'We borrowed on our credit cards.'

'Oh Lana!'

'No one's in any major debt,' Lana insisted, 'we started small. Plus we sold some of our own things and someone gave us a loan.'

'Oh, but Lana, Svetlana is going to ... going to completely ...' Annie didn't like to think about what Svetlana might do. 'This will cause

335

unbelievable trouble . . . I mean, it's her label. And she said: NO.'

'Mum, look at the dresses first before you say anything else. Will you please just look at them? It's too early to know if they're selling yet, but the buyers really like them.'

'But how will we make this work with Svetlana?'

'We're not exactly sure,' Lana admitted.

'No. Neither am I. Where can I see the dresses? Have you got anything up online?'

'We haven't put them on the company website yet.'

'No. I suppose it's a bit early for that since you might be starting your very own company pretty soon.'

'Mum!'

'Well, I'm just saying . . . you might. Svetlana could have a total meltdown and kick you all out!'

'Mum, we're relying on you to help us win her over.'

'You're relying on me? But you've not even told me! You've not even phoned once since you left London in a great big huff!'

Silence at the other end of the line.

Annie was now approaching the kind of twisting mountainous road that would require all her concentration.

'If I felt I could trust your judgement, I would have told you,' Lana said finally.

There was the heart of the problem and it still hadn't been solved. All of a sudden, Annie didn't know what to say. She was still angry with Lana about their row; in fact, this news about unauthorized dresses was making her feel even more annoyed.

The girls hadn't asked her if they should go ahead, but they were expecting her to somehow put it all right with their very scary boss.

'I suppose it's too late to call the dresses back?' Annie asked. 'If you could get them back, you could show them to Svetlana and maybe she'd change her mind when she actually saw them.'

'No. It's too late.'

'Good grief!' Annie exclaimed. 'So you've just gone and put out unauthorized dresses for sale under our label.'

'It's NY Perfect Dress, a diffusion range,' Lana replied.

'That doesn't exactly make it all better.'

Annie was trying to restrain herself, trying to stop herself from shouting down the line. Why had the girls done this? They had forced the issue and it was going to cause a very big fuss. Svetlana might sack them all and close the company.

'You shouldn't have done it,' Annie told her daughter.

'Why not? If we'd stuck with your boring old stuff, the company would have gone down the pan anyway. We had no major orders, we had nothing to lose,' Lana stormed.

'I need to concentrate on driving,' Annie said, wanting to buy herself some time, to avoid saying something furious and regrettable down a long-distance line. 'I'll talk to you later. Meanwhile, stay right out of Svetlana's way. Don't let her find out about this or she will completely freak out.'

'Fine.'

Clunk.

The line went dead and Annie signed with frustration. Just how was she supposed to solve this?

Chapter Thirty-Nine

Italy

The café owner:

Red and blue tunic (Topshop)
Tight bright blue capri trousers (Armani)
Wooden-soled leather sandals (little shop in Florence)
Gold necklace (a secret admirer)
Coffee-coloured nail varnish (Chanel)
Total est. cost: €180

Another hour into the drive and Annie had passed through the worst of the mountains. The sun was shining in an unbroken bright blue sky and the scenery spread before her was a glorious tapestry of green, gold and brick red with the silvery lakes shimmering ahead in the distance.

This was stunning. Finally, despite her latest worries, she could feel a sense of relaxation creeping up on her. She was starting to feel like someone on a holiday ... not someone enduring a series of stressful events.

The road was taking her through yet another beautiful hillside village where every house was more charming than the last, with pale blue doors and window boxes bursting with pink geraniums.

As she drove past a café with pretty white tables and chairs set out on the pavement, she decided that she had to stop; the lure of a caffeinated top-up was too strong.

She brought the Bentley to a halt on the side of the road, and after a fresh touch of lipstick, Annie walked back to the café, where she chose a sunny seat and ordered an espresso.

A friendly Italian woman of around Annie's age, maybe the owner of the café, brought the coffee and exchanged a little chitchat in accented English. As they talked, Annie couldn't help but notice how perfectly turned out she was, right down to the caramel-coloured tips of her fingers.

As she sipped her coffee, despite the undoubted strength of the treacly liquid, Annie suddenly felt incredibly tired. All the driving, the tension, all the lack of sleep of that last twenty-four hours had taken everything out of her. So she decided to lean forward on the table, head on her arms and treat herself to just a tiny little catnap.

'Hello? Are you all right?'

Annie felt as if she was being shaken from the deepest, darkest sleep. She opened her eyes and saw a tiny white coffee cup with a deep chocolaty trickle running down its side. Lovely colours, she couldn't help noticing. White with chocolate . . . a white linen suit with chocolate leather accessories . . . maybe.

'Are you awake?' the accented voice asked. 'Maybe you should have another coffee?'

'Yes,' Annie croaked. 'And some water too, please.'

'No problem.'

She lifted her head from the table and for a moment or two had no recollection of where she was, how she had got there, or why. Golden sunlight streamed into her eyes, making everything look back-lit and hazy.

The Italian woman set the coffee in front of her, pulled up a chair at the table and, after asking 'May I?', sat down beside her.

She was lovely, Annie saw, in a totally elegant, totally together, Italian way. Her dark hair fell in a classic blunt cut to below her shoulders. Her tanned skin was set off by the deep red and blue of her striking graphic top. She wore a tiny golden chain around her neck. She was that perfect combination

341

of serious, professional, classy and just the right pinch of sexy which only women who'd grown up in the southern Mediterranean could manage effortlessly.

'Your top is beautiful,' Annie croaked, her voice not fully woken up yet.

'Thank you. A tunic I think you call it. I bought it in London,' the woman replied with a white-toothed, brown-lipsticked smile.

There was another Italian classic: brown lipstick, a shade which only looked good against beautiful, tanned, olive skin.

'A tunic?'

Annie had to have a little laugh at herself. Hadn't she sworn eternal enmity to all tunics and here she was complimenting this stranger on hers.

'Yes.'

The woman stood up. The top draped gently past her waist and ended just below the hip bone where it met tight blue trousers and . . .

Now Annie felt compelled to look under the table.

There she saw a pair of wooden-heeled, peep-toe sandals in nude-coloured leather. The toes too were coated with the fudgy brown nail varnish.

Totally chic and: inspiring. No other word for it. For the first time in months, Annie was really look-ing at an outfit, noticing all the details and feeling the stirrings of enthusiasm.

She looked down at her coffee cup and saw

the brown swirl gently around the cream, with the toffeeish shades in between. A symphony in taupe, cream and neutrals was going on right in her cup. She couldn't help staring.

'I put in milk,' the woman explained: 'is not so strong on the stomach.'

'Thank you.' Annie took a reviving sip.

'I'm Isabella.'

'Hello, I'm Annie, I'm on holiday at the famous Villa Verdina.'

'Oh yes, resting from a very tiring job I think.'

Isabella smiled. She didn't seem too ruffled by a stranger exiting a Bentley and promptly falling asleep at one of her tables.

'Yes . . .'

'In which business do you work?' Isabella wondered.

'Fashion,' Annie replied, because that was the straightforward answer.

'Oh, how lucky, I love fashion. It keeps us young, it keeps us interested in the world and in love with ourselves.'

'Yes, all of these things . . . in love with ourselves,' Annie repeated. 'They're very important.'

'Very important. How can you love anyone else if you don't love yourself?'

'I like that,' Annie said and smiled at her new acquaintance.

'I think this is called: café *filosofia*.'

'Café philosophy – perfect. I used to love everything about new clothes and the latest fashion, but I've been feeling out of love.'

'I think you have been feeling too tired,' Isabella pointed out.

'Maybe, but I've forgotten what I used to love so much.'

'Perhaps you need to remember your favourite things. Why not tell me about your best dress.'

Annie didn't have to consider her answer for long: 'It's bright pink, the colour of those geraniums over there – silk, with a big flouncy skirt, a tight top and then a halterneck; no shoulders, you understand? And a big bow tied here, behind the neck. I feel like a star in that dress. I feel happy and loved. I love pink and I love red, even together.'

'Yes, wonderful together, pink and purple too,' Isabella agreed, 'so why are you wearing brown?'

'Oh . . .' Annie looked down at the well-worn, rather grubby brown linen sundress, 'I've not been in the mood for pink or red – not for some time.'

'So you come to Italy to rest?'

'Yes. Well, that was the idea. What about your best dress? I want to know about that.'

'Oh, no question, it is made from purple velvet,' Isabella confided. 'It is to the knee and a little tight, but not too tight, with bare arms and a low neck.

344

But because it is rich velvet, it is very sexy and womanly.'

'It sounds wonderful. It sounds like Dolce & Gabbana,' Annie guessed.

'And you would be correct!' Isabella smiled. 'Is wonderful to save up and once in a while spend some money on a real label, a beautiful piece of clothing.'

'What's your best bag?' Annie asked.

'A Fendi envelope.'

'You own a Fendi bag?!'

Annie knew Italians took their luxury label purchases seriously but still, it was surprising to be sitting chatting with a Fendi owner in a tiny café in a village in the middle of the countryside.

'Yes, but it cured me. It was so obvious when I take this bag anywhere, now I never buy anything again which is so clearly expensive.'

This made Annie laugh.

'Who is your favourite designer?' Isabella asked.

'It has to be Viv,' Annie decided after just a moment's consideration. 'If I could only shop at one place for the rest of my life, it would be Vivienne Westwood.'

'Ah, yes, very English eccentric.'

'Perfect for the fashion-forward, funky, fat lady.'

Now it was Isabella's turn to laugh: 'But you are not fat!'

'I'm not exactly a model.'

'How did you manage to stay at the Villa and not turn into a supermodel?' Isabella wondered. 'Everyone round here makes jokes about the hotel. They feed you just vegetable juice and put water into your . . .' her eyebrows raised and her meaning was plain: 'No?'

'Yes! It's torture. I ran away – but now I have to go back to return their car.' Annie gestured to the Bentley further along the road.

'You run away?' Isabella cackled with laughter. 'I think before you return to the Villa, you have to eat a delicious meal.'

'That sounds like the best idea ever. Oh, you have no idea. I've had no sleep for two nights in a row. I've had nothing but water, coffee and chocolate for the past . . . I can't even remember how many hours. I am practically delirious, my love. You could be a figment of my imagination, for all I know. A spirit sent down to guide me back to fashion enlightenment.'

Isabella made a quizzical face, as if she hadn't understood all of this, but then she said firmly: 'No, I am here and I will bring you some lunch.'

After a truly magnificent lunch, Annie drove back to the hotel feeling that her faith in human nature had been restored and her eyes had been freshly opened. Suddenly everywhere she looked there was something truly inspiring to see: startling, fresh colour combinations or zingy new textures jostling for her attention.

Silvery olive leaves shimmering against the impossibly blue sky ... a box of bright lemons stacked against a red stone wall ... a group of grannies in black lace against shady grey limewash. There were bright, brand new colours, ideas, outfits, details and inspiration everywhere ...

For the first time in years, she parked and took random photos with her mobile phone as ideas piled up in her mind. Bright blue and yellow, how had she forgotten how mouthwatering those colours looked together?

Italy was the land of yellow: bright yellow, dusty yellow, ochre yellow, honey, pale baby lemon ... click, click, click, she was totally trigger happy until she'd filled up the memory card.

Her road to Damascus moment had come in a tiny café on the road to Milano. Her wearied eyes had been reopened and her jaded palette had been revived. Once again, she was bursting with ideas and enthusiasm for life.

When she couldn't take any more pictures, she got back into the car and drove through the now familiar country road towards the hotel gates. Even if they made her eat vegetable broth for dinner, she was beginning to realize how much she longed to get into the little pink and golden floral bedroom with the heavenly bed.

There was no way she could even think about flying home tonight. She'd already spoken to Ed and assured him she would be on a plane first thing tomorrow, just as soon as she'd slept for a full twelve or maybe even fourteen hours.

As the big electric gates began to open, Annie suddenly remembered the state of the car and an ominous feeling started to grow in the pit of her stomach. As she reached the top of the driveway, she saw Carlo step out of the front door and stand, very seriously, awaiting her return.

She parked the Bentley, opened the door and stepped out of the car hesitantly.

'Ah ... Mizzzzzzz Valentina, welcome back to our hotel,' Carlo began, with a smile which didn't look perfectly genuine.

Then the smile faded and Annie could no longer say that Carlo even looked pleased. No, definitely not pleased.

In fact it might be fair to say ... as he walked slowly towards the car and then, even more slowly, around it, taking in the dents, the scratches, the scrapes and the crushes ... yes, it would probably be fair to say that he looked, well, utterly horrified.

Chapter Forty

New York

Lana's more Lana-ish office look:

Grey short-sleeved jersey tunic (Perfect Chic sample)
Black footless tights (Bloomingdale's)
White sneakers (Keds)
Black hairband keeping fringe from face (drugstore)
Skull and crossbone earrings (same)
Darkest purple lipstick (Maybelline)
Total est. cost: $45

Lana ran her hands along the rail of NY Perfect Dress items once again. She looked at each of the garments in turn, carefully.

The red one was gorgeous, with punky studs and very clever styling. The black was also totally edgy and funky. The tunics made up in Parker's designs were stunning. She loved the orange with swirls of red, the black with emerald green, but the blue and yellow – the one she'd worn on her night out with him – now that she was looking at it again carefully, there was something troubling her about this one.

It was undoubtedly a totally fashion forward print. But something tugged just a little, the way it had from the moment she had first seen the print.

'Who's getting the dresses?' she asked Gracie, who was tapping out address labels madly at her computer on the other side of the office.

'Let me just call up the full list, Elena sent it through just before she went out. OK, let's see: six boutiques in New York have four items each . . . ten dresses went out by express delivery to London, to the style-setter stores there, so they should have them by now. Then two stores in Paris and one store in Milan are all taking samples from this capsule collection.'

'Right, and any news about sales yet?'

'No . . . but Elena said it was too early to worry.'

'Ha! Haven't we all been worrying about sales ever since we had this mad idea?'

'But just look at those dresses, girl, and do not tell me they're not going to sell.'

'You've not had a furious mother on the end of your phone yet.'

'No. That's true. But that's because my mom thinks I'm working in a lawyer's office and if she ever found out about this—'

'Really?'

'Really.'

'When are you going to tell her?'

'When these dresses . . .'

With a grin, the two girls chimed together: 'Fly from the rails!'

But still, an hour or so later, Lana went back over to the dress rail. She pulled out the blue one with the yellow swirls and looked it over carefully.

'What is it with you and that dress?' Gracie wanted to know.

Lana couldn't explain. It was like an undercurrent of doubt. A seed. An inkling. There was just something about this blue and yellow print that gave her a feeling of déjà vu.

What did she mean exactly: déjà vu – seen before? Was that really what she thought? Had she honestly seen this pattern before Parker had shown it to them? Exactly the same? Or just something like it . . . but where?

She looked at the shape of the paisley pattern. The way the strange stretched ovals flourished to a point and the swirl of pattern inside the shapes. She concentrated hard. There was somewhere . . . somewhere right at the back of her mind she knew she'd seen exactly this pattern before.

She closed her eyes and tried to let her mind go blank, hoping the answer might just suddenly appear. It didn't.

Back at her desk, she typed in 'paisley pattern' and searched through many, many results. She was no wiser. It was no use. She hated to have to do it, but she'd have to call in expert fashion advice.

So Lana went to the dress, took a photo of the print and sent it to her mum.

'What are you doing?' Gracie asked.

'You promise you will not freak out. Not even slightly.'

'I promise.'

'I've just sent a picture of that dress to my mum.'

'So she knows all about NY Perfect Dress?' Gracie asked, her tiny tadpole eyebrows shooting up into her bright orange fringe.

'Yes! Didn't I tell you she was yelling down the phone at me at five this morning? She knows and she's not happy. Especially as we're hoping she can break the news to Svetlana and save us all from getting fired.'

'Does Elena know that your mum knows?'

Lana nodded: 'She heard the phone ringing at 5 a.m. But Svetlana doesn't know yet and really, my mum has to be the one to break it to her. None of us can handle that scary lady.'

'No,' Gracie agreed. 'So what's with the blue and yellow dress?'

'I'm sending my mum a picture of this print because it looks familiar to me.'

'Yeah well, no wonder, you wore it to your date with PB.'

'No, I know that. But ever since I first saw this print I've had the feeling that I've seen it before.'

'Don't be crazy!' Gracie dismissed the suggestion. 'You know how serious that would be – Parker knows how serious that would be. If he'd copied someone's print, we could get sued! We could be ruined. He knows that, he's a professional designer.'

'Well, fine, I'm probably completely imagining it, but I've just sent it for a second opinion, OK. My mum knows stuff.'

For a moment, Gracie looked as if she was about to cry.

'I'm sorry . . .' Lana began, 'I know how much you like him . . . and there's no reason not to trust him. I just want to be really, really careful.'

'Don't be sorry,' Gracie replied, tilting her head up. 'We're businesswomen, aren't we? We can't let some dumb little crush get in the way of our future careers. Do you think your mom will reply soon? Isn't it, like night-time in Europe?'

Lana picked up her phone. 'We'll see. If she doesn't reply, I'll give her a call. We need an answer and I kind of hate to admit it ... but my Mum knows fashion. If anyone can tell us if that print has been used in a big way before, it's going to be her.'

Lana couldn't know that thousands of miles away, under a pink bedspread in the Villa Verdina, Annie was lying in the deepest sleep, dreaming of toenail varnish and tunics, Fendi bags and brightest lemon yellows.

On her bedside table lay her mobile phone but it was switched off.

Chapter Forty-One

London

The pavement fashionista:

Green tight cropped trousers (Oasis)
Pale grey leather jacket (AllSaints)
Graffitied vest top (Portobello market)
Yellow wedge-heeled espadrilles (holiday buy)
Total est. cost: £270

Annie burst through the arrivals gate with a delighted smile on her face and took in a big lungful of warm, second-hand, London air. She had slept for fourteen hours and rushed to catch her Svetlana-paid first class flight home to London. She had her all-important fashion mojo back; now she was touching down in her town and it felt fantastic.

No one could make her drink courgette juice, or commandeer a Bentley, or take on Eastern European hard men armed with switchblades. She was back! The new, improved Annie: fitter, slightly fatter than the ideal, but so much more fashion-forward.

A quick glance at her watch told her there was still plenty of time until she had to be at Ed's school for the concert of the season and still hours to go before the twins' birthday party this afternoon. She was on a mission to buy presents. The long Italian shopping trip she'd planned for herself had never happened, but never mind – she was at the airport and there was no shortage of shops.

Her zest for the new had returned. Her eye was in and she didn't doubt for a moment that her once unsurpassable shopping skills were back.

First stop was the toyshop where she powered on through until she had a mini mountain of gifts for Micky and Minette.

Next, she hit the surfer style shop and, thinking of Randall, bought Owen a pink T-shirt and a pair of board shorts. Ed got a linen shirt, pink with loud checks, Italian label, so that she could pretend she'd brought it all the way back from Milano.

Bulging bags in hand, Annie walked through the airport with a happy, springing feeling in her step. She was back! Wherever it was she had been for the past few months – miserable and uninspired, overworked and under-appreciated – it didn't matter any more, because she was back. Life felt shockingly good all over again.

She would take a taxi home and ask the driver to pass through all her favourite shopping stretches as he went: she wanted to gaze in windows, watch the passers-by, see the new looks and feel inspired.

Her mind turned to Nancy, the unfortunate woman who'd been on the live event just before Annie had run away to Italy. The knitted shorts – eek! The metallic jacket Annie had inflicted on her! Annie would come up with a whole new look for Nancy and they would re-shoot.

She was back and she was never going to let anyone go on screen looking anything less than amazing. Otherwise, it would all become a compromise and a waste of her talent and their time.

As soon as she was back in the studio tomorrow morning, she would set that mistake right. And as for the Perfect Dress situation: she would help to sort that out too.

She settled back into the cab and watched London unfold outside her window. The magic Italian goggles were still working; everywhere she looked she saw inspiration.

There was a girl with long, dark hair sporting a deep fringe and grey leathers, so very chic and Left Bank, loving her bright green satchel. There was a black guy with his hair in braids and his torso wrapped in a tight pink polo shirt, completely cool.

She loved that blue and white striped awning over a flower shop where red roses were bursting with life in the windows boxes . . .

'I'm back, I'm home, it's all going to work out just wonderfully,' she told herself, but under her breath, in case the cabbie chucked her out for being a crazy lady.

They passed a perfectly turned out woman with a scruffy dog on a bright blue lead. The dog was wearing a polka-dot blue neckerchief and looked adorable.

Even Dave could be beautified. That's what he needed, a neckerchief! Then instead of looking like a mongrel, he might look like a sort of cheeky pirate dog: a rascal rather than a lost cause.

In her tote bag, Annie's phone began to bleep.

She pulled it out and read: 'Still on for meeting? My office 11.40 a.m.? Tamsin.'

She read that again. Meeting? Tamsin? Her office at 11.40 a.m.?

'Today?' she texted.

Back came: 'If ur still on.'

How could she have forgotten? Well maybe kidnappings, Bentleys and hair-raising mountain drives could be blamed . . . but today she was supposed to be meeting Tamsin, to prove she was all set to return to work and brimful of new ideas. She checked her watch . . . in forty-eight minutes.

'Yes fine. See u,' she replied because – in this mood – she was more than ready to prove herself.

The cab was approaching the stylish streets now. The outskirts of Knightsbridge where blondes flicked their £200 blow-dries and stalked up and down the pavements in nothing less than £500 shoes, clutching designer bags under their arms to ward off evil glances.

And just then Annie's eye caught the red dress in the window. Red: her signature colour. Dress: her signature item. In fact, this wasn't a dress . . . it was one of the dreaded tunic dresses.

But even from the back of the cab, she could tell it was a quality piece. It looked soft but substantial, fitted but draping, cool but well made. The shop window model wore it with black leggings and a black leather cap.

Annie liked the wide sleeves, elbow length with one of those strap and button arrangements holding the softly rolled-up fabric in place. Would that be a good outfit to wear for a showdown with her producer? A meeting to prove she was back on track?

The taxi was crawling forward, the light red again on the busy junction ahead.

Was Annie finally going to embrace the tunic? Wouldn't a funky red tunic with the perfect sleeve be exactly the right thing to wear for this meeting and then on to the school concert this afternoon?

Dressing for school events was always fraught with difficulty. Too mumsy was bad, too fashion was bad, too designer was bad, too inconspicuous and mousy was all wrong as well.

How not to embarrass your children (and in Annie's case, husband) while not being upstaged by every other yummy mummy in the audience was a very tricky look to pull off. In short, a minefield.

Stopping to buy the red tunic would involve getting all her luggage and shopping bags out of the cab, hauling it all into the shop and then having to flag another cab down later.

Not stopping would involve a protracted outfit crisis in front of her wardrobe as the time ticked down to concert hour.

The lights changed to green and the cab driver put his car in gear.

'Hang on a second,' Annie instructed him. 'I think I want to get out here instead.'

The cabbie pulled over and helped her to unload her bags while she settled the fare. Then, laden down with shopping and luggage, Annie made a beeline for the shop with the tunic in the window.

Pushing open the door, she found herself in a boutique she hadn't visited for several years, but she still remembered it well.

'Hello.'

She gave the sales assistant a big smile. 'I love the dress in your window so much I made the taxi driver let me out.'

'Isn't it fantastic? Very new,' the assistant replied. 'I only put it in the window this morning. But we've got three in. What's your size?'

Annie was directed to the changing room to wait. When the assistant reappeared, she had the tunic in red and in bright blue and she also carried a pair of shiny black leggings and spike-heeled black sandals.

'I think you need to try it on with these, to see the whole look in action.'

'Good idea,' Annie agreed, recognizing a fellow saleswoman.

She stripped off, pulled on the tight, shiny black leggings, not really loving what they did to her legs. Sausages about to burst from their skins was the image that sprang to mind.

But she put the sandals on, which at least gave the sausages a little length, then she slipped the red tunic from its hanger and pulled it on over her head.

It was good. In fact, it was very good. She felt the material between her fingers: just right, just thick enough, just thin enough, a touch of stretch, but beautifully matte so that it really carried the red.

She loved the sleeves and the stud detailing – an

edgy stroke of genius. The studs were punched all around the wide neckline and ran in a line over the shoulders and the top of the sleeves, transforming the dress from chic to punkish.

The flattering cut meant she didn't need a belt or anything complicated. Wearing this, Annie wondered what her resistance to the tunic had been about for all this time.

It was a great look. It was a long top, or a short dress – loose around the pesky bum and tum areas, putting the focus on neck, cleavage and arms.

It made her look very fashion, very current without a hint of the dreaded dressing 'too young'. Oh, who knew what that meant anyway? Some 50-plus women looked downright fabulous in vest tops and skinny jeans ... some 70-year-olds wore bikini bottoms on the beach with long grey plaits and nipple rings. You could look far too staid and old if you didn't dress a little too young.

'How is it going?' the assistant asked from the other side of the curtain.

'It's great ... I love it.'

Carefully, she looked herself over from all angles. It was a yes. It was absolutely definitely a yes. Isabella, her café fashion guru, would say yes, wouldn't she?

'Two questions: how much is it?'

The assistant told her.

'Pretty reasonable,' was Annie's verdict: 'and who made it?'

She'd pulled the tunic on so quickly, she'd had no chance to glance at the label.

'A little company, quite new, this is one of their diffusion pieces: NY Perfect Dress.'

For a moment, Annie just stared, mouth a little open.

'NY Perfect Dress?' she repeated, her voice sounding weak.

'Yeah, have you heard of them?'

'You could say that.'

Chapter Forty-Two

London

Boss Tamsin:

Crisp white shirt (Thomas Pink)
Pink and grey print skirt (Marni)
Grey suede heels (LK Bennett)
Chunky pearl necklace (Topshop)
Total est. cost: £420

Wearing the new NY Perfect Dress tunic, the shiny black leggings and the foxy black sandals – because they fitted so well, it would have been criminal not to take then too – Annie gathered up her bags and hailed another cab.

It was time to get to Soho and thank Tamsin for the strange holiday, which had nevertheless shaken

Annie out of her rut. But meanwhile, in the back of the cab, there was another urgent phone call she had to make.

It was 11.12 a.m. Early to call New York, but given the circumstances ... finally, she heard Lana's bleary voice at the other end of the line.

'It's me, Lana. I have to talk to you. I'm in London, where NY Perfect Dress is hanging in shop windows!'

'In shop windows?' Lana repeated, waking up rapidly.

'Yes. I'm driving past this shop and I see an outfit in the window which is so good that I have to stop my cab and get out there and take a look.'

'So *good*?' Lana said, just to be sure.

'Yes, it's so good I do in fact buy it: red, covered in studs, amazing. But—'

'But it *is* really good, isn't it?' Lana chipped in.'So, the punky red, is that the one you went for?'

The enthusiasm in Lana's voice was infectious.

'Yes, it really is incredibly clever, Lana, and I look one whole lot less middle aged – but it doesn't make me any less angry.'

'Yes it does, Mum. You already sound a lot less angry.'

'Well, I'm not!' Annie insisted, but really, she was much more hopeful. The dress she was wearing was really good. It might be a lot easier to get

Svetlana on side now that she knew these new dresses were brilliant.

'Did you see a blue one with a yellow print?' Lana asked.

'The one you sent a picture of? Asking if I recognized the print? Sorry, I only picked that message up this morning.'

'Right. Did you see it?'

'No, there wasn't one in the shop. I can't say hand on heart I've seen the print before, but there is something familiar about it.'

'I know,' Lana agreed.

'Babes, if you're uneasy, if you've got any doubts, you've got to grill the designer and maybe you should just recall all the dresses with that print. You know how much trouble a copied print could cause.'

'I know!' Lana almost squeaked her reply.

'What does Elena think?'

'I haven't mentioned it to Elena. She's so stressed, she's so worried about the whole thing . . .'

'Well, wise up, girl. You have to talk to Elena. You've got yourselves into this, now you have to be big and decide what to do.'

The cab pulled up in the Soho street where the TV production company had its sleek headquarters. Annie buzzed the door and was soon being ushered in to her boss's all-white office, where Tamsin was at work behind her desk.

'Annie, hi!' Tamsin greeted her cheerfully, 'you're looking great.'

'Yeah, feeling great too,' Annie added and vigorously shook the hand offered. 'A break was a great idea. I can't tell you how much better I feel. Full of enthusiasm, *bursting* with enthusiasm, sweetheart.'

'A long weekend in an Italian spa – I am totally jealous,' Tamsin added.

'The spa was beautiful and I was more pampered than the wife of an African dictator, but there was *no food*! Not a shred,' she confided, sitting down in a dainty Perspex chair and reaching over for one of the vast muffins waiting in a basket for attention: 'it was barley broth once a day and vile green vegetable juice. Courgette, I ask you? Like drinking pond water. There are limits to what a girl will do to shrink her derrière. And quite frankly, buying a nice new pair of Spanx is about as far as I'm prepared to go.'

Annie bit into the muffin. It was blueberry, utterly delicious and she was starving.

'So . . . any thoughts about the show?' Tamsin asked.

Annie swallowed her mouthful and decided to go for it: 'I'm so sorry about the live event. I panicked.

I thought I didn't understand fashion any more so I sort of went label crazy. I made that terrible mistake of thinking a blizzard of designer labels would do the fashion thinking for me. It was madness . . . that poor woman. I think we need to contact her and re-shoot.'

'Yes, I've sweet-talked her into coming back next week. We won't have an audience, but we can improvise.'

'Perfect. I've been having nightmares about making her cry on stage.'

'I'm sorry we've worked you so hard. Next season we'll rethink the filming schedule and make sure you get more time off.'

Annie grinned at her: 'Next season, Tamsin. Now, those words are music to my ears.'

'What do you think we should be doing next season?' Tamsin asked.

Suddenly Lana's words, even Randall's words, were ringing in Annie's ears: 'We need to get creative, arty – maybe even messy!'

Tamsin's eyebrows rose, but she was still smiling.

'What we're doing now you can see on every single makeover programme: we get someone in, we tell her what to wear, we marvel at the result. I don't think it's ringing my bell.'

'So how do we get more creative?' Tamsin asked.

'Why don't we get the guests to show us their

favourite thing at home . . . their favourite painting, or fruit bowl, or something that makes their heart lift – and then we base their new outfit around this inspiration. So we make it much more about finding their real style rather than shoving them into what's on offer on the high street.'

'Right . . .'

'And what about tracking down much smaller designers? You know, people who are making hand-knitted jumpers or printed scarves. Show how much care and thought and art goes into making clothes? Can't we tap into the creative side of it?'

Annie was on a roll now, and thinking of Inge and the trip round the Italian ribbon shop, she added: 'I'd really like a "make do and mend" strand. Someone brings in a tired outfit and we spruce it up for them with ribbons, or a braid trim, give it new buttons – dye it a different colour, sew on flowers. I think that would chime with the times.'

Tamsin gave her a quizzical look and Annie felt a little chill of fear. Had she gone too far? Had the Randall hippie-trip gone to her head? She wasn't really an artist . . . she was a TV presenter. It wasn't her job to be creative, it was her job to pull in viewers, make sure Tamsin's show got re-commissioned and Annie's contract got renewed – wasn't it?

But really, she did have a feeling that her viewers

would want a more interesting show, one with real passion and heart. Everyone could buy women new clothes from the high street and do their hair nicely, but what did that say? What did that inspire?

Wasn't it better to try and help everyone to relight their creative fires? As Isabella had said, wasn't fashion all about keeping interested in the new and staying in love with yourself?

'I want to help everyone to get creative,' Annie added. How had Isabella put it? 'Fashion should be all about staying young at heart, keeping an interest in the new and being in love with yourself.'

'Well . . .' Tamsin began in her usual unruffled way.

Annie held her breath. Had she gone too far?

'Sounds very exciting. Now go away and write up some fresh proposals.'

Chapter Forty-Three

London

The St Vincent's Yummy Mummy:

Fitted beige shift dress (Gerard Darel)
Sensible beige pumps (Hobbs)
Tasteful gold studs (Ernest Jones)
Black and pink demi-cup bra (Agent Provocateur)
Black and pink knickers (same)
Total est. cost: £650

Annie brushed her hair carefully and applied bright red lipstick in the back of the cab. There was no longer any time to go home. She'd have to head straight to the concert at Ed and Owen's school or miss seeing both of her boys in action.

Unfortunately, this meant she would have to tow

all her shopping and her luggage with her, but she had a vague hope that St Vincent's was the kind of school which might just be able to provide luggage storage for jet-set parents.

It was a very smart school: fee-paying, old-fashioned and self-important. The kind of school where, in amongst the fairly ordinary, hard-working parents, were a handful who rocked up to events in Ferrari convertibles and looked put out to find there was no valet parking.

Annie paid her cab, charmed the receptionist into stashing her luggage and headed for the main hall, greeting parents that she knew en route.

'Annie, hello, you're looking well! I love the red.'

She turned towards the familiar voice and was caught up in a hug and a kiss with yummy mummy, newly divorced, Tessa, who was sporting her latest winning outfit: a figure-skimming beige dress with just a hint of blush pink bra.

It wasn't what Annie would have picked for a concert at her children's school, but there was no denying that Tessa looked good in it and maybe school concerts were a gold mine of single dads.

To confirm this, Tessa added in a low voice: 'I have my eye on Miles White, Charlie's dad. I think he's keen. Over there . . . have you ever noticed his shoulders before? A former Cambridge Blue. Magnificent.'

Annie smiled encouragingly, although really this felt perfectly teenage. She didn't want to be talking about Miles White's undeniable fit dad status, she wanted to crow about the fact that Tamsin loved her new ideas and the new series was going to be amazing.

She also didn't want to be looking at Miles White when she was so desperate to see Ed, but she would have to wait until after the concert for that first reunion hug.

Finally, the audience was seated, the orchestra came in, and there was Owen at the back manning the oversized drums. He scanned the crowd for his mum and shot her a huge grin when he finally saw her.

Not wanting to mortify him, she risked a little wave, and then Ed was striding towards the front, conductor's baton in hand.

It was perfect to see them both again, just perfect. She kept smiling, beaming in their direction. Ed, with his back to the audience, didn't have the chance to look for her, so she tried to read as much as she could from this rear view. He'd had time to iron his shirt and sort out his hair – that was good; obviously the twins hadn't driven him to complete distraction.

She was a little bit uncertain whether a dark patch on the back of his trouser leg was a shadow or some sort of juice stain, but thought it might be best not to fixate on that.

The orchestra tore through a whirlwind of pieces for a full hour and a half. Annie was no classical music buff but it seemed pretty impressive to her. Owen's face had turned pink with effort and concentration while Ed's impassioned baton waving had untucked his shirt and ruffled his hair.

After the thunderous applause at the end, it was time to wait for Ed in the library, sipping at a glass of lukewarm fizzy wine with the other parents.

'Hello Mrs Leon, how are you doing?'

For a moment the question startled her, because no one ever called her Mrs Leon; well, apart from the headmaster, who was approaching for a quick, sociable word or two of small talk: 'Wasn't Mr Leon brilliant at leading from the front, and your son is always so demonstrative on the drums, isn't he?'

She smiled proudly. Good old Mr Ketteringham-Smith. Despite all the difficulties there had been in the past with Lana, Owen and even Ed, he always liked to act as if nothing very serious had ever happened between them, but . . . well, maybe it was more true to say that he acted as if he didn't bear a grudge.

Annie's phone began to trill loudly. Phew . . . whoever it was on the other end of the line, even an insurance cold caller, would get her full and devoted attention if it meant her strained chat with the headmaster was over.

'I am so sorry about this – lovely to see you, a fantastic concert, but I'm just going to quickly deal with this call . . .'

Phew!

As Annie brought the phone out of her bag, she clocked the caller's name and braced herself and her eardrum.

'ANNAH!' came the screech down the line.

'Hello, darlin' . . .'

'What is happening in New York? What do you know and why is no one telling me?!'

Svetlana sounded wound up and furious. Now was not the time to fill her in on the NY Perfect Dress story. It wouldn't work: it would blow up.

With Svetlana right against her ear, waiting for a reply, Annie felt as if she was tiptoeing round the edge of a volcano.

'I don't know much, I'm trying to find out, I'll let you know everything just as soon as I know more,' she said, keeping her voice low in this milling crowd of pushy parents, everyone busy worrying about which *conservatoire* their child should aim for if it didn't work out with Oxbridge.

'Why do they not tell me?' Svetlana asked. 'I call and call for Elena, but she not reply to me.'

'Look darlin', you have quite enough on your

plate. How are the boys doing? Have you had a chance to speak to Igor yet? I hope Harry has well and truly lawyered him.'

'Igor and I are having dinner tonight like two civilized adults.'

This sounded so implausible that Annie couldn't help laughing.

'Dinner?!' she exclaimed. 'But he snatched your boys and tried to put them into military academy in Russia!'

Did Svetlana really need to be reminded?

'Well, he offer dinner in the Capital Restaurant, best lobster and champagne in London. He said we need to talk this out like grown-ups.'

'Do you think he's going to offer you a deal? He might try to take Michael and leave Petrov in London.'

'Oh no! I will never let him take Michael or Petrov. I make offer to Igor,' she said with admirable deter-mination: 'I offer to send the boys to a different school in London. One where there is optional army training. Cadets, I think you call it. I think if Michael does cadet training in London, Igor will be more happy.'

'Right . . .'

Annie wasn't really up on military training for boys. Owen would have taken one look at her, rolled his eyes and run a mile; well, no, he would

376

have sauntered a mile and definitely without a backpack. Playing violin and being super-shy were the things Owen had done when he was Michael's age. Now it was footie, German, eBay trading and banging drums so hard that the house shook.

'If Igor is happy with their education, maybe he will stop pulling these silly stunts,' Svetlana went on.

'Hope so,' Annie said, keeping to herself the thought that 'silly stunts' was playing it down a little. Those boys were kidnapped! Driven across Europe! By men with switchblades!

'Igor is very impressed I got the boys back from him. I knew this. I think he is a little afraid of me now.'

'A little *more* afraid, I think you mean. He's always had a very healthy respect for you, darlin'. Why do you think he's not remarried when there's no shortage of willing candidates? You've scared the living daylights out of him.'

'He ask if I have new bodyguard,' Svetlana laughed.

'Do you mean *me*? He thought I was your bodyguard?'

'Yes. He knew someone kick the knife away from his army-trained thugs. He also know someone rip out the tyre of his BMW. Maybe you could think about this as new career.'

This made Annie laugh properly: 'Now you are joking. I was so frightened, I just about peed my pants.'

Ooops. She remembered where she was: in the rarefied atmosphere of St Vincent's library, sipping a post-concert fizz. A startled hush had fallen over the knot of parents immediately beside her.

She felt a tap on her shoulder, turned and found herself looking straight into Ed's eyes, his eyebrows way up above them. Unfortunately, it looked as if he'd just heard that last remark too.

'I should go—'

'NO!!!' Svetlana protested. 'What about our daughters? If they have rebelled and made their dresses – oh, I am furious! I will throw Elena out of job, out of flat, out of country.'

'Svetlana . . .'

Ed rolled his eyes at this name.

Annie had to go. Any moment now she would lose Ed to the throng of parents wanting to pat him on the back, congratulate him for the performance and get a detailed critical run-down on how extremely well their child had performed and how they were expected to do in their next music exam, and should the parents start saving up for *conservatoire* fees right now?

'You can't talk like that,' Annie told her friend firmly. 'Weren't you telling me in Italy that you wanted to be a good mother? Well, stand strong. Whatever our daughters have done, we'll have to stand by them. We're going to have to help them, not punish them. They are headstrong, determined girls – just like their mothers. So calm down, my love, calm right down and I'll call you back when I have news.'

For a moment there was silence. Svetlana hated to be told what to do and Annie knew it.

Finally, Svetlana replied with a chilly: 'I await your call.'

Then the line went dead, so Annie could look at Ed and, regardless of the pack of parents circling like hungry wolves desperate for a piece of him, she smiled wide and fell against him, wrapping her arms right round him.

He smelled just like himself: a touch of soap and fresh air with a little bit of concert nerves and school dinners thrown in.

Face towards his soft neck, she put her cheek against the scratchy tweed of his jacket and allowed herself to rest there for a moment. Right here, in his arms, everything felt totally all right once again.

'Hello you,' he said, his arms tight around her. 'Busy holiday?'

'Hello you, I'm not sure you'll believe the half of it.'

Chapter Forty-Four

London

Minette's birthday outfit:

Bright pink, orange and red dress (Oilily)
Pink tights (John Lewis)
Red T-bar shoes (Start-rite)
Chocolate icing on face (Ed's homemade cake)
Total est. cost: £120

One hour and seventeen minutes into the twins' second birthday party and Annie was seriously considering locking herself into the bathroom, burying her face into the stack of fluffy towels and screaming.

Toddler parties were in so many ways so much worse than teen parties. First of all, there was the endless amount of booze and drugs: sugary fruit juice and caffeinated chocolate cake covered with chocolate icing and Smarties. Despite Dinah's warning, Ed had apparently made this last night, insisting it was only once a year and it would be fine.

Then there was the bad behaviour: Micky had of course pulled the hair of the most fragile, darling little girl in a velvet dress, who had dissolved into tragic tears. Meanwhile Minette and a gang of admirers had broken away from the crowd to amuse themselves by floating Lego pieces in the toilet then trying to sink them with the toilet brush.

Naturally, the poshest mummy had turned up to reclaim her treasure and found her in Minette's gang, clinging to the toilet rim, wide-eyed with wonder.

But somehow the remaining forty-three minutes of the party had passed, rescued mainly by Dinah and her tireless stream of games, songs and distractions. Then finally the last child was out of the door and Annie could collapse straight on to the sofa while Minette sat on her chest and Micky tried to feed her cake from the assortment of half-finished plates lying around on the floor.

'And welcome home,' Dinah said, collapsing into the armchair opposite. 'How did I manage to forget what hordes of two-year-olds can be like? Billie's last party was all about super-sophisticated nine-year-olds making pizzas and discussing how uncool Justin Bieber is.'

'You didn't forget – you've just repressed the horror,' Annie told her.

'Tea, coffee or several large glasses of brandy?' Ed called from the doorway.

'Yes please,' Dinah and Annie answered together.

'The twins are so well and have survived brilliantly without me, thank you so much, my perfect Mummy-substitute,' Annie said gratefully from the sofa with her eyes shut and her temples throbbing – the after-effects of the noise or the cake. Or maybe both.

'Ed? Maybe I'll just have warm water and a paracetamol,' Annie added weakly. 'I think I need to detox.'

This made both Dinah and Ed laugh.

'Listen to spa girl,' Ed said, 'she just can't handle the chocolate the way she once could.'

'I was hardly even in the spa! I was cheated of the spa!' Annie protested. 'I could have stuck it. I could maybe even have coped with an enema or two. But oh no, I have to drive across half of Europe in search of Britain's most valuable boys. If I'd stayed I could have lost 15 kilos – that must be at least half of my big bum.'

'Big bum,' Micky repeated solemnly.

Annie held out her arms to him and cuddled him

in close despite the layer of luminous icing around his lips.

'Don't say that in front of your friends' parents. OK?'

'Big bum,' Micky repeated.

'Big bum, big bum, big bum . . .' Minette chanted as she crawled down from the sofa. Now the twins were standing in front of her doing a demented 'big bum' chorus.

'Annie,' Ed said as he came in bearing a tray of tea mugs, 'what have you done? You've only been back here for two hours and look at them!'

'Big bum!'

'How's Mum?' Annie asked her sister as the mugs were put into their hands.

'Really looking forward to seeing you this weekend. Well, so long as you keep on reminding her,' Dinah replied. 'Phone again ten minutes before you arrive. That really helps.'

'But no other news, nothing to report?'

'Her blood pressure is a bit high. Stefano has done three readings in a row, all over 160. I'm not an expert but apparently that's not great.'

Annie sat up, sploshing tea onto her shoulder.

'So what does she need to do? Does she need medicine?'

'She needs to stop fretting so much – which is a bit hard because you know how much she frets over all kinds of things at the moment. She's supposed to switch to a low salt, low fat diet. But if nothing improves, she'll need tablets.'

Annie and Dinah exchanged an anxious look. They worried about their mother almost all the time at an acceptable low level, but news like this always brought a spike of fear.

'I've looked it up and everything,' Dinah said, 'there's lots she can do to improve things.'

'But she's all forgetful and she hardly remembers to have lunch most days, how's she supposed to remember a special diet?'

'We'll all look after her,' Dinah soothed. 'Stefano, the home help and us.'

'OK . . . you're right. Must not fret.'

'No, or you'll be the next one on the low salt, low fat diet.'

'Which would mean no crisps,' Annie sighed tragically.

'Yeah and you'd have to cut right back on the caffeine too. In fact, when did you last get your blood pressure checked?'

Dinah looked at her, face full of concern.

'At the spa by Dr Delicioso and it was fine.'

'Dr Delicioso?!'

'Totally dreamy, I would go there again, just for him. But he made me give up coffee for two days . . . and oh my God,' she rolled her eyes, 'talk about a wrecking ball on the rampage inside my skull.'

'It's a powerful drug,' Dinah said.

'OK, saintly drinker of peppermint tea.'

'I occasionally allow myself a little Earl Grey,' Dinah said, pulling her teasing face.

'Shut. Up.'

Annie's phone began to ring.

'Oh no, it's going to be Svetlana. I have to phone her, but I can't face it yet. Could you answer?' she asked Ed, 'tell her – I don't know, I've been hit and run by a toddler party and I may not pull through.'

'Hello, Annie's phone,' Ed obliged. 'Hey Connor! How is it going?'

'Oh it's OK,' Annie said, holding out her hand, 'I can make an exception for Connor.'

'She told me to say she was dying and not to put anyone through, but apparently this doesn't include you.'

Annie took the phone: 'Hello darlin', is this not a bit early for you? I thought you board-treaders only got up half an hour before the curtain?'

Connor snorted at this.

'Nine a.m., my lovely, I have been up since 9 a.m. working out, meeting and greeting, networking, having a facial to steam that horrible stage make-up right out of my pores.'

'Stage make-up? Surely you can demand Clinique or Chanel and nothing less?'

'You're right, I should. But I don't like to be too much of a diva.'

Annie snorted at the thought. Connor was *born* to be a diva.

'Chanel probably do a special make-up for the stage,' she added. 'Couleurs pour les bigheads,' she said in a properly French accent.

'Oh yeah. You found that one to use on your show, did you? And have you got the matching perfume: L'air du Trashy Television?'

'Miaow, miaow, miaow. I don't know if I can cope with this, I've just survived the twins' second birthday party. It was a Malteser massacre. There is chocolate icing on the ceiling and Lego down the loo.'

'When can I come round to deliver their presents?'

'I don't know, it depends what you've bought. If it's the two life-sized toy tigers you were threatening me with at Christmas, then the answer is: never. Same goes for your full-sized billiard table idea.'

'I've got them a little wooden train set,' Connor said, sounding hurt, 'with a bridge and a station.'

'Oh I'm sorry!' Annie said, sincere now. 'You are a lovely man, that sounds perfect. When would you like to come?'

'Tomorrow? Maybe in the morning? What are you doing? Oh, I met someone . . .'

'No, Connor,' Annie groaned, 'please! Not the latest instalment in the saga of the McCabe love life, I can't take it. Really, I'm too tired. But tomorrow would be fine.'

'Ahem . . .' Connor cleared his throat, 'any chance you could let me finish? I met someone last night who was wearing a dress made by your company and she's hoping to buy more, for her HUGE ONLINE RETAIL EMPIRE.'

Now Connor had Annie's full attention.

'Which dress was she wearing?' Annie asked, feeling a little dizzy and breathless all of a sudden.

'Something very short and orange and surprisingly funky. I thought you and Svetlana's thing was all about those classy shirtwaisters?'

Bless. He even knew the correct term for a button-down dress. This was why she had been friends with Connor for so long.

'This looked different. It looked cool,' Connor added. 'Whatever you're doing there, it's working. Arlene loved it.'

'Arlene? Not Arlene Henderson?! Do you mean the woman who runs catwalktoyou.com? *She* loved the dress?'

'Yeah. She was wearing one. Said she'd just bought it, said she was going to get in touch with your office.'

'Arlene Henderson' Annie repeated, stunned.

'But how did you meet her? When did you meet her?'

'Last night, after the performance I was invited out to some swanky celeb-studded party, I was standing next to her and we got talking. I complimented her on her dress like you do when you're a charming urbane man-about-town and we chatted about dress designers and I realized it was one of yours. Made me feel pretty in the loop, Annie, chatting to Arlene of catwalktoyou.com and being able to say: 'Oh yeah, my friend Annie runs that company.'

'I don't run it; I'm a minor partner but . . .'

Annie's breathing was now shallow and excited.

'Connor . . . this could be big.'

As soon as Connor had rung off, Annie scrolled to Svetlana's number. Finally she could make this call, finally she could tell Svetlana the NY Perfect Dress story in the hope that it was going to be OK.

'Annah?' the phone was answered almost immediately.

'Hello, sweetheart, it's me. Yes, I've got news. I've got the full story. You're not going to like the start, but I have a feeling that you're going to love the end.'

Chapter Forty-Five

Ed making an effort:

White, pink and blue checked shirt (Boden sale)
Navy chinos (Gap)
New, clean trainers (borrowed from Owen)
New, clean socks (discovered in drawer)
Pour Monsieur aftershave (Chanel, via Annie)
Total est. cost: £95

Annie was bent low over Micky and Minette's twin beds, patting both toddlers on the back and soothing them off to sleep.

'Are they away?' Ed whispered from the doorway.

'Yes,' Annie whispered back and tiptoed carefully out of the room.

In the hallway, she was pleased to see that Ed had showered and changed into a fresh shirt. There was also a cloud of her favourite aftershave hovering around him.

'You look good,' she told him, moving her arms around his waist.

'Do I look like your dreamy Dr Delicious – or other assorted Italian stallions you've been hanging about with?'

Annie kissed him on the lips, then broke off to admit: 'My Italian stallion was actually American . . . a surfer dude, very fit, very tanned and very blond . . . aged about twenty-three—'

'What?!' Ed exclaimed. 'Should I be asking about this? Do you have a confession to make?'

'No, don't be an idiot, of course not,' Annie told him, instantly remembering two breathless hugs and a bottom slap – but hardly enough to feel guilty about.

'My American surfer dude helped,' she admitted.

'Helped? How, exactly?'

'He helped me get my fashion mojo back. He reminded me that I'm a creative person and I need to mix it up a bit and not get stuck in a rut.'

'Were you in a rut?'

'Of course I was in a rut! I was a tired, strung-out harpy who couldn't even pick an outfit from a clothes rail any more.'

'I never noticed,' Ed said, but his voice was gently teasing.

'But my Italian fashion gurus have put me back on track: Inge, Isabella and Randall.'

'Randall . . . sounds like an interesting guy. I hope you got his email address.'

'No, I didn't get his email address! He said good-bye and wished me a nice life.'

'He's probably looking for you on Facebook right now. And what about your other mojo – the one we were trying to revive before you left for Italy?'

Ed pulled her in a little closer and kissed the side of her neck.

'Oh, my other mojo . . . ?'

'Mmmmm,' Ed agreed, landing a kiss on the sensitive skin just below her ear.

'Maybe it's time to head to the bedroom and see if Italy has worked wonders there too,' she said and reached up to kiss him.

This was good: standing in the hallway, kissing a minty clean Ed and thinking of all the things they might like to do in the bedroom.

'Please tell me you've moved the laundry pile?' she broke off to ask.

'So, you've not been into the bedroom yet? Just like I asked you?'

'No, but Owen might have sneaked in to dump a

fresh pile of football kit on the floor. In fact, fresh is not the word I want there.'

'No, he won't have. I think the condition for staying over at Andy's house tonight was that he had to clean, tidy and put away everything he's ever owned.'

'So just what am I going to find in there? One hundred and one dirty nappies?' Annie teased. 'Or maybe some dried dog sick that Dave left there earlier?'

'No!' Ed shook his head and smiled. 'It's a surprise . . . but a nice surprise.'

'Ooooh . . . the babies are in bed, Owen's out for the night and Ed has a nice surprise. The evening is really looking up.'

Ed pushed open the bedroom door and turned on one of the bedside lights. As Annie stepped into the room and looked around, she couldn't quite believe what she was seeing.

'Is this the same room?' she asked, amazed.

'Yes, this is the same room.'

Somehow in the short time she'd been away, Ed had organized a complete redecoration.

'How?' Annie asked. 'By yourself?'

'No, I got some help in,' he admitted, 'but I did the walls and it's my styling.'

'Styling?!' Annie repeated, smacking his arm. That was such a non-Ed word.

All the woodwork had been repainted and the walls were now a glowing, calming, muted, beige-meets-pink. New curtains hung from a brand new rail and the clutter, the junk, the broken chair, the laundry mountain, the collection of fungal mugs – it had all vanished . . . evaporated, hopefully never to be seen again.

Instead, there was calm, tidy space, plus their bed loaded with snowy white pillows and linen, twinkling with fairy lights, which Ed had strung over the headboard.

'Wow . . .' she said, running her fingers over the nearest chest of drawers and wondering at the pristine surface. 'Where did it all go?'

'I sorted and stored, I threw away – just the rubbish, though. Don't start worrying.'

'*You sorted and stored?* You – the king of clutter?'

'I can be surprisingly tidy and organized when I put my mind to it.'

'You can. It's amazing. It looks totally, totally beautiful,' she gushed, 'I'd have picked this colour myself. It's absolutely perfect.'

'Annie, I've seen the paint charts lying around. Your hints were getting a little loud.'

On one of the bedside tables, more fairy lights had been artfully arranged in a large glass vase.

'Tell me that was Dinah,' Annie said, and pointed, 'or I'm going to worry about you. I'm going to worry that you're about to leave teaching, burn all your tweed jackets and become an interior designer.'

'That . . .' he leaned over to kiss her, 'was definitely Dinah.'

'It's so beautiful and so clean! I can't take it in.'

'I was hoping you'd think it looked very, *very* sexy. I was hoping you'd walk in here, be bowled over by all my hard work and think: "I must reward this man right now".'

Ed put his arms around her waist and pulled her in close.

'I was thinking that . . .' she took a proper close look at her husband, teasing smile in place, 'I was thinking just how inviting that fluffy white bed looked.'

'Sexy,' Ed reminded her.

They kissed and she felt her body melt against his. It was so good to be home, back with her family, right back at home with Ed. The very best thing about getting caught up in a Svetlana adventure was that it made normal, safe, sane home life feel just fine.

'Just absolutely fine,' she said.

'What?'

Ed ran his fingers between her shoulder blades and that was enough to send a shiver of pleasure down to the base of Annie's spine, and now she definitely wasn't too tired.

'One more thing,' he said, breaking off from the kiss: 'I haven't shown you the best bit.'

'No, you definitely haven't.'

He stepped away from her and walked towards the bedroom door.

'Look,' he said, turning the handle and pushing the door shut.

To Annie's surprise, it stayed closed and the handle didn't disintegrate and fall onto the floor.

'I can hardly believe it!' she told him. 'But you didn't mend it yourself this time, did you?'

'No, a handier handyman than me may have been involved.'

'A closed door . . . a mended handle, a dog and toddler-free room . . .' Annie said, letting herself fall backwards onto the plump and inviting bed, 'what more could any girl want?'

'Just let me know,' Ed offered.

'Come over here . . .'

'We need to start practising for our mini-break,' he said, moving to the bed and lying down beside her.

'I will book us a mini-break. I promise.'

'You've already promised. Now I need locations, Annie, plus dates and reservations.'

'Definitely . . .'

Just as the kissing began, Annie's mobile, abandoned on the bedside table, burst into life.

'Ignore,' Ed said, as she pulled away from him.

'Shouldn't I just . . . ?'

'No. I can promise it will be your fascist production assistant. Have you forgotten about her and her late-night schedule-anxiety phone calls?'

'It's a bit late even for her.'

Annie pulled out of his arms and reached for the phone, 'I'll only answer if it's . . . Lana?'

Annie sat up and gave the phone her full attention now: 'What's up?' she asked her daughter. 'How are you?'

For a moment, Annie only heard gasping, choking sounds as Lana struggled to talk through a storm of tears.

'What's wrong? Are you OK?'

Ed was sitting up too now, face full of concern.

'It's the print!' Lana managed. 'We got him to tell us. It's a copy. That East End designer: PoliPolka. You gave Dad a scarf, remember?'

'Oh yes . . . oh no! That's it!'

'That's why we'd seen it before. *He* thought he'd changed it enough. He thought he was paying *homage*, not copying. I don't think he meant any harm. Oh the stupid arse! I could just kill him! The print is too like the original. Some of the dresses have already sold. It's a disaster. It's a total disaster. What are we going to do?!'

For several moments, Annie just let the news

register. Hadn't Svetlana said that Lana would come running back to her after their argument? Now that it was happening, there was nothing good about it. Annie didn't feel like gloating or saying 'I told you so,' or 'I knew this would end in tears'.

She felt really sorry for Lana. She didn't just want to make it all right: she wanted to help Lana make it all right.

After listening to Lana vent her full upset and anger, Annie couldn't offer an easy solution. The best she could suggest was that they all tried to think of a good way out.

'I'm going to go now so I can think too, but I'll phone you back just as soon as I can.'

'OK . . . soon, Mum,' Lana said tearfully.

Once Annie had ended the call she looked at her husband and put a hand tenderly against his cheek.

'Oh dear . . . I get the gist, big trouble in the Big Apple,' he said.

She really did owe Ed a mini-break and her absolute full attention.

'I love you,' she told him, 'and I take you totally for granted. But that's family life, isn't it? We're pulled in fifteen different directions every minute of the blinking day.'

'Uh-oh, this doesn't sound good . . .'

'I think Lana and NY Perfect Dress need my help.'

'Not in New York?' Ed groaned.

'Maybe in New York . . . very likely in New York, but right now, I need you,' – she landed a kiss on his mouth – 'so can we just try and concentrate on that?'

Chapter Forty-Six

New York

Lana fully Lana-ish:

Tight grey skinny jeans (Diesel)
Latest white chiffon tunic (NY Perfect Dress)
Grey pinstriped waistcoat (flea market find)
Pendant in silver with semi-precious stones (Monica Vinader)
Black peep-toe, so cool, heeled sandals (Shoe Warehouse)
Clips to hold fringe out of face (drugstore)
Total est. cost: $128

As Annie stepped from her yellow cab on Fifth Avenue, Manhattan, all traces of jet lag were blasted away by the breathtaking *wow* of this city.

Even though she'd visited many times before, New York was always bigger, better, louder, brighter, brasher than she remembered: like an adrenalin shot direct to the heart.

She wanted to throw up her arms and '*woooo hoooo*' at the vast skyscrapers, the jammed lanes of traffic, the jangle of noise and the wide sidewalks packed with New Yorkers marching purposefully along on this gorgeous June day.

But instead of shouting, Annie grinned from ear to ear, paid her cab fare, shouldered her handbag, clicked out the handle of her trolley bag and began to speed straight for the Perfect Dress office.

According to her body-clock it was 9 p.m., but stepping out onto the sunshine of Fifth at 3 p.m. New York time, she felt instantly revived, all set for work and a whole evening of cocktail bar hopping afterwards.

As soon as she was buzzed through the doors of the office block, she took the lift – no, make that elevator – up to the 47th floor. Then she walked along the corridor looking for the door to office number 4712. When she found it, she gave a little tap, but walked in without waiting for an answer.

'Hello and how is everyone at Perfect Dress?'

'Oh Mum!'

Lana leapt up from her desk and rushed over to greet her.

'Lana, babes,' Annie sighed, throwing her arms around her daughter, 'it's so good to see you.'

And it was. For a moment, Annie kept a tight hold, telling Lana: 'Look at you, I can't really bear that you're over here doing all this growing up without me.'

Her face was pressed against Lana's silky hair and as Annie thought of all the love, all the hugs, disagreements, conversations and all the time that had passed between them, the angry argument dissolved. She and her daughter would always, always find a way back to each other. No matter what might have been said or done.

'It's lovely to see you,' Annie croaked because of the lump in her throat.

'But it's so sad,' Lana said when the hug was finally over. 'Look at us, we're packing up. It's all over! Perfect Dress is finished. The copied print was the final straw for Svetlana; she's pulled the plug and closed us down.'

Now Annie looked properly around the office and saw Elena and Gracie at their desks packing files into boxes and dismantling the computers. Everyone had long, glum faces and Gracie's eyes looked tearful.

'You're joking!' Annie exclaimed. 'Was this decided while I was on the plane?'

'We get the call an hour ago,' Elena said.

'But I've come up with an answer,' Annie protested, 'I've thought of a way to solve the print problem – and what about Arlene Henderson? Hasn't she been in touch? Doesn't she still want to order dresses from the new line?'

'Svetlana says we are to finish. She's not going to back the company any more. It's over,' Elena replied.

'You're joking . . .' Annie sat down on the nearest chair and tried to take in this news.

'You're too late, Mum.'

'But I can't be too late!' she insisted. 'Do you have any idea how much schedule arranging I've done to get here for three days?! Filming's been rearranged; Dinah's been rearranged . . . Ed . . . even Owen has given up drum practice to babysit! It can't be too late.' She clenched her hand into a fist: 'It's never too late, not when catwalktoyou.com wants to buy into your line.'

'Too late, Mum,' Lana repeated, 'it's too late. I'll have to come home . . . I'll have to go to Dagenham Technical College.'

The defeat in Lana's voice made Annie want to cry. But seeing her daughter look so lost and unhappy also made her want to jump into action.

'Now girls,' she began, 'you are just going to have to listen to me. It's time to put up a fight. If something's worth having, then it's worth fighting for. No good thing ever came easy – well, not in my experience anyway. You're right on the brink of success here, you can't just fall at the last hurdle.'

'But we could be sued over those dresses,' Gracie protested. 'Svetlana said if we're not in business then we can't be sued. Oh, I wish I'd never, ever met Parker Bain. If I ever see him again, I'm going to punch him in the face!'

'And he so likes you,' Lana chipped in, 'And he's so sorry—'

'Forget it,' Gracie replied.

'We can't be sued if the designer of the original pattern thinks it's flattering to be copied,' Annie replied. 'So that's our first mission.'

'Flattering? But how . . . ?' Elena began.

'OK, Lana,' Annie interrupted, 'I have the number for PoliPolka headquarters. You are going to phone them up and ask to speak to the boss, she's called Susie Fellows and apparently she's incredibly nice. Tell her that a "homage" to one of her designs has made it onto a small run of your dresses by mistake. And assure her it won't happen again because next time, you're going to commission her directly to design a print for you – and mention that catwalktoyou.com are buying.

'Just to keep her totally sweet, I want you to tell her that you have a brilliant contact on the TV pro-gramme *How To Be Fabulous*. There's a new guest slot for small designers and you're sure you can get her on.'

Lana gasped: 'Really? You think it will work?'

Annie nodded. 'I'm sure it will work.'

'I don't think I could make that call,' Lana hesitated. 'You'd be much better at it, Mum, or Elena. Surely it should be Elena?'

'Lana, you want to work in fashion, right?' Annie asked. 'You want to be going places with a company that's really going places?'

Lana nodded.

Annie gave her daughter a loving and deeply encouraging look. Lana was getting older, growing up; she looked sophisticated and beautifully dressed, but she had to let go of all her little girl insecurities and step up to adult-sized responsibility. Annie was right here to give her the push.

'OK, babes, you're making the call,' Annie said, handing her the card with the phone number: 'time to man up.'

Lana took the card and her face changed from doubtful to determined.

'Gracie, it could be time to unpack,' Annie suggested. 'Start getting the office ready for business again.'

'OK!' Gracie replied with a grin.

'Elena, my darlin', you've got a difficult call to make too.'

'Not Svetlana . . .' Elena protested.

'Yes, Svetlana. You've got to ask her for one more

404

chance. You've got to tell her that we're all going to work together, no more bolting off to do things on our own. We're a team now.'

Everyone nodded solemnly.

'We'll put the copied print right,' Annie added, 'and call a meeting with catwalktoyou.com. We need our best negotiator at that meeting and we all know who that is: the only person in the world who can get Igor Wisneski to do exactly as she wants.'

'I do not think Svetlana will give us another chance,' Elena said, 'I think we already blew our last chance.'

'Yes, you probably did. But we're the Mothers, we're always, *always* going to want you to pick yourselves up after you've fallen down again.'

'I don't know . . .'

'Elena – if your mother even thinks about not agreeing, then remind her that she owes me one favour,' Annie said. 'She promised I would get one favour, which she wouldn't be allowed to refuse, no matter what it was. So I'm asking her to give NY Perfect Dress a chance. And the best chance for NY Perfect Dress is to have the three of you in the New York office and Svetlana leading the negotiations.'

'C'mon,' Annie clapped her hands, 'what are you all waiting for? Time to make it happen!'

Chapter Forty-Seven

New York

Arlene's high fashion rules:

Peach satin sleeveless dress (Hussein Chalayan)
Peach metallic ballet flats (Lanvin)
Pale grey leather jacket (Rick Owens)
Tan boxy shoulder bag (Reed Krakoff)
Diamond spider ring (Irit Design)
Total est. cost: $12,000

'She's late!' Lana wailed, 'How can she possibly be late? This is the most important meeting of my entire life and my boss is late.'

Annie risked a peek at her watch, although she had a feeling she knew what it would say.

It was 10.02 a.m. She felt sick.

Annie had been listening to Elena lecture them all on the American obsession with punctuality for the past seventeen minutes. That's how long she, Elena and Lana had been standing outside at the foot of the vast stone staircase which led to the soaring tower block where catwalktoyou.com HQ was located.

'We are dead. This is over,' Elena said, her voice simmering with rage. 'Svetlana strikes again. That woman! She must have changed her mind! Maybe she still wants to close down Perfect Dress but she wants to humiliate us one last time!'

'Shhh . . .' Annie said, trying to be calming. But after seventeen whole minutes of trying to soothe rapidly fraying nerves, she was all out of calming. Plus, it was infuriating. And *so* Svetlana. Annie didn't think Svetlana could have changed her mind – surely not now, at the very last minute? But the Queen Bee of drama queens always had to make an entrance.

Annie took in a deep breath and let it out slowly. Maybe there was a perfectly reasonable explanation. No one had been able to reach Svetlana by phone, but maybe she had a genuine excuse.

Maybe the boys . . . ?

Her heart gave a momentary flutter of anxiety. No. Surely Annie couldn't be asked to join in with a kidnapper chase again? No, it just couldn't be the boys. Igor had been placated, the boys were safe.

Annie looked round at the Perfect Dress team. They were all in their absolute best. Everyone had made a huge effort for this meeting and they were completely worthy of an interview. They had assembled at the Perfect Dress office two hours earlier where Gracie had styled everyone's outfit, tweaked make-up, added accessories and wished them all the very best luck in the world. She'd decided to stay and man the phones because she was too nervous to come to the presentation.

'Already puking with fear,' she'd told them. 'Please make this work or you know I will be looking for that job in a lawyer's office.' Plus, she'd admitted there was one phone call she had to make: 'If it all works out, maybe I'll call Parker and listen to his grovelling apology and accept the offer of a date – but only *if* it works out!'

Annie and Lana were in Perfect Chic tunics, dressed up with careful hairstyles, best make-up, leggings and seriously good shoes. Lana wore her lucky, dotty Mary Janes and Annie tottered on electric-blue suede sandals which were manna from shoe heaven but when it came to actually walking; well, they were presenting a challenge.

Elena, perhaps to please her mother, had gone Perfect Dress 'classic' with a slubby taffeta button-down dress in a shade of lime green which made her clear skin, blonde hair and grey-green eyes dazzle in an extraordinary way.

Where was Svetlana?!

'Do you think we should go on ahead?' Annie wondered. 'Should we let Ms Henderson know that something has happened?'

Elena shrugged. 'I don't think she will even take our call. She is an extremely busy lady and we are LATE.'

'Do you think this could be Svetlana?' Lana asked, pointing to a sleek silver limousine nudging its way through the traffic. All eyes fixed on the car. Sure enough, it peeled away from the inside lane and pulled into the waiting area near where Annie and the girls were standing.

A chauffeur jumped out and before he'd even opened the door for her, they could see that Svetlana was beyond the tinted window, flashing a megawatt smile.

As she stepped gracefully from the car, Svetlana, even by her own standards, looked quite extraordinary. She'd chosen a black Perfect Chic tunic, spray-on leather trousers, the highest, pointiest purple sandals ever invented and over this outfit she'd thrown lashings of diamonds: ropes, chunks, hunks of diamond, plus a furry purple waistcoat which was probably made of finest Mongolian baby yak underbelly or something equally rare.

Completing the billionairess look were gigantic Chanel shades and the kind of priceless handbag that took an entire village of Italian master craftsmen several years to complete.

'You're late!' Elena complained, obviously not as dazzled into silence as everyone else.

'No, no, I am perfectly on time and it is wonderful to see you. Everyone looks so beautiful,' she countered.

'It's nearly five past ten!' Elena exclaimed.

'Ah Elena, I know I am a very difficult mother, I know, I know, I know . . .' Svetlana held up her hands in protest, 'I know I often make life difficult for all my three beloved children, but I can promise you that today, I am on time.'

She stalked over in her skyscraper shoes and actually kissed Elena's troubled brow, something Annie had never seen her do before.

'This time you can trrrrrust me,' she purred soothingly at her daughter. 'Today, I am doing everything I can to help you.'

Meanwhile, the chauffeur had walked around the car and was now opening the door on the other side. Annie, Elena and Lana tried not to let their mouths fall open with astonishment as Arlene Henderson stepped out in an outfit of show-stopping fashion meets elegance and began to walk towards them.

'What's going on?' Elena whispered.

'I invite Arlene for breakfast at the Carlyle Hotel before the meeting. Everyone love breakfast at the Carlyle. Is a wonderful place to talk a little beeeeeezness away from the power games of the office, no?'

Svetlana gave the breezy, charming smile she had perfected in her Miss Ukraine days; the smile which brought millionaires to their knees and made anger, reprisals or recriminations just about impossible.

'She loves our dresses, *loves* them,' Svetlana added in a whisper, 'but we have to hold out for a huge order and a big price. Never give in easily, girls. Igor always tell me the number one rule of negotiation is: always be prepared to walk away.'

'Hello Perfect Dress. How wonderful to meet you all.' Arlene approached and gave the dazzled team brisk handshakes all round: 'a mother and daughter business. I love that!' she enthused, jangling bracelets and ignoring the urgent trill of the phone in her other hand, 'I love that you're making dresses which are multi-generational. I might get mother and daughter models for the catalogue. Yes! That could be fantastic. OK, team, shoulder your sample bags and follow me in.'

Lana and Annie picked up the plastic garment bags, Elena gripped the case with the collapsible garment rail. Then they followed on up the huge set of stone steps.

'Do you think we're going to land the big order here?' Lana asked her mother in an excited whisper.

'This could be immense, my love, and you made it happen.'

'No Mum, YOU made this happen.'

Annie gave a little laugh and linked arms with her daughter: 'I can't help thinking about that afternoon in The Store when I was convinced I was shopping with the enemy. It's nice to be back on your side again, Lana.'

Up through the marble hall they walked, then into an elevator with a liveried bellboy. On the 78th floor they were shown to a waiting area while Arlene assembled her team in the boardroom.

Annie took a seat in the middle of a long row of white leather chairs. Lana joined her on one side, Svetlana on the other.

'You could have told us about the power breakfast,' Elena protested before sitting down beside her mother, 'we just about died of nerves out there on the forecourt waiting for you to appear in your limousine.'

'My darling Elena, I am properly sorry for all the trouble I cause you,' Svetlana replied sincerely. 'You are a wonderful girl.'

As Elena turned to look at her mother, Svetlana gently took hold of her daughter's face. 'Just like your mother,' she said. 'Too like your mother.

I'm sorry, Elena that I didn't see you grow up . . .'

Just a handful of words, but suddenly it felt as if there was a break in the impressive, glacial façade.

'I did leave you with a good woman,' Svetlana added.

'You did . . .' Elena's voice was husky.

'Everything I am learning about being a good mother, I am learning from my friend, Annah.'

'Oh sweetheart,' Annie slipped her arm round Svetlana's waist in thanks, 'we're all just doing the best we possibly can.'

Annie wound her other arm round Lana's waist and added: 'the hardest thing is that one day, we have to push them out of the nest and hope with all our hearts that they will fly.'

Quietly into Lana's hair, she said: 'We're so very proud of you. And you know, don't you, that your real dad, he would love to be watching you take New York by storm.'

'Mum . . . we're about to go into a meeting. Get it together,' Lana whispered back but with an irrepressible smile on her face.

'Yes. I will and I am,' Annie insisted.

'We wouldn't be here without our mothers,' Elena said, giving Svetlana's arm a grateful squeeze.

'No, no . . .' Svetlana began.

'We wouldn't be here without you,' Annie finished the thought.

At that, the boardroom doors were opened and they saw a vast window with a breathtaking view of the Manhattan skyline – the city was spread out before them.

'Ladies, come on in. We are ready for you.'

THE END

The fashion-fabulous *Personal Shopper* series

New York Valentine

'Annie Valentine is a wonderful character – I want her to burst into my life and sort out my wardrobe for me! Escapist summer reading at its best'

Jill Mansell

Celebrity Shopper

'Outrageously funny... filled with shopaholic fabulousness'

***Now* Book of the Week**

How Not To Shop

'Sexy, fun and flirtatious. Reading Carmen Reid is the most fun you can have with the lights on!'

Katie Fforde

Late Night Shopping

'As fun and frothy as a poolside pina colada'

Heat ****

The Personal Shopper

'A satisfying slice of escapism and more heartwarming than an expensive round of retail therapy'

Daily Mail

A fabulous read. A sexy read.

A *Carmen Reid*

Laugh, cry and read until you drop . . .
Carmen's standalone books

The Jewels of Manhattan
'This rom-com with a twist of criminality is brilliantly fun. ****'
Closer

Up All Night
'Cleverer than the average and much more entertaining too'
Heat

How Was It For You?
'Her previous bestsellers were only a delicious taste of how
brilliantly she can tell a story'
Daily Record

Did The Earth Move?
'Full of love, hope and a dash of sadness, it's a great
summer read'
Sunday Mirror

Three In A Bed
'An entertaining and insightful tale of a 21st century working
motherhood with a bittersweet edge'
Cosmopolitan

A fabulous read. A sexy read.
A Carmen Reid